Praise for *Faking It*

'Gabrielle Tozer nails it with *Faking It* — it's fun, sassy, endearing, and an accurate account of magazine life with a hilarious twist.'

Lucy Cousins, *Dolly* and *Cleo*

'Entering adulthood is tough and Tozer nails the feelings of fraud, phoniness and faking it. Two books in and Josie Browning is still the awkward hero you can't not root for. You'll laugh, you'll squirm, you'll thank god eighteen didn't last forever.'

Mel Evans, *Sunday Style*

'*Faking It* presents teens with a main character who is smart, loveable, hilarious and discovering life (and love) on her own terms. This is all wrapped up with gorgeous writing. What a gift this is for girls of all ages — I devoured it in one giggle-fuelled sitting!'

Dannielle Miller, co-author of *Loveability*
and CEO of Enlighten Education

Praise for *The Intern*

'If you loved *The Devil Wears Prada*, I have a sneaking suspicion you'll dive right into *The Intern* … I loved this fun, cheeky read, as well as the genuine heart at its core.'

Lauren Smelcher Sams, *Cosmopolitan*

'It is an upbeat tale with a loveable heroine who is both physically clumsy and academically clever, which sets it apart from the usual teen fantasy fare.'

Kerryn Goldsworthy, *Sydney Morning Herald*

'Funny and entertaining with an element of real-life challenges and issues, *The Intern* is smart chick-lit for mid-teens and older.'

Susan Whelan, *Kids' Book Review*

'*The Intern* is a page turner that left me wanting more of Tozer's work.'

JJ McConnachie, *NZ Booklovers*

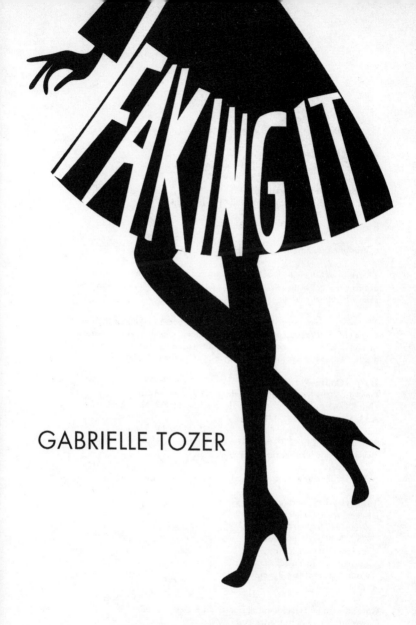

FAKING IT

GABRIELLE TOZER

Angus&Robertson
An imprint of HarperCollins*Publishers*

Angus&Robertson
An imprint of HarperCollins*Publishers*, Australia

First published in Australia in 2015
by HarperCollins*Publishers* Australia Pty Limited
ABN 36 009 913 517
harpercollins.com.au

HarperCollins*Publishers*
Level 13, 201 Elizabeth Street, Sydney NSW 2000, Australia
Unit D1, 63 Apollo Drive, Rosedale, Auckland 0632, New Zealand
A 53, Sector 57, Noida, UP, India
1 London Bridge Street, London, SE1 9GF, United Kingdom
2 Bloor Street East, 20th floor, Toronto, Ontario M4W 1A8, Canada
195 Broadway, New York, NY 10007, USA

National Library of Australia Cataloguing-in-Publication data:

Tozer, Gabrielle, author.
  Faking it / Gabrielle Tozer.
  978 0 7322 9706 0 (pbk.)
  978 1 7430 9949 0 (ebook)
  For secondary school age.
  Journalism—Juvenile fiction.
  Women journalists—Juvenile fiction.
A823.4

Cover design by Hazel Lam, HarperCollins Design Studio
Cover images by shutterstock.com
Author photograph by Simona Janek, gm photographics
Typeset in 10.5/17pt Sabon by Kirby Jones

To my darling JT,
who bravely rode the roller-coaster again

FAKING IT

1.

We still hadn't done it. You know: *it*.

James and I had been together for approximately three months, two weeks, one day, ten hours and five minutes and we still hadn't said 'I love you'.

I figured the words would come eventually, and when they did I wanted everything to be perfect. Preferably with baby bluebirds following us around chirping and singing a love song. James was my first proper boyfriend — I didn't count being mouth-mauled by Pete Jordan last year, especially as his kissing technique had rated ten out of ten on the scientific Sloppy Pash Scale — so 'I love you' was a big deal. In eighteen years, I hadn't used the L-bomb to describe anything other than my affection for my family, friends, food and overpriced stationery. The pressure was on and my expectations were high. So high, I was semi-convinced that when I spoke that magical trio of words to James, fireworks would go off and a mariachi band would appear out of nowhere, sparking a flash mob of people shimmying in the streets from the sheer romance of it all.

But spilling the beans on my heart-thumping, distracting love for James wasn't my only concern. There was something else we hadn't done together yet. Something big. Something huge. Something life-changing.

We hadn't done it.

You know, *it*.

Okay, the *other* it.

James and I were going slow and, thanks to my lifelong guy drought and lack of experience, I was fine with that. The fact that his ex-girlfriend Summer had cheated on him meant that he wasn't in a rush either. Besides, every other area of our relationship earned gold stars, high distinctions and A-plus-pluses. We sniggered over the same YouTube clips, texted and talked on the phone for hours, and had a mutual aversion to dried food, pickles and ferrets. We even shared a borderline-obsessive enthusiasm for Christmas, which we discovered when we both wanted a cheesy photo with a flushed, potentially drunk Santa during the holidays. James's kisses switched between sweet and hot, and his hugs were the warm, bone-crunching type that let you know everything was going to be okay. He was my perfect guy and *it* was going to be worth the wait.

But that didn't stop me feeling pressure from everywhere. From the colourful magazine covers lining the newsagent's shelves to the gossiping girls I'd hear in the juice line at the local café — everyone had an opinion on doing it. Or on who was doing it with who. Or on where they were doing it and how many times. It didn't help that the moment people (friends, acquaintances, the local seamstress who specialised in taking up denim jeans and giving unsolicited love advice) heard I was part of a twosome, the knowing smiles began, leaving me feeling like I was the last virgin on the planet rocking a jewel-encrusted chastity belt. Even Mum was on the case, bluffing her way through the-birds-and-the-bees talk using a stumpy carrot and an over-ripe melon to demonstrate, turning me off orange fruit and vegetables for life.

Somehow I'd gone from not worrying at all to freaking out that if I wasn't careful I'd end up as an 80-year-old virgin with frizzy grey hair, a walking frame and a thirst for Saturday-night Scrabble sessions. So I'd gone to the shops and, suffering from an epic brain-fart, had splurged on lacy black lingerie. Expensive lacy black lingerie. The kind that showed off every curve, freckle, hint of chest and thigh dimple. The kind that said 'Hello, sailor'. The kind that would make James's jaw drop, if I ever had the guts to show him.

One Wednesday morning before heading off to my job as junior writer at online magazine *indi*, I was staring at my black lacy lingeried reflection in my bathroom's full-length mirror. The knickers had wriggled their way between my butt cheeks to form a wedgie, and I'd stuffed tissues down the bra to fill it out.

I turned to look at my butt in the mirror when a loud banging on the door caused me to jump and stub my toe against the bathroom cabinet.

'Aw, crap!' I yelped, huddling over to clutch at my foot.

The knickers slipped even more, taking the wedgie to an atomic level. I had to be the unsexiest person ever to wear sexy underwear.

A nasal, high-pitched voice rang through the door. 'Josephine, are you going to be long?'

'Just a minute!' I called out, rubbing at the fresh red mark on my foot before yanking my towel off the rail.

'We've talked about this,' the voice whinged. 'How many emails do I need to send to make everyone realise I need the bathroom at this time to make it to the lab on schedule.'

The voice belonged to my housemate Prue, a second-year medical student who ran her life according to a colour-coded timetable that accounted for every minute of her day. Prue kept two copies of her insane schedule in our crummy little terrace — one on her bedroom door, and one on the fridge to keep her life functioning 'like clockwork'. She also left Post-it note reminders on the kitchen bench and bathroom wall, such as *Who's on shower-cleaning duty this week?* (when she knew full well who it was) and *Happy for you to use my stainless-steel knives, but please rinse, wash and dry thoroughly afterwards* (which was her way of turning you off ever borrowing her cutlery again).

Prue's strict life-plan was proof that my living arrangements had changed since I'd moved to the city. Gone were the days of home-cooked dinners, Mum clipping her hair up in clothes pegs while she did the washing, and daydreaming in the herb garden with my little sister, Kat. Thankfully Prue, the med-student-moonlighting-as-a-military-official, wasn't my only housemate. The terrace, which technically only had two and a half bedrooms, had recently become home to my friend Steph, who I'd met interning at *Sash* magazine last year. The ultimate free spirit, Steph had set off on the overseas adventure of a lifetime to India with my cousin Tim a month before, only to have her credit card cancelled by her rich and powerful father. Her dad, who judged people on their job, social status and connections, wanted her close to him so he could set her up for the future — or in Steph's words: 'Set me up for a snoozefest life — no, thank you!' Steph wanted fun, love and adventure, so she flew home, scored a job waitressing at a café to earn enough money to return to Tim in India, and refused to move back in with her parents. Instead, she and her giant backpack had made themselves comfortable in our 'half-bedroom' — the teeny-tiny space that Prue and I had been using to store unpacked boxes and my unused ironing board.

The terrace in the city wasn't exactly home, but it had grown on me — especially now Steph was in the room next to mine. I had enough space to store my books, only sometimes heard the neighbours fighting through the paper-thin walls, and the hot water lasted long enough for a shower every second day. The main downer was sharing one bathroom between three people — one of them being a bigger clean freak than my Aunt Julie, who had designed her own chemical-free cleaning range.

Prue pounded on the door again. 'Josie, hurry up.'

'I'm coming, I'm coming,' I said, and opened the door to find Prue tapping her foot on the hardwood floor.

'Took you long enough,' she snapped.

'Sorry.' The towel slipped down, revealing a tissue poking out the top of my bra. I shoved it back into place.

'Work it, Josie!' Steph announced with glee as she came out of her bedroom and stood behind Prue. 'What's with the Victoria's Secret? I always pictured you going to bed in one of those neck-to-ankle onesies with a bumflap.'

'Gee, thanks,' I said, making a mental note never to admit I'd been the proud owner of three pairs of onesie pyjamas, each with a bumflap, until I was thirteen.

'I'm late,' Prue said. 'Steph, I hope you don't need the bathroom, I'm going to be a while.' She squeezed past me and closed the door.

'Hey!' I said. 'My stuff's still in there.'

'So uptight,' said Steph.

'I can hear you,' Prue called out over the sound of the shower running.

I stifled a laugh and Steph and I hurried into my bedroom.

'Seriously, what's with the lace?' she pushed. 'I didn't know sex goddess was in your repertoire.'

'I knew I couldn't pull this off,' I groaned, glaring at my reflection.

'Please, you look crazy-hot,' she said. 'But that's enough compliments for you. I haven't even eaten breakfast yet.' She yawned, reminding me she'd worked the late shift at the café the previous night. 'Hey, don't you have a features meeting this morning?'

'Crap on a stick!' I shrieked. 'What's the time?'

'Almost eight thirty — you better run,' said Steph, yawning again as she attempted to smooth down her short, shaggy blonde hair. 'Nighty-night. Hey, I'll cook us tacos for dinner — I can't remember the last time I ate a proper meal.'

As she left my bedroom, I slipped off the fancy lingerie, dragged on my usual plain bra and undies, followed by a polka-dot dress that had been lying in a crushed heap on the floor. I sprayed myself with perfume, layered on a coat of eye shadow and mascara, and looped my handbag over my shoulder. On the way out, I noticed my dishevelled brown mane in the hallway mirror, so I dragged it up into a messy ponytail.

I had twenty minutes to get to work. It wasn't an impossible feat — not if I powerwalked for two blocks, caught the bus for ten blocks, jogged for one block, sprinted for four blocks, and was happy to arrive at the *indi* office in a hot, sweaty mess.

I glared at the buttons on the work lift as we chugged up each level. Faster, go faster. I couldn't afford to be late, not now, not today. My editor, Liani, was awesome — she'd even brought in a communal lolly jar for our office — but something told me that missing the 501 bus due to 'trying on lingerie to seduce my boyfriend' wouldn't cut it.

I glanced at my phone: 9.07 am. Being late was a new sensation; I was usually unfashionably early. The lift finally arrived at level nine. *Ding!* The doors strained open (almost stopping halfway from the effort) and I sprinted towards *indi* HQ, my handbag bouncing on my hip so hard that I wondered if it would bruise.

When I slid open the office door, the lights weren't even on. I fumbled for the switch. White light flooded the room, except for one faulty bulb that flickered on and off in rebellion. I walked to Liani's desk. There was no sign of her signature bright-red handbag, her computer wasn't on and her usual 'Don't mess with Mum' coffee mug wasn't steaming away.

Soaking in the eerie quiet, I wondered whether I'd missed a memo or group email.

Our online producer, Harrison, worked from home a few days a week so I wasn't surprised to see his empty desk. It looked like something out of a furniture-store brochure. The only evidence he worked there was a black-and-white photo of Ryan Gosling pinned to his bulletin board, and a pencil sharpener in the shape of a cat which was perched next to the computer mouse. But our features and beauty director, Sia, who had cut her (perfectly polished and straightened) teeth at *Sash* too, was also absent. As usual, her desk looked as though a kitsch party shop had vomited pink and purple decorations all over it. Even her chair was stacked with boxes and bags of make-up and stationery from adoring public-relations consultants.

When Liani offered me the junior writer position at *indi* a few months ago I was ecstatic. (Confession: I never told anyone, but I sobbed with happiness in the foyer. And a little on the train home.) My journalism lecturer, Professor Fillsmore, was supportive and happy for me to study long distance, as long as I checked in regularly to 'tick the boxes' for my degree. It was the ultimate win: I was a paid writer (on a crappy salary, but still — money!) with a column of my own, complete with a by-line and a head shot, in an office with a communal lolly jar that never ran out.

Though during the first month of the job, there hadn't been much writing. Organising, filing, researching, interviewing and photocopying, however? Oh, yes. The most writing I got to do was proofreading the emails Liani sent to her boss, a micromanaging high-flyer called Mya, who worked remotely and had never bothered to visit us.

Thankfully things had changed. Sure, I was still the team's go-to printer whisperer — no one else seemed to be able to keep it purring quite like I did — but I'd also been writing my weekly column, as well as copy for the entire website, excluding Sia's beauty pages. Having a by-line (a by-line I was actually paid for) made me feel like a real writer — like Carrie Bradshaw, just without the string of hot guys and walk-in wardrobe of designer threads.

I was nervous when I saw the clock had ticked over to 9.27 am, but still no one had arrived for our meeting. I'd already seen one magazine go down in flames as the industry played 'survival of the fittest'; I didn't want to be on another sinking ship before we'd even had the chance to set sail.

I re-read my notes, jotted down an extra page of ideas, sent a few email replies to pushy PR consultants, and practised my pitch while pacing back and forth through the office, but still the smiling faces of my colleagues didn't appear. Bored, I rearranged my desk, which had become cluttered with personal knick-knacks. I put the photos of me, James, Angel, Steph, Kat and Mum in order, then lined up a neat rainbow-coloured row of nail polishes that Sia had given me.

Finally, with no Very Important Meeting taking place, no printers to soothe, no more tidying to do, I had no option but to fixate on Mission Drop The L-bomb And Hook Up With James. I would have given anything to have someone to talk to right now, but I couldn't call my best friend, Angel, because she was off the grid backpacking her way through Europe; Steph was still heartbroken after her and Tim's Indian path to spiritual enlightenment (and goal to eat twice their body weights in curries) had been axed; and I wasn't close enough to open up to my uni classmates, many of whom had the personalities of used hankies. Mum couldn't talk about guys without embarrassing everyone within a two-kilometre radius; and I didn't want to give my 16-year-old boy-crazy sister any ideas. I was so desperate for advice I almost considered typing *Help! I want to say 'I love you' and I'm still a virgin, what should I do?* into Google.

I was halfway through an email to my contacts list calling for case studies for a column idea, when I realised there was another way to reach out to Angel. *Email.* She'd apparently lost her phone during a messy bar crawl in Florence, but she still tried to log on at an internet café about once a week. Email gave me the perfect opportunity to lay out the problem and tell Angel my fears. No interruptions, no judgement, no worries.

I bashed away at my keyboard, writing Angel the mother of all emails. When I pressed send on it, along with the case-study call-out, a sense of relief overwhelmed me and pushed away my doubts for the first time that morning. My worries about my personal life were now out there in the internet abyss, rocketing away from me and growing smaller and less important by the millisecond.

2.

The office door burst open and a flushed Sia raced in, her huge designer handbag hanging off her shoulder. She was chewing a large mouthful of food, which prevented her saying hello as usual. Instead, she careened straight to her desk and turned on her computer. Throwing the envelopes strewn on her chair on the floor, she planted her curvaceous body down and sniffed out a PR goodie bag brimming with brownies. I hadn't seen anyone this ravenous since the cool group at school dared Bobby Milton to smoke pot at lunchtime in the Year Twelve common room. He'd ended up with a mega case of the munchies in maths class, stole Mr Salliway's sandwich from his top drawer, and muttered 'Who else can feed me?' on repeat until the bell rang. Sia wasn't far from pulling a Bobby — she had barely swallowed what was in her mouth before she was tearing the plastic packaging off a brownie and biting into it.

'I know, I know, don't say a word, Josie … I'm an hour late, I'm a terrible person,' she said, chewing like a cow working overtime on a bale of hay. 'I'm so hungry again —

like, murderous hungry. Toast didn't cut it this morning, and neither did cereal, or a muffin, but this brownie may work! It smells so good and tastes …' Her face whitened; a striking contrast to her bright red lipstick.

'What? What is it?' I asked.

'I think I'm going to be …' Sia stood up and covered her mouth, searching around for something, anything, to be sick into. She looked inside the bags piled on her desk only to discover, like I had, that they were filled with lovely beauty products. Without a second to spare, she crouched down on all fours, her head over my garbage bin, and vomited.

'Sia! Are you okay?' I said, willing my sympathy spew reflex to ease up. 'I want to hold your hair back, but I can't come any closer.'

'All good, I'm done,' Sia said, still wrapped around my bin. She sighed, then, using an elastic band that had been wrapped around her wrist, pulled her long, brown hair into a bun. 'Maybe the brownies were rotten? Although, I've been feeling off for a while with all the anxiety of trying to get this website off the ground. I can't even remember the last time I ate properly … or exercised! Seriously, stress must be so bad for your body.'

'I know what you mean. It could be a bug — unless you're pregnant,' I joked.

'Ha, nice try, but Scott and I broke up ages ago.' She stood up. 'Anyway, that was officially the grossest thing

I've ever done — in this office anyway — so I'm going to clean it up and go and brush my teeth. Let's never speak of this again.'

I nodded. 'You're the boss ... Are you really alright?'

I hadn't known about the break-up, but realised now that I hadn't heard her mention Scott's name for a while.

'Peachy,' she said. 'Hey, where's Liani?'

'I was going to ask you.'

'Weird ...' Sia rustled through her bag and pulled out her phone. She held it up to show me three messages, all from Liani. 'Oops.'

We read them together. Liani's baby, Dylan, had weed on her leg, pooed on her arm and spat up over her shoulder just when Liani was about to walk out the door. The final message read: *Sorry, I'm running late. I'll see you both soon. Liani x PS The timing of this kid!*

'Pooed on her arm?' Sia groaned. 'Babies are disgusting ... not that I'm much better.'

She picked up my bin and strode off to the bathroom to clean it — and herself — up. When she got back to her desk, she turned on the radio, opened up her email inbox and started typing, her long polished nails click-clacking on the keyboard.

'This is not my week, hon,' she said. 'On top of this bug, I have so much to write for Liani and Mya, but there's a beauty launch on a private yacht, tomorrow of all days. I mean, are they trying to kill me?'

My jaw dropped. 'For work? That's amazing.'

'Networking, canapés and champagne on a fancy boat sounds amazing to you?'

'Well, yeah.' It would sound amazing to anyone.

'I guess the launches blend into each other after a while,' said Sia nonchalantly. 'I have to start watching myself though. I love my curves, they're killer, but I'm getting fatter than ever from all those canapés. I mean, everyone knows about the beauty-editor five-kilo spread — it's impossible not to gain weight in your first job — but seriously, I've been doing it for years now and my arse hasn't stopped spreading. I'll probably need my own lifeboat on the yacht!'

'Your arse is fine — and I mean that in a completely reassuring friend-type way,' I said.

'Got it.' Sia grinned. 'Hey, I have eighty-seven emails. Who are all these desperados sending me rubbish? I mean, don't they realise I have important things to do and ... What the hell is this?'

I looked up, startled by her shriek. 'What?'

'Josie, honey, sweetie ... I can't even ... Get your tiny tushie over here now.' Sia pulled up a chair and gestured for me to sit down. 'Um ... I'm trying to think of the mature, senior-management way to ask you this so I don't get reported to HR ... Not that we even have an HR department ... or any departments, really ... but ... look! Just look!' She stabbed her pointer finger at the email on her screen.

It looked long — so long I couldn't see where it began or ended — so I dived in and read out a random line. '*I can't help thinking I'm the last virgin in the galaxy. I bet even space aliens are getting more action than me and* … Holy crap! My email!'

My stomach tossed and turned, probably in a failed attempt to make an escape through my throat. I couldn't tell if Sia had taken pity on me, was judging me or whether she was fighting back laughter. Maybe a little of all three.

'Put it away … I'm humiliated,' I said, cringing. 'How did you get it?"

'*You* sent it to me,' she said. 'Look, it's in my inbox.'

'No, I sent it to Angel — only to her,' I insisted.

'I feel like, as your senior, I should ask if you're planning on using protection?' Sia said. 'There's the Pill and condoms and —'

'Sia, geez!' I said. 'This is the most embarrassing thing that's ever happened to me — and that's saying something. Please forget you ever read it.'

I stormed back to my desk to open up my sent folder, confused about how Sia had received the email. I read down the list: three emails sent to individual PR consultants, one email to Angel, and one email to all contacts. My heart beat faster. The notes to the PRs were as expected: I'd politely declined their offers to include their products on the website. When I brought up my email to Angel, however, I was greeted with a succinct four-liner: a call-out for 'real-life stories from girls aged sixteen-plus'. Wait, what? That's not what I sent to Angel, that was what I sent to all contacts … wasn't it?

By now my heart felt like it was trying to punch its way out of my chest. I opened the email titled 'Real-life call-out', which had been forwarded to all one hundred and nineteen of my contacts. Fellow journos, PRs, experts, real women, Sia, Liani, Harrison. Everyone who mattered to me in this industry.

Dear Angel, today goes down as the day I tried on sexy (and painful) lingerie and daydreamed about hooking up with James. I sit here, writing this email to you (missing you hopelessly by the way, so write back and stop ignoring me, woman!), still a virgin and still yet to tell him I love him, even though I have for longer than I'd like to admit …

'No, no, no!' I cried out, my eyes retracing the words 'sexy lingerie' and 'still a virgin'.

Sia spun around in her chair. 'Sweets, it's okay, I won't show anyone. And if you ever need to talk —'

'No, it's the email, the email …' I didn't want to finish the sentence. It would make it real — and it couldn't be real. I couldn't have accidentally sent an excruciatingly personal email to every contact I'd made over the past few months. I couldn't have. I rechecked the sent folder.

'Liani got it too,' I blurted out.

'Shut up!' said Sia, standing up.

'And other people,' I spluttered. 'Important other people.'

I was going to have to get a face transplant, change my name, start a new life somewhere else. Somewhere far away like Botswana. Or the North Pole.

'Half of the city will have heard of this by lunchtime,' Sia said.

'Maybe we could try recalling it?' I suggested. 'Is that still a thing?'

'A shitty thing,' Sia said. 'It rarely works. People are going to get this email. We can't change that, it's the nature of the beast. But maybe we can prevent Liani from finding out. I know her password …'

'You mean hack into her computer?' I was worried about Liani walking in to find me and Sia huddled at her desk on an email-deleting spree. On the other hand, I was even more worried about her walking in to find this email snuggled in her inbox. 'Let's do it.'

Sia raced to Liani's desk and fired up the computer. As I watched it struggle to load I cursed our low budget — if we'd had better computers this wouldn't be taking so long. (Or I could have not sent the email in the first place, but this wasn't the time for logic.)

'Click here, then here …' Sia said. 'Damn. Her password didn't work.'

'You've got caps lock on! Argh! Could she fire me for this?'

'Writing the email? Nah. Breaking into her inbox? Sure!'

'Crap, oh crap, oh crap,' I muttered, wondering how Sia had talked me into it. I'd experienced some ridiculous moments during the past year — kissing a pop star, spending a day trapped in a fashion closet, butt-planting the floor too many times to count — but hacking into my boss's computer to save my reputation took the prize.

'Now, dirty little email, where are you?' Sia said. 'Got it! And ... deleted!'

'Delete it from the trash folder! Delete it from the trash folder!' I knew repeating it wouldn't help Sia go any faster, but I was so revved up that the words flew out.

'All done!' said Sia.

We cheered and high-fived like two characters in an eighties television sitcom.

'Sorry I'm late, girls,' piped up Liani's cheery voice behind us.

We spun around and chimed 'Morning' in sync, reminiscent of naughty children who'd been caught painting the school's pet budgie. Luckily, Liani didn't seem to notice the beads of guilt-induced sweat forming on my brow.

'Oh, you got the computer fired up for me,' she said. 'After such a crappy morning, literally, I'm lucky to have you two on my side.'

'Our pleasure,' said Sia, her voice sweeter than a bag of pick and mix.

I mouthed 'Thank you' to her, then asked Liani, 'Did you want me to get ready for our meeting?'

She clapped her hands together. 'We'll get to that, I promise, but first I have the most exciting news to share. After all our months of hard work, I'm so thrilled to announce that Mya has given me the go-ahead to throw a proper launch party for *indi*!'

'Sweet, should I book a table at that fancy-pants restaurant around the corner?' Sia said. 'Harrison said the polenta chips are to die for.'

'Polenta chips?' Liani said, her brow furrowed. 'Girls, I don't mean a team party. No, we're throwing something big, something memorable, something that will get the media buzzing about *indi* — and you're both going to help me organise it!'

My eyes widened. I could barely organise my own breakfast. When it came to event management I was as useful as a nail without a hammer. Once I'd tried to help Mum arrange some last-minute entertainment for Kat's thirteenth birthday party and we got stuck with the local accountant who moonlighted as a clown every second Saturday. Only problem was (besides the fact Kat was thirteen years old and he was a creepy *clown*), he got stage fright and burst into tears, his make-up ran all over his face and all her friends ran away screaming. Kat still refused to talk about that birthday, except to blame it for her now being the *second-most* popular girl in her year and to warn us she'll need therapy in her thirties.

'I'll need both of your inputs on the VIP guest list, and I'll get you negotiating with celebrities' managers on *indi*'s behalf,' Liani said. 'Yes, this is going to be a big learning experience for all of us, but I need your help to make it a night to remember.'

'So ... so ... there'll be celebrities at the launch?' I asked. 'And you want me and Sia to talk to them?'

I was failing to play it cool, but I'd already had one brush with fame and it had maxed out my stress quota for the next decade.

During my internship at *Sash*, a minor — very minor — kissing incident with Billy, a famous pop star from the boy band Greed, had become common knowledge — in the magazine office, on social media and even on national television. At the time, Billy had just got a girl pregnant, but was still seeing other girls as well. For some reason, all that wasn't enough drama for him. No, he also had to kiss me. In public. On the night of my eighteenth birthday. And our picture got snapped and did the rounds of media.

Now Liani was telling me I'd be liaising with a whole VIP guest list of celebrities. Commence nerves of mammoth proportions.

'Wow, Liani, it all sounds awesome,' I fibbed. 'So ... this launch ... When will it be?'

'Three weeks,' she said, clapping her hands together again. 'Isn't that great? We'll go live with the new look and content tomorrow, then launch with a real bang! Mya will be in Dubai on the actual date, but she trusts us to make it a memorable event.'

'Um, only three weeks?' I said, swapping a concerned look with Sia.

'Actually, that's not quite right,' Liani said.

I was relieved I didn't have to tell her it would be impossible to pull it all together in twenty-one days.

'We've only got eighteen days,' Liani continued. 'Fewer if you don't count weekends. Mya wants us to dominate this first quarter — get in before anyone else does. Timing is everything in this business.'

I'd never met Mya in real life, but according to Sia she was a ball-breaking businesswoman who reeked of expensive perfume and had a hint of a moustache. She was the boss of all bosses, the walking piggy bank who made Liani's life hell — and giving a tiny team of amateurs eighteen days to plan a revolutionary launch looked to be another display of her unreasonableness.

'Oh,' I said, trying to think of something less panicky to say than, 'This sounds scary and hard, so can I cry now, then eat some fudge?'

Sia put an arm around me. 'Liani, I think what Josie's trying to say is that it sounds like a wonderful challenge and we can't wait to get started. Right, J?'

I nodded. It was going to be a challenge alright. I didn't know anything about launches. I imagined roaming the city's A-list hot-spots and lassoing celebrities with a long brown rope, hauling them in and throwing them in the back of a ute destined for our party.

'Um … it sounds great,' I told Liani. 'Great for the website, great experience for us. And of course I'm happy to help in whatever way you need.'

Liani cheered. 'That's my girl. Don't worry, we'll all share the load with the organising. Of course we'll need to think about the entertainment, venue, decorations, save-the-dates, catering, but first let's start with the basics — the guest list. There's no point getting too excited about the rest until we have an idea of how many people might show up. Oh, and before I forget, you're welcome to invite a friend each if you like? And Sia, I'm sure you have some contacts you can pass on?'

'You bet,' she said, shooting me a wink.

Writer. Printer whisperer. Event planner. I could barely keep up. The only soothing part was the news that I could invite James for moral support.

Sia's hand suddenly grabbed my shoulder and her eyes bulged from their sockets. 'Something's wrong … I need to throw up,' she barked, standing up and knocking things everywhere.

'Again?' I said, scrounging around my desk to unearth something for her to use as a sick bucket.

'Did you say *again*?' asked Liani.

I thrust a plastic bag into Sia's hands. 'Quick, take this!'

But it was too late — Sia had already run off and vomited into one of the bags of hair products on her desk.

3.

After all the craziness of the morning, the office had returned to its usual quiet ambience. Liani had sent Sia home, so our dream team was temporarily whittled down to two.

'So ... when do you think Sia is coming back?' I asked, my voice a little shaky.

'Not today, she's off to the doctor,' Liani said.

I wasn't surprised. After Sia had vomited, she'd burst into tears and hurried from the room with Liani in hot pursuit.

'Right, let's talk features,' Liani said. Her phone beeped and she groaned while reading the message. 'Mya's hassling me *again* for launch numbers, figures and spreadsheets.' She put the phone aside and looked at me expectantly. 'Okay, so ideas. Hit me with them.'

I rattled off a few while Liani nodded along. Even when I could tell she didn't love an idea she'd grin, but her eyes darted as she waited for the next — hopefully better — suggestion. We agreed on two: a profile piece of a 19-year-old woman who owned nineteen properties, and a bigger feature on Photoshopping in the media. Liani had refused to let Harrison Photoshop her picture that accompanied her editor's letter on the website, which was practically unheard of. Editors usually had a team of minions who worked overtime to preen and primp them, disguise all their flaws, coax their body into a painfully flattering position, then retouch the image anyway. But not Liani: she did her own make-up (Sia helped her with eye shadow) and demanded no retouching on her freckly shoulders or hint of crow's-feet. She was determined the *indi* team would practise what we preached and I loved it. The more we reminded the world that the photos of celebrities and models we saw every day weren't real, the better.

'Jose, this all sounds great, but keep an eye out for some really juicy stories too,' Liani said. 'Make a start on these — I'll run them past Mya to be safe — and we can go from there. Sound good?'

Writing always sounded good to me.

I returned to my desk to get started on the new articles, then held my breath when I saw Liani checking her inbox. Even though I knew Sia had deleted the email, the universe and I had always been more foes than friends. Five minutes later, there had still been no gasps of horror or peals of laughter so I figured I was in the clear.

The next morning, not even a solid night's sleep and steaming cup of hot chocolate could ease me into the day. My body felt stiff, hardened, strained, like my joints needed softening with the help of the Tin Man's oil can. I stared at my computer screen so hard that it felt like my eyeballs might burst into little blobby messes. My flagged emails about the launch were threatening to overtake me, one by one, and I didn't know where to begin. Not to mention that embarrassing email that had rocketed into the inboxes of the city's coolest media types; a to-do list that spilled over every page of my brand-new notebook; and no idea of the right time to drop the L-bomb.

Was this life as a grown-up? Responsibilities, changes, choices, mistakes, pressure from all angles? It made sense why adults looked so serious all the time; why they rarely smiled when they walked down the street. Why their words were often tainted with worry, or panic, or flakiness because their minds had already shuffled onto the next task or obligation.

As much as I liked parts of my new life — renting a terrace in the city, having a boyfriend (who had brains, dimples *and* a scooter!) and working as a paid writer — in that moment I wished for simpler times, when the only things on my to-do list were: (a) read a book; (b) ask Mum what she was cooking for dinner, then complain about it for an hour; (c) sneak chocolate biscuits from the top shelf in the pantry; (d) repeat previous three steps.

Adrenaline pumped through my body so hard that I figured if anything else changed, or went wrong, or got added to my workload, I'd bounce right out of my chair and land on the floor with a clunk.

'Geez, Josie, you got ants in those pants of yours?' asked Harrison, who'd graced *indi* HQ with his presence to upload the new website. 'I can hear you huffing and shuffling your teeny-tiny bod from over here.'

'I'm not huffing,' I said. 'Or teeny-tiny. I'm ... busy and ... distracted and ...' More stressed than the time I thought I was allergic to cheese and would never be able to eat Hawaiian pizza again, I wanted to say, but I squashed the words down. Harrison always seemed so together, and I wanted him to think the same about me.

'Take the compliment, pipsqueak,' he said. 'In a decade you'll pash someone because they call you small. It's been *that* long since anyone's commented on my rock-hard buns.'

I swallowed. 'Oh ... do you want me to? Because from where I'm sitting you look —'

'No, Jose. No.' Harrison rolled his eyes. 'Anyway, you're too young to be stressed — it'll give you premature lines. What's going on? Spill, I don't have time to bully it out of you.'

'Fine, so the ants in my pants ...' I started, wondering how much to reveal to him. 'Well ... did you get my email? You haven't said anything about it.'

'The one you sent this morning with the new monthly schedule?' he asked. 'I wasn't going to say anything, but you *have* to stop colour-coding everything with that sickly green and purple.'

'No, not that,' I said, trying not to take offence. '*The* email? The one I sent to everyone? About wanting to ...'

Harrison raised his eyebrow. 'What?'

'Do it,' I hissed. 'Where I admitted I was confused and worried about doing ... *it.*'

'Oh, that.' He shrugged. 'What about it?'

I hurried over to his desk, all attempts to seem 'together' forgotten. 'I've revealed *that* and you're just ... shrugging!' I whispered. 'What's that about?'

'Well, it was kinda tame, and I'd figured as much, Jose. You have a stuffed toy on your desk.'

'That was a gift! Look, Sia knows, but just ... don't say anything to Liani. She can't find out. It's too humiliating.'

'Don't fret, pet, it was cute,' he said. 'How did Liani skip out on all the teen-romance goodness if you sent it to everyone?'

I paused. 'Don't ask.'

Harrison grinned. 'You may surprise me yet.'

The sound of someone banging on the office door snapped me from my worrywarting. I looked up to see Sia's tear-stained face peeking through the glass. I rushed to open the door and Sia trundled through, pulling me into a hug that almost sent us both sprawling onto the floor.

'I didn't know where else to go,' she said, wiping away a tear. In one hand she clutched her handbag and the other held something small and white. Her face was smudged with mascara — it was the first time I'd ever seen her make-up ruined. Media girls usually didn't have a hair, eyelash or freckle out of place.

'What's happened?' I asked. 'What did the doctor say?'

'Your stupid joke was right — I *am* pregnant,' she said, waving the small white thing, which I could now see was a pregnancy test. 'I've weed on three of these and it's showed up positive every time. The doctor took a blood test yesterday and we're waiting on official results, but … I am. I know I am.'

'Really?' Harrison blurted out.

Liani gasped and stood up from her chair.

'Congratulations …' I started, but my voice trailed off as I noticed Sia's bottom lip was trembling.

She walked to her desk, rifled through her latest delivery of beauty bags and pulled out that day's freebie: a box of mini iced strawberry cupcakes. She took one and shoved it into her mouth.

'How am *I* pregnant?' she said, crumbs flying. 'I had no idea. None! I've been so busy, I can't even think when I would've found the time to make a baby. I could have been one of those freaks you read about in trashy magazines — you know the type: "I gave birth, but I didn't know I was pregnant".'

'Bloody hell,' Harrison said. 'You're lucky you didn't go to the toilet one day and have a baby fall out!'

'Not helpful,' Liani said, rushing to Sia's side. 'Sweetie, I know this is a lot to take in.'

'I am one hundred and fifty per cent alone in this,' Sia said, her voice rising. 'Scott took that job interstate. Me and a baby, *alone*. I've never even changed a nappy! How have I gone from being a beauty director to a single mother in twenty-four hours?'

'You have us, doll,' Harrison said. 'Me, Li, pipsqueak.'

'Hey!' I said. 'But he's right: babysitters at your service.'

'Urgh, I appreciate that, but there's already too much going on with *everything*,' Sia said. 'This job, and the launch, and about a hundred events, and bills to pay, and what's Dad going to say about a baby out of wedlock? And my career, I had all these plans — oh no —'

'Take a deep breath,' said Liani, her maternal instincts firing up. 'First, your career is fine, so don't give that another thought. Sia, honey, you have options, so take it all in before you make any decisions. Does the doctor know how far along you are?'

'Maybe three or four months,' Sia whispered. 'I'll know in a few days for sure. Urgh! How could I be so stupid? Scott and I were safe every time ... or at least I thought we were. I've been a bit off, but I didn't even consider that it could be ...' Her voice broke again. 'I didn't even notice any missed periods because I've never been that regular anyway. Maybe I'm just getting fat and the nausea's from anxiety. I am stressed, there's no doubt about that. Maybe it's a brownie baby.'

'You're beautiful,' I said, at the same time as Harrison said, 'Stuff the brownies — you're a minx.'

'What those two said.' Liani rubbed Sia's back. 'You're *pregnant* — don't talk about yourself like that. Everybody's different and your body's going to keep changing. The most important thing is you're okay.'

'But my boobs!' Sia threw the pregnancy test on the floor. 'They'll get huge and I won't even have a boyfriend to appreciate them. But at least I have an excuse to eat for two now.'

Liani stroked Sia's hair, Harrison stared at the ground, and I awkwardly patted her on the shoulder, hoping she didn't feel too much like a labrador. I wanted to squeeze her tight and tell her everything would work out, but I couldn't, because: (a) I was worried that I'd squeeze her too tight and hurt the mini Sia brewing in her belly; and (b) I had no idea if everything would work out. None at all.

Unsure what else to do, I passed around Sia's box of cupcakes and the four of us sat together in silence, licking off the sweet, headache-inducing icing.

Twenty minutes later, I was ploughing through my to-do list when Liani appeared next to me. 'Can I grab you for a second?'

I nodded, collected my favourite notebook (okay, *one* of my favourites) and followed Liani into our makeshift meeting room — the kitchen. Talking here, next to the whirring fridge and the temperamental kettle, rather than at her desk in our open-plan office, meant she needed to tell or ask me something that she didn't want Sia and Harrison to hear. After a few seconds of small talk, it didn't take long for her to get to the point. And once I'd heard what she said, I almost pinched my arm to see if I was dreaming.

'You want me to step into Sia's role? As the *director*?' I stammered, half-excited, half on the verge of losing my breakfast.

Liani paused and I could tell I'd missed the mark. 'No, not exactly ... Sia's our director, that hasn't changed, but when she's feeling off-colour and can't come in, or needs to leave early, I need you to step up — big time. Technically you're still my junior, but there'll be more writing and sub-editing — we can talk about that. I'll also need you to take on a much heavier load with the launch planning. That means liaising with our contacts and more ownership of the finer details, especially with the entertainment, guest list and invites. Oh, and have you heard of Maxxy? Mya and I want her top of the guest list, ideally as a performer on the night,' Liani said. 'How amazing would that be?'

I nodded. 'Yeah, it would be great.'

Maxxy, a 16-year-old singer, was all over the charts with her latest song, 'On Your Side', plus Kat had flooded her Facebook stream with her other folky pop-rock YouTube music videos. She was outspoken and social columnists followed her wherever she went, so it was no surprise that Liani wanted her at the launch to guarantee a strong media presence.

'Now, I know this is all a lot of work, so I'll commission some freelancers to free up your time and take over Sia's bigger fashion projects, but I'll still need your help,' Liani continued.

I swallowed, wondering if I should have been taking notes — and then realised Liani wasn't finished explaining my new workload. Yep, should have taken notes.

'Josie, I realise I'm asking more from you than I ever thought I'd have to in your first few months, but as a start-up we're low on resources — really low — and that's often the way in the media. And there's more ... I need you to schmooze for *indi*.'

'Schmooze?' I asked. Was that a new dance move?

'Yes, I need you to schmooze like you've never schmoozed before,' Liani said.

A small laugh escaped my lips. 'That's fine because I don't think I *have* schmoozed before.' I wasn't sure what it meant, but it sounded funny rolling off my tongue.

'Sia has a number of engagements with potential advertisers and contacts, but the poor thing can't be running out of the room to throw up every five seconds,' Liani said. 'I'm too swamped with the logistics of the launch, so you'll have to attend some events on *indi*'s behalf and charm the pants off everyone. That's what schmoozing means.'

'Me?' I asked. Didn't Liani remember I was missing the charm gene? I came from a long line of non-charmers. I wouldn't know charm if it curtseyed, offered me tea and scones, then showed me to my seat in a fancy restaurant.

'Yes, is there a problem?' Liani asked.

'No, no, of course not,' I said in a rush. 'Um, does Sia know the plan? I don't want her to think I'm … trying to … you know …'

Liani pursed her lips. 'Sweetie, Sia's got other things going on. She's in the hallway on the phone to her dad sharing the news right now, then she has to call Scott. By the way, keep her news quiet, because it's hers to tell when she's ready. Gallivanting around at events is the last thing on her mind, trust me, at least until she works out her next move. But it's top of mine. I need a face — an *indi* figurehead — out there raising our profile and promoting our brand in the lead-up to our launch. You've got what it takes, even if it doesn't feel like it right now. I hired you, and I want it to be you. So, *can* you do this for me?'

Hearing Liani's confidence in me was what I needed, especially as I was so overwhelmed I felt as though the blisters from my ballet flats, the pimple on my forehead, and my bladder were about to simultaneously combust.

'Of course,' I said. My voice didn't tremble, but my hands were clammy. 'I'll represent *indi*.' Those three little words sounded ridiculous spilling from my mouth.

'Great, because your first beauty launch is today,' Liani said. 'Sia's not up for setting sail, so I hope you've got your sea legs ready.'

'You want me to go to the launch on the yacht?' I asked, remembering my conversation yesterday with Sia. Canapés. Champagne. Fancy boat. Maybe my new responsibilities wouldn't be so bad after all.

'You bet I do, sailor,' Liani said. 'Maxxy and the launch planning will have to wait because the car transfer arrives in twenty minutes.'

'But ... my hair?' It looked like a lion had stuck its paw in an electrical socket.

'There's a straightener in the beauty cupboard.'

'And my face?' I'd seen how much make-up magazine editors caked on and I'd barely remembered to put on mascara that morning.

'A little gloss and you're good to go. There's no need to hide that clear complexion of yours.'

'My shoes?' I panicked. 'They're old, and Sia always looks amazing at events.'

Liani looked at my well-worn ballet flats. They didn't exactly scream 'Hello, please hand over all your cash to us and make our website famous and stupidly successful'.

'Give me a minute, I'll see what I can find,' she said, heading towards the fashion closet. 'You get started on … everything else.'

I opened the beauty cupboard to hunt around for the hair straightener, and gasped at how many products filled the shelves. Box after box of lipsticks, eye shadows, glosses and nail polishes; bottles of shampoo and conditioner lined up two by two; and a pile of sleek styling products. Among the hairdryers and curling tongs I spotted what I was searching for — the hair straightener. I plugged it in to heat up, wondering if now was the time to tell Liani I wasn't exactly a pro at wielding one.

Before I had time to Google *How to use a straightener without burning my hair/hands/office*, my phone buzzed. It was James, texting me from his music production course: *JB: Iron Man vs Thor. Who would win? Discuss xx*

I smiled. James and I loved superheroes — and he knew Iron Man and Thor were my favourites.

Don't make me choose, I texted back. *They'd agree to disagree, shake hands and become best friends, then they'd invite me, Spidey and Batman to join their group. It would be awesome and we'd totally kick arse. PS: Off to board a pirate ship with a bunch of mega babes. Wish me luck xx*

His reply fired back quickly. *Trade places? PS: Sorry, Batman's already my wingman. PPS: Don't fall overboard, pretty girl, I kinda like you.*

The fact that James complimented me in a PPS text message only made me fall for him more.

'Jose, what's your shoe size?' Liani called out.

'Seven, thanks,' I said, snapping back to attention. I snatched up the hair straightener and ran it over my wild mane, ignoring the faint sizzling sound and hoping I wasn't adding 'Burns off hair before beauty launch' to my growing list of achievements.

'One of these will have to do,' Liani said as she burst out of the fashion closet waving a pair of size-eight patent-leather cream peep-toe heels in one hand and a pair of size-six floral-pink wedges in the other. 'You've only straightened half your hair! I hope your schmoozing ability is better than your styling skills.'

I forced a laugh, not about to tell her they were probably on a par.

Now it was time for Liani's phone to buzz. 'Argh, the taxi's downstairs,' she said, conceding that the blunt, straightened look wasn't going to happen for me that morning, and spritzing sea-salt spray into my hair instead.

'Here's your lip gloss, kick off those flats, take these heels to put on in the car, and remember: be nice, make small talk about whatever product they're flogging, and most of all, make *indi* sound incredible,' she said, giving my hands a quick squeeze. 'You can do this, Jose. I know you can.'

4.

Water lapped against the side of the yacht, while the sun blazed in a sky littered with crisp white clouds. Media girls were on parade, each more polished and groomed than the next — and then there was me, clomping around in a pair of one-size-too-big designer heels, like a little girl playing dress-ups in her mum's closet.

Each girl had a signature feature — thick and symmetrical eyebrows, a cheekbone-highlighting topknot, pouty red lips — but together they blurred into a mix of oversized clutches, fake tans and body-con dresses that stopped halfway between the hip and knee. An invisible cloud of perfume enveloped us, and the cocktail of fruity, flowery and woody smells made my head spin. I breathed through my mouth as soft jazz music played in the background.

Five waiters in matching white shirts and black bowties ducked and weaved between the guests, holding trays of cocktails and platters of grape-sized canapés. One waiter raised his eyebrow when I loaded three

canapés — a sushi roll, a mini quiche and a spring roll —
onto my serviette. It was like he'd never seen someone eat
at a function.

The media pack had quickly broken up into smaller
groups, who were whispering and sniggering like
schoolyard bullies. No one cared about the awkward-
looking girl with half-straightened, half-wavy hair
whose too-big heels were slipping up and down against
the back of her ankles, burning monster blisters into
her skin.

Needing a hit of courage, I devoured the sushi roll
and smiled across the deck at a girl with a bright-red
twenties-style bob who had separated from the pack and
was standing by herself at the bar. She smiled back — a
real, honest, let's-be-friends smile. It was so wide and
welcoming, I almost ran straight into her arms, ready to
spill over with compliments about her hair, pretty navy
dress and emerald necklace. But I reined it in. The new
me wasn't needy or in-your-face. The new me was cool,
collected and mysterious. I was no longer Josephine
'Brown Pants' Browning, a nickname bestowed on me
in primary school after an ill-fated overdose of liquorice
allsorts. No, I was Josie Browning, acting features writer
at *indi*, a new online magazine doing amazing things for
young women.

Liani's pep talk ran through my mind: *You can do this,
I know you can.*

I sauntered towards Red Bob to introduce myself. She strutted past me, her mouth stretched into a clown-like grin, and swapped air kisses with two other girls before joining their exclusive huddle.

I looked around, hoping no one had noticed Red Bob snubbing me. They hadn't. No one was even peeping in my direction, not even the waiters. I was surrounded by people, but I'd never felt more invisible.

Unsure what else to do, I hurried towards the women's bathrooms to seek refuge. The little cartoon lady on the door was inviting me in, offering me a shoulder to cry on. I wobbled towards her with one shaky foot in front of the other. Head lowered, I rummaged through my handbag for my mobile, in part so I could make an SOS call to James, but mostly to look occupied. But, in all my efforts to seem busy, I was distracted. That's when I crashed into something — or someone — with one of the snarkiest tones I'd ever heard.

'Ow! That was my foot,' the voice snapped. 'This isn't a Topshop sale, sweetie. No need to rush.'

Three girls stood before me: all looking like they'd strutted off a fashion runway, all wearing high heels, all smirking. The girl who'd spoken had the biggest smirk of all, as well as long, jet-black hair that could only have achieved its gloss through brushing one hundred times each night (and forking out for expensive hair treatments and blow-dries). To her right stood Red Bob; to her left was a girl with a blonde shaggy mop who seemed more interested in the pot plant next to us.

'Ah, hey there,' I stammered. 'I'm so sorry, are you alright?'

They didn't fill the silence. This wasn't schmoozing and I was dangerously close to reclaiming my 'Brown Pants' status.

'So, um ... what do you guys do in the media?' I asked.

Big Smirk pursed her lips even more. 'I'm a features editor, but I also do a bit with fashion, health and beauty ... everything really,' she said, eyeing me up and down. 'This is my features writer and my beauty assistant.'

Red Bob gave a little wave, but Shaggy Mop wasn't even listening. The pot plant was no longer proving interesting, so she'd moved on to texting.

'Features editor? That's amazing!' I said. 'I bet you love it.'

'Well, I work fourteen-hour days with endless deadlines for a tough editor, but someone's got to do it, right?' She sniffed. 'I kid ... of course I love it.'

I didn't know how to reply. If my previous attempts to mingle with the cool kids were anything to go by, I should have slapped gaffer tape over my mouth and marched myself off a plank there and then to avoid any further embarrassment. But despite what I'd jokingly texted James, this wasn't a pirate ship. It was far more terrifying.

'By the way, I like your heels, they're really something,' Big Smirk said. 'Aren't they something, girls?'

Her little pets nodded, and I shuffled in my shoes, trying to disguise the fact they were a size too big.

'Thanks ... they're newish. So ... this launch is brilliant, huh?' I said. 'Not a bad way to spend a work day.'

'It's pretty gorgeous,' Red Bob agreed, and for that I wanted to high-five her. Finally, the boat was off to Schmoozeville.

'Yeah, the view's nice, but the lipsticks they're promoting are cheap and tacky, and those canapés look horrible,' Big Smirk whispered, pointing at a waiter circling with a platter of the mini quiches.

He caught us staring and came over. 'Food, ladies?'

I cleared my throat to hide the fact my stomach was growling.

'Oh, no, thank you — I couldn't possibly eat another thing,' Big Smirk said. 'But they look delicious — please give my compliments to the chef.' Once he was out of earshot, she added, 'The canapés were *so* much better at that other launch last month. You know, the ones with the goat's cheese? Oh, and what about that junket three years ago when they gave us truffles with flecks of gold in them? Now, *that* was spectacular.' She sighed. 'Don't you think the service here is pathetic too? Like, if he hadn't heard me whispering, he wouldn't have even come over. I've had better service at a drive-through.'

It took me a moment to realise she was waiting for me to answer. 'Yeah, it's ... rubbish,' I said, eager to fit in. 'So, where do you all work anyway? A website, newspaper, blog, magazine or ...?'

'*Marilyn*,' they replied in unison.

I couldn't believe it. *Marilyn* was *the* fashion mag in the country. Everyone who worked there fitted a certain mould — polished, glamorous, stuck-up — and these girls were no exception. I'd heard the perks included trips to international fashion weeks and free couture outfits. But, most of all, it was *Marilyn*'s editor who came to mind. Her name was Rae Swanson and she was a powerhouse in the industry. From her sleek bob to her piercing glare, she had a reputation for style, perfectionism and fierce, ballsy decision-making. I should know — she'd fired me last year when I stuffed up during my internship at *Sash*. It wasn't surprising that thinking of her got my stomach churning away like a washing machine on spin cycle. But I couldn't let these girls know that.

'I love *Marilyn* — it's a great read,' I trilled. A great read? Activate brain filter, then speak, Josie.

The trio didn't bother replying. They didn't need some junior nobody telling them *Marilyn* was a big deal. They knew it, I knew it, the freshly shucked oysters being passed around knew it.

'And what about you?' Red Bob asked. 'Where do you work?'

'Um, at *indi*,' I said. 'It's a newish magazine — well, a website really — and we've just gone live with new content and a fresh look and —'

'That's with Sia, right?' Big Smirk interrupted. 'Where is she? I haven't seen her all week.'

'Ahhh ... yeah. It's a long story, but I'm filling in for her today.'

Big Smirk raised an eyebrow. I could almost see her invisible gossip detector switch on.

'Yep, so *indi*'s fab,' I babbled, not that they'd asked. 'The editor's Liani, who used to work at *Sash* with Rae actually. Small world and all that.'

'Freakishly so,' Big Smirk replied. 'Rae doesn't dwell on her *Sash* days, though. Anyway, how terribly rude of me — I'm Edwina.'

The other two didn't introduce themselves, and Edwina didn't bother on their behalves either.

'Well, I'm Josie, Josie Browning,' I said, my voice cracking with nerves.

'Browning?' Edwina cocked her head to the side, her eyes narrowing into slits. Her eyelashes, which were so long they had to be extensions, fluttered. 'Like the colour?'

'I guess.'

Why couldn't my father's legacy have been something exotic or glamorous, like Onassis, Taipan or Séduisant (which meant 'glamorous' in French)? Even Mum's maiden name, Smith, would have been better. It was plain, but at least it didn't have 'brown' in it, which was the ugliest colour in the world, only one-upped by poo brown and baby-poo brown.

'So … *Josie* Browning, you say?' Edwina stared at me. 'Have we bumped into each other at one of these before?'

I doubted that, considering this was the first one I'd ever been to. 'Maybe,' I said.

'Girls, doesn't Josie's name sound awfully familiar?' Edwina continued, turning to the others.

'I'm not sure. I know, like, eight Josies,' Red Bob said. 'Anyway, it was nice meeting you. I need another drink.'

She walked away and Shaggy Mop scurried after her.

'Those two are about as useful as an appendix,' Edwina said. 'Oh my … Josie, I think I've worked out where I know you from!'

'You have?' I replied, confused.

'My best friend, Susie, is a hairstylist and she does all this work for a photographer called Kevin, although everyone calls him Vin, I think the "Ke" is silent. Anyway, his assistant is cousins with a girl in PR called Trish, or Mandy, or Mindy … whatever … and she forwarded on this email she received earlier this week. It was hilarious.'

Uh-oh.

'Yeah, it was about a girl thinking about losing her virginity to a guy called Jeremy or Joshua or one of those clichéd J-names,' Edwina continued. 'It was kind of sweet in a made-for-TV-movie way, but *so* cringe-worthy. It had clearly been sent by mistake.'

'What a loser,' I muttered.

Edwina raised an eyebrow. 'Well, the girl who wrote it was called Josie and I'm sure her last name started with B. Thinking about it, maybe it was even Browning ...'

'Sounds like a crazy coincidence,' I said.

'It's pretty embarrassing stuff,' Edwina went on, her smirk back again. 'If it were me, I'd throw myself off this yacht and let the sharks put me out of my misery. Anyway, it was *so* nice chatting, and *indi* sounds amazing. I'm sure I'll see you at a hundred more of these time-wasters, but I'd better keep circulating. You know how it is at these things — all work, work, work.'

Edwina strutted off towards a group of women. She whispered something to them and suddenly shrieks of laughter rocketed around the yacht. One girl peeked at me while the others shushed her, scolding her amid muffled giggles. I was trapped on a luxury yacht with mega bitches and no hope of dry land for another hour. Escaping on a life raft had never sounded so appealing.

If only Edwina hadn't mentioned the sharks.

5.

The next morning was a flurry of talking catering options with an increasingly frazzled Liani, putting finishing touches on my columns, and sending emails to our list of two hundred and fifty invitees. Sia had a fair few contacts in her little black book, but finding the leftovers and entering them into a spreadsheet was up to Detective Browning. Liani had suggested starting with the celebrities' websites, and I was shocked to see almost a third of them had contact details either for themselves or their manager. It was information that Kat would have instantly abused.

Once I'd drafted the perfect save-the-date email message and spent an hour refining it, I was ready to press send. Now I had to wait to see if I got any bites, especially from my 'big fish' Maxxy and her manager, a woman called Darlene Wright.

I walked into the office kitchen. It was empty, quiet; the perfect place to take a minute to call James.

'Hey, I'm at work,' I whispered down the line when he answered. 'How *are* you? I feel like we haven't spoken for ages.'

'I know, stranger,' he said. 'I'm good … busy. How was the pirate ship yesterday? See any wooden legs?'

'Er, not quite,' I said, thinking of all the beautiful people aboard. 'It was fun … mostly. Free food, free yacht ride, free lipsticks. I can't complain, although some of the girls were unhappy the food didn't contain "flecks of gold".'

'What? Douche alert,' James said. 'Was the whole event free? That's awesome.'

'It sounds fancy, but it was almost not worth it,' I said. 'I had to pretend I cared about lipstick for hours, it took up the entire afternoon, and now I've got *so* much work to catch up on. Liani mentioned something about a wellness event on Monday that she wants me to attend too. You should've seen the e-vite she forwarded me. How am I supposed to fit in writing as well?'

'I think you'll find a way to cope with all the pampering and free stuff,' James said with a laugh.

I paused, realising I was bitching about first-world problems, just like Sia and Edwina had. 'Crap. That's strike one on my douche-o-meter. You better keep track for me.'

'You got it, JB.'

I smiled. 'Hey, so I rang because I wanted to see if you have any plans tonight? I know it's last minute, but after your text yesterday I was thinking we could go to that new superhero movie?'

I turned to face the wall so Harrison, who'd wandered into the kitchen to heat up his lunch, couldn't hear me. Not that it worked.

'Oooh, is that loverboy?' he cooed, letting out a long, low whistle. 'Tell him I say hi.'

'Loverboy?' James chuckled. 'Is that what you're calling me?'

'Among other things,' I said, thankful he didn't know what I'd really been saying — and accidentally emailing — about him. 'So ... movies? Superheroes? Popcorn tubs the size of your head? Yes?'

'Sounds awesome, but me and the guys are going out. You can come if you want?'

'That's okay,' I said, feeling a twinge of disappointment. 'I should catch up on some launch planning anyway.'

'Just chill tonight. You work too hard.'

'Maybe ... You do too.'

'Yeah, I never thought I'd see the day,' he said. 'The only upside is Dad heard how many assessments and group projects I already have this year and has started taking the course more seriously. He still dislikes me doing it, but he no longer *hates* me doing it. That's progress, right?' He yawned. 'I don't know where my head is half the time ... probably still on holidays. I even have to go to the library tomorrow, on the weekend!'

'No way. You're a student and you have to go to the *library*? Shocking!' I said.

'Righto, Miss Academic ... Well, maybe you could come with? Show me how it's done?'

'Are you asking me on a library date?' I teased. 'That's so rock'n'roll.'

'It's lame — I'll cop that — but we could make out in a study pod. I'm just saying.'

I paused, my thoughts running over everything that had been plaguing my mind all week. The lingerie. The L-bomb. The V-plates. The self-inflicted pressure. 'Intriguing. One more proviso and you have a deal.'

'Chips, right? You want me to bring chips? They're already on the list. So you heard what I said about the study pod?'

I lowered my voice. 'I did.'

'Good. Hey, we're about to lay down a track so I better go. I'll pick you up tomorrow about nine.'

'Back it up ... did you say "lay down a track"? That was kinda hot.'

'Yeah, apparently I am incredibly hot and awesome, and have a cute butt. Some girl called JB keeps telling me that.'

'She sounds smart, and also hot and awesome,' I said. 'Bye now ... cute butt.'

I hung up, a grin plastered from ear to ear. I sighed with relief, calm at last about the state of my relationship. We didn't need to rush anything, or prove anything, or do anything we didn't want to. We were great just as we were.

As I turned to walk back to my desk, I heard Harrison slurping his soup. 'Cute butt? Really?'

I wrinkled my nose. 'Oh shut up.'

'Josie, there you are!' Liani's voice sang out. 'I just heard from Sia — she's got a meeting for an upcoming fashion shoot, but she's at home sick and I'm stuck on a conference call. Could you meet the visitors in the foyer and keep them company while I wrap up? Thank you!'

Liani rushed off without giving me the opportunity to ask her anything else.

'Who does she mean?' I asked Harrison. 'Are they photographers?'

'What you're about to see will blow your mind,' Harrison said. 'I just hope you've brought your stilts and something to put your brain back together.'

I went to the foyer, sans stilts, to see what all the fuss was about. Harrison hadn't been kidding. Within seconds my mind was blown, then reblown, then somehow blown again at the sight of the creature staring back at me. She was at least six feet tall, and that wasn't including her stilettos. Her hair was long, strawberry-blonde and lush (although I noticed the split ends in her severe ponytail didn't quite match the rest of her polished look) and she had tinted lashes, a slender build and flawless pale skin.

'Hey, you're young for a magazine director,' she said, her eyes pausing on my worn-down sandals.

'Um … sorry, what did you say?' I stammered, trying to collect my thoughts. I'd been meaning to buy new clothes since Liani hired me, but my low salary often meant choosing between fashion and food.

'Are you Sia? I'm Sophie, I'm here for my go-see.'

She looked at me like I was from a different planet. Which, based on our significant height difference and level of attractiveness, was a real possibility.

The lift door opened and another model, this one dark-haired and dressed in a tight T-shirt and distressed skinny jeans, glided across the foyer to join Sophie on the couch. Together, they were a sight: all gangly long legs, voluminous hair and oversized black folders no doubt containing shots of themselves looking even more stunning.

'Hello, Sia, I am here to see you,' the brunette beauty chimed in with a sharp French accent. 'My agent told me it was urgent.'

I sat down in the chair opposite them, noting that they still towered over me in this position. 'Hi, so I'm not Sia, I'm a writer at *indi*. In regards to this go-spree —'

'It is go-*see*,' interrupted the French model.

Sophie cleared her throat. 'I'm in a bit of a rush, so do you know if Sia's around or —'

'Of course, sorry … Sia's unwell, but we would still love to see your work and … um …' I racked my brain for something else to say, but nothing came.

The other model started checking her phone.

'My agent's locked me into another casting this afternoon,' Sophie continued. 'If Sia's not here then maybe I should go and —'

'I know this is unorthodox, but it's happening, I promise,' I said.

I searched frantically for a topic of conversation, but the only thing of interest was the jar of lollies on the coffee table — and models didn't eat lollies. My brain was frozen, so I decided to give small talk a miss and soak in the stillness. I counted the fine dusting of hairs on my arms as a distraction, but only made it to fifteen before I broke my vow of silence.

'So … much on for the weekend?' I attempted.

'Work for me,' Sophie offered, glancing at her watch.

The other model didn't look up from scrolling through her text messages.

'More modelling?' I asked Sophie.

'No, actually I'm starting a personal stylist company — you know, decluttering people's wardrobes, helping them choose the right colours and outfits for their shapes and styles, going shopping with them … all that.'

'Wow.' I struggled to shop for myself, let alone help other people do it.

'You learn a lot about fashion after modelling for ten years,' Sophie said. 'For example, with your skin, hair and eye colour, you should wear a more spring palette.'

'Thanks, I'll remember that.'

Suddenly the brunette squealed, causing me to jump in my seat. 'E's having a party tonight!' she said to Sophie. 'She's just announced it. Are you going to go?'

Sophie shrugged. 'Tonight? Bit last minute …'

'Her parties are fabulous and you know it.'

'Yeah, but she called her last one a soirée. *Please.*'

'Maybe the nose job changed her?' the brunette asked. 'People don't know how to handle life with a perfect face. It's hard when you're not used to it.'

I searched for a trace of sarcasm or humour in her voice, but there wasn't any.

'Not all of us can be born with a perfect nose crafted by the hand of God himself,' joked Sophie, rolling her eyes.

'The last shoot I did with her, she was yelling at people like she ran the place,' the French model said. 'It was horrible.'

'Come on, I heard she got her heart stamped on pretty bad a year or so ago,' Sophie said, obviously trying to soften the conversation. 'It's not a great excuse, but a bad break-up can change someone, for sure.'

'Well, her career may be on fire, but Edwina's no Rae Swanson. I do like her new nose though.'

I interrupted. 'Are you guys talking about Edwina from *Marilyn*?' Otherwise known as Big Smirk from the yacht.

'Don't tell me *you're* going to her party too?' Sophie asked.

'No, I ... I, ah, have something on tonight.' Eating a plate of grated cheese for dinner while watching trashy television counted, right?

'You know what, I can't be bothered,' Sophie said, making the French model gasp. 'I've been pulling so many hours trying to get this business off the ground. I think I'll chill with my sewing kit and a cup of tea.'

'Sophie, it's a Friday night and she's getting a super-hot DJ from Ibiza to perform. You are so boring.' The brunette jammed in her earphones.

'Anyway ... can I grab a lolly?' Sophie asked, then caught the look of surprise on my face. 'What?'

'Ah, nothing,' I said. I unwrapped a lolly of my own, much to the displeasure of the other model, who'd screwed up her nose.

'You know,' said Sophie, as she sucked on her lolly, 'My agent got forwarded the strangest email from someone who works here — a girl called Josie Browning. Do you know her?'

Here we go again. This email was following me around the city like a bad smell.

'Um, loosely,' I stammered.

'Well, tell her it was so ...' Pathetic? Childlike? Desperate? 'Sweet,' Sophie concluded.

'Sweet? *Really*?'

She shrugged. 'Yeah. She talked about feeling scared to say I love you, and it gave me goosebumps. It could have been from my own diary a few years back — well, a fair few years back. Those three words are huge, and it was refreshing to see someone taking them seriously.'

'I'll, ah, pass on the message.'

'I have no doubt she'll eventually tell this guy how she feels and they'll be madly in love for forever and a day. Made me happy, and a little jealous.'

'But you're beautiful,' I said, popping another lolly in my mouth. 'Men must worship at your feet. I bet you have fifty guys telling you they love you just in one day!'

'Fifty's a slow day,' Sophie cracked. 'Look, I'm human. Don't buy into the whole beauty-means-you'll-get-everything-you-want myth. Those three words don't mean a thing if they're not coming from the right guy. If someone finds the right person, they should make sure they know it and never let them go.'

'You're a romantic, huh?'

She winked. 'Only in secret.'

'Ladies!' Liani chimed behind us, almost causing me to choke on my lolly. 'Sorry for the hold-up — that call took longer than expected. Now, what did I miss, Josie?'

Sophie shot me a wry smile.

'*Josie* was just filling me in on a great idea she had for an article,' Sophie fibbed, as I attempted to thank her telepathically for keeping her perfectly plump lips sealed. 'It sounds fabulous — love, sex, virginity ...'

'Juicy!' Liani told me. 'I'll talk with Mya, and you and I can flesh out the details later.'

'Ah, great,' I said. 'I better get back to work. Good luck with the new business, Sophie. It sounds cool.'

'Best of luck with ... *everything*, Josie,' she said, drawing the word out so I didn't miss the point. 'Don't forget — spring colours, okay?'

I nodded, and left Liani to talk the models through the fashion-shoot brief. Harrison was right: I had been blown away by my close encounter with the modelling kind, but not for the superficial reasons he'd expected. Sophie's comments about love had hit a nerve, especially the tender way she'd spoken about me and James. For a moment — just a quick one — I wasn't ashamed of what I'd sent out into the universe.

6.

The thought of eating a plate of grated cheese for dinner lost its appeal on the bus ride home, so I stopped off at the local convenience store to grab a bag of salt and vinegar chips, a block of chocolate and a banana (my attempt to be healthy).

'Not your usual, Miss Josie?' asked Amir, his bushy eyebrows wiggling. We'd swapped names one evening when I'd come racing in to grab toilet paper for a panicked Prue because Steph had forgotten to buy some — a mistake that resulted in an evening of passive-aggressive text messages, yelling and door-slamming.

'My usual? I don't come here *that* often.'

'One cookie-dough ice-cream on a stick and a packet of mints, no?' He grinned. 'And your boyfriend likes those sugary red drinks — he gets one every time.'

I had a usual. Looked like James and I needed to branch out.

'You win this round, Amir. Have a great night,' I said, waving goodbye as I left the shop.

Hugging my wares, I walked the few metres home, crossing everything — down to my strands of hair — that Steph and Prue were out. Since moving into the share house, my treasured quiet time had been whittled down to stolen moments while they were out, in the shower or sleeping in.

I walked into the terrace and, for once, my wish had been granted. The house was quiet. The couch was free. And, most importantly, the remote was all mine. My night of escapism via trashy television and even trashier food could begin. First up: chips. I licked the salt off each chip until my tongue was stinging, then pecked the soft, soggy edges into a wonky heart shape, before gobbling it whole. As I tore into my next victim — the block of chocolate — my phone blasted to life.

'Hello?' I said, trying to speak through a cube — okay, a row — of chocolate.

'It's me, loser,' Kat's voice laughed down the line.

My sister hadn't called in ages, to the point where I was convinced she'd become allergic to picking up the phone.

'Hey ... what's going on? It's been a while,' I said. Then it hit me. Why *was* she calling me now? 'Oh crap, is it Mum? She didn't get upset and have another fall, did she?'

Mum had hurt herself pretty bad last year and it had rattled us all.

'She's great. What about, "How are you, Kat?" Well, I'm good,' she went on before I could speak. 'Thanks for not asking.'

Kat was as infuriating as ever. I'd thought me moving to the city would bring us closer together — absence was supposed to make the heart grow fonder — but it hadn't worked. Despite us pulling together when Mum had melted down and needed extra TLC, our relationship was back at square one — only this time I couldn't storm into her bedroom to hash it out. Living so far away meant we struggled through cryptic, confusing phone calls that never went anywhere. But at least we were talking, I told myself.

I tried again. 'So ... What's up? Met any nice guys lately?'

'Is that all you think about since getting your first proper boyfriend?' she said. 'James *is* real, right? Not that I've been introduced or anything. I still think you've made him up — the guy doesn't even have Facebook! Is he, like, a hundred and you guys have matching Snuggies?'

'I'm hanging up now.'

'No, don't!' she said, immediately making me suspicious. Kat was never this keen to talk.

'James is real,' I said. 'You and Mum will meet him soon — I'm bringing him home in just over a week.'

I'd told them we'd be home on the Saturday morning, but we were planning on surprising them on the Friday night. Steph was doing a road trip in the same direction that weekend with one of her friends, a girl called Alex who I hadn't met yet, so James and I were planning on catching a ride down with them and getting the train back together on the Sunday. I didn't want to get ahead of myself, but I had a feeling Mum was going to be so chuffed that I'd go down in family history as Favourite Daughter and Surprise-Planner Extraordinaire.

'If James is a blow-up man-doll, I'll never let you live it down.'

'Kat!'

'I'm joking,' she said. 'Meeting the mum and the sister — this is big. I bet Mum'll get the fancy china out. Aww, I wish I had someone to bring. This town needs some fresh meat because the guys here are walking fails.'

Walking fails that she'd dated ten of in the past year.

'What about that guy whose dad drove the green —'

'Clammy hands.'

'Oh, but there was that cinema guy who was kinda —'

'Boring? Yeah.'

'And that tall guy from the watch shop?'

'Rubbish kisser.' She sighed. 'I need a city guy. An older guy, maybe. Those pics you showed me of James — if that *was* him and not some random on the internet — he's not bad-looking for a dork. Maybe he has a friend for me.'

Not bad-looking? Dork? James was perfect. Well, except for his bad habit of chewing his fingernails and commenting through every TV show we watched. And I wasn't going to encourage my little sister to meet an older guy — knowing my luck, she'd end up with a

35-year-old divorcé with a failing shares portfolio, bad teeth and three kids under five.

'Maybe you need to chill for a while?' I suggested.

'You're doing whatever you want in the city and you expect me to chill?' Kat shot back. 'No way. This place is a hole and school already sucks. Whatever, let's not forget how far you've come.'

'Hey!'

'Jose, c'mon,' she said. 'Don't make me bring up the Year Twelve formal — people still laugh about you and that spiked punch. Now you're rubbing shoulders with hot famous people and scoring free beauty products on a daily basis. Urgh, I could vomit with jealousy.'

When she put it like that, it did sound awesome. But Kat didn't realise that despite everything I had on paper — the job, the boyfriend, the share house in the cool city terrace — I was exactly the same person underneath it all. The same school joke; the same girl who doodled hearts in her notebook when interviewing people at work, who cried when a lecturer gave her a credit when she'd expected a high distinction, who got butterflies every time her boyfriend texted her. If anything, I was even more neurotic since moving to the city because I was only one embarrassing email, magazine-event encounter or failed hook-up from losing everything. But it was too complicated to explain to my little sister, so instead I listened to her rant about, of all things, the upcoming *indi* launch.

'Mum told me about it, and she said that Maxxy might be there,' Kat said. 'I love her. Like, really love her, Jose. She's such a babezilla and I'm playing her song right now. Can you hear it?'

'Nothing's definite yet,' I said.

'The launch is in a few weeks, right? Get me an invite.' There it was — the real reason for the call.

'It's not that type of event, and you're sixteen,' I said. 'You have so much cool stuff to look forward to — don't rush it.'

'You suck!' she snapped, and went on to bitch about her lame social life ('This town is such a drag. Can I come visit you?'), Mum's new interest in yoga ('She thinks she's a pro already!'), and her best friend's boyfriend ('I saw him pick his nose!'). Finally, after six minutes and forty seconds — I'd started watching the clock — she drew a breath. 'So, you wanna talk to Mum?'

'Yeah!' I said. 'Our last chat was pretty rushed.'

Mum's social calendar was packed since she'd found a new confidence in herself after her counselling sessions. She was now a 'yes' woman — she no longer refused invites or shied away from experiences — which meant pottery class on Tuesdays and aqua aerobics on Thursdays. She'd become hard to track down for a decent conversation.

'Put her on, that would be great.'

'I can't,' Kat said.

'But you asked if I wanted to talk to her.'

'Yeah, but I didn't say you *could*. She's not here.'

'Well, why would you ...?'

I didn't even bother finishing the sentence. Kat's motivation always came down to three possible reasons: (a) to impress a guy; (b) because she was bored; or (c) to piss me off. It didn't take a genius to work out this was a tasty combination of options (b) and (c) — maybe with a splash of hidden option (d): just because.

'I'll fill you in on a secret,' Kat offered. 'She's out on a date. With a guy.'

I paused. Mum was dating now?

'It's their third one too,' Kat dropped in with the subtlety of a wrecking ball.

'Um ...'

'I knew you'd flip!' Kat said. 'Listen to you — flipping out. This is why Mum didn't tell you.'

'I didn't say anything!' I retorted.

'*Exactly.*'

'I'm happy for her, I am, but ... how can you be so cool with this? She's still technically married to Dad and —'

'He's a dick, Jose.'

'Yeah, but —'

'He's not coming back, and I don't want him to. Who cares about "technically"? You have a boyfriend — why shouldn't Mum? You're not the only one who deserves happiness.'

I hated it when my little sister sounded so wise and left me feeling like a bratty baby on the verge of a tantrum.

'I know,' I said. 'Hey, Kat … do you really think he'll never come back?'

I'd wanted to ask that question for so long, and couldn't believe it'd slipped out, tonight of all uneventful nights.

'Yeah,' Kat said without hesitation.

'Me too …'

'Maybe he's dead.'

'Jesus!' My eyes welled up at the thought. I'd never even considered that he mightn't be alive any more.

'I don't know, maybe!' she said. 'You hear about that kind of stuff on the news. Or maybe he has a double life, or he's living in the Bahamas, or has a new kid on the way. Who cares? He's a coward. He doesn't deserve us giving him any more oxygen.' She had another bomb to drop. 'Jose, did I ever tell you I tried to contact him?'

'No! When?'

'Right after that letter arrived for my birthday. I needed answers.'

The letter on Kat's birthday (he'd missed my eighteenth) was the first and only time we'd heard from him since he'd left over a year ago with nothing but two suitcases, a cricket bag and an esky, never bothering to tell us why. For a while Kat and I were convinced he'd show up again on our doorstep, weeping and overflowing with apologies, regrets and flowers. But enough time had passed for us to realise that wasn't going to happen, so we stopped saying his name out loud.

'Oh my god …' I said.

'Yeah … I Googled him and found him on Facebook — thought he'd started an account. The profile pic was his footy team's emblem. It seemed legit, so I gave it a shot and messaged him.'

'And?'

'I said "How dare you run off on us!" I said way more stuff too. I was dropping F-bombs left, right and centre — must have given him a heart attack.'

I couldn't believe it. 'What did he say?'

'Um, well, that's the thing … turns out it wasn't him. It was a guy from Perth who happened to have the same name and rooted for the same team. He didn't even have kids, but I think I scared him into believing he had a whole family he didn't know about. Such a fail.'

'Oh my god, oh my god, oh my god!' I repeated like a broken record. 'How have I never heard this story?'

'Doesn't matter. Our real dad's not coming back. He missed your eighteenth. Even if he is alive, he's dead to me, and to Mum.'

After such an intense, surprising conversation, I didn't know whether to laugh or cry. So I didn't do anything. I had to admit, I agreed with Kat and felt the same anger towards Dad. While I couldn't picture Mum dating — I almost didn't want to try — it was comforting to hear she was happy enough to get back out into the world and start living again.

'Say something, Jose! Are you trying not to bag me out for what I did to that guy on Facebook?'

'Kinda,' I admitted. 'But I love you for trying.'

'Ew, don't get clingy, you always ruin these moments,' she said. 'And Mum doesn't know, so keep your gob shut. Hey, I've got another call coming from Matty so I should go. I had, like, a thousand missed calls from him before. Total stalker, but he's hot so …'

'I thought you hated country guys?'

'Did I say that? Don't forget to send me an invite for the launch.'

'It's never going to happen!'

'Gotta go — bye, Jose!' Kat said, hanging up.

Drained, I lay back on the couch and sucked on another cube of chocolate, letting it melt in my mouth until the brown, gooey goodness was caught between my teeth. So much for my relaxing Friday night.

7.

I woke up to the sound of arguing rattling through the paper-thin walls of our terrace — no phone alarm required this morning. Prue's voice was loud as usual, and squawking in an attempt to get her point across. Rubbing my eyes as they adjusted to the strips of sunlight shining through my blinds, I heard Steph defending herself, but couldn't make out what she was saying.

I fumbled for my phone to see if I had a message from James. *Morning, study-buddy.* I laughed and texted back *See you soon, nerd-face*, then wriggled into a jumper. I didn't bother changing out of my boxers — Steph and Prue wouldn't bat an eyelid at me in my PJs. Well, not until they noticed the rubber ducks wearing top hats that were printed on them.

I walked into the lounge room and a piece of toast went flying past my head, before bouncing off the wall behind me.

'Hey, watch it!' I yelled. 'Steph, what's the matter with you?'

'Sorry, babe, I was aiming for Prue,' Steph said, as though that explained everything.

Prue huffed. 'You better clean that up. I don't pay my share of the rent to deal with this kind of drama.'

'Can someone tell me what's going on?' I asked.

'Steph came home last night and ate all my leftovers — they were meant to be my lunch today,' hissed Prue. 'It's the final straw. I've been holding it in for weeks, but I can't handle it any more!'

'*You* can't?' Steph said. 'This is like living with a drill sergeant! I was going to offer to make you dinner tonight to even things out, but you didn't give me the chance. This is called a *share* house, right?'

'Well, what about the fact that you never clean around here?' Prue continued. 'Do you even know where we keep the vacuum cleaner? Josie manages to find it every now and then, but you — I don't think you've even met!'

Steph tried not to laugh, which was like a red flag to Prue. She launched into another tirade.

'Well, this isn't how I imagined spending my morning,' a male voice drawled behind me, causing me to jump in fright. I wasn't expecting company.

For a second I thought my cousin Tim had teleported himself back from India, but instead I turned to find a guy with medium-length wavy brown hair, olive skin and a sleeve tattoo sprawled on the couch with my childhood heart-covered blanket (named Benji, if you must know) draped around him. I gulped. He looked like a rock god. A gorgeous rock god. A gorgeous rock god who had spent the night on our couch. And if I knew anything about gorgeous rock gods, they were trouble.

'That's my blanket baby — er, baby blanket,' I blurted out. I'd never seen Benji wrapped around another person before, especially someone who was male, six feet tall and covered with tattoos.

'So it's vintage,' said the handsome stranger. 'You're lucky, it's probably worth a fortune.'

'Yeah ... totally,' I said, plopping down on the chair adjacent to him while the girls continued to lash out at each other.

'I was joking,' he said, breaking into a big grin that softened his whole look. 'It's probably worth, like, fifty cents. You're kinda gullible, huh?'

'No, I was, ah, kidding,' I insisted. 'Anyway, I'm ... um ...'

'Hey, Um,' he said, readjusting his position on the couch and wrapping himself tighter in the blanket.

I didn't know how to talk to this guy, especially when he was simultaneously teasing me, making dad jokes sound cool and staring at me with big brown eyes. Not wanting to seem shy or intimidated, even though I was feeling both, I forced myself to make eye contact, and I noticed his lips were still curled into a warm smile.

'I'm Alex,' he said, extending his right hand.

I paused. *This* was Alex? The amazing friend Steph raved about? The Alex she had sleepovers with? The Alex I'd thought was a girl?

I shook his hand, gulping at his warm grip. Nervous again, I slid my hand free, but not without noticing my palm was tingling.

'You're looking at me like I have three eyes,' he said.

'Ah … yeah … you're a guy. Sorry, I guess I always assumed that … Never mind. Um, I'm Josie, Steph's friend. And housemate. And former journalism intern rival, I suppose you could say,' I rambled. 'But we're just friends and housemates now.'

He nodded. 'Sounds simpler. So *you're* Josie the journo who we're doing the road trip with, huh? Steph was saying one of her friends was a writer.'

'I suppose that's me,' I said. Even though I was paid for writing, it felt so unreal, so grown-up, to say it out loud. 'How do you know Steph? Are you friends or …?'

'Or what? Are we more than friends?' Alex said, reverting back to teasing me. 'Do I *like-like* Steph? Well, that's a story and a half.'

'Doesn't matter, it's not my business,' I said. Surely Steph wouldn't be cheating on my cousin? She wasn't afraid to play by her own rules (case in point: throwing toast in the middle of a ridiculous share-house fight), but I couldn't imagine her deliberately hurting anyone. Steph was kind and loyal, and her heart was full of Tim. But the nosy journalist in me couldn't resist. 'Actually, yeah … are you and Steph seeing each other behind Tim's back?'

Alex roared with laughter. 'Steph!' he called out, almost choking. 'Hey, Steph!'

'What?' she said, pressing pause on her argument with Prue about whether or not it was okay to eat peanut butter from the jar with a spoon. (One guess who thought what.)

'Josie wants to know if we're going out? And if you're cheating on Tim? Should we tell her?'

Steph rolled her eyes. 'Goddamn, I leave you two alone for one second … Yeah, tell her everything, Al, I think my girl can handle it.' And she returned to debating with Prue over her right to double-dip from the communal PB.

Was it true? Was Steph cheating on my cousin?

'Brace yourself, Josie,' Alex said. 'Here it comes … drumroll … She's my … fake little sister! Ta da! Bit of a letdown, huh? I touched down from an overseas media junket a few days ago and, as we go way back to toddler days, I thought I'd see what Smelly Socks was up to.'

'Smelly Socks?' I raised an eyebrow.

'Told you we went way back. You see that dirty look she's shooting your other housemate?' I noted Steph's furrowed brow, pursed lips and dark eyes as Prue lectured her on the benefits of scrubbing the shower weekly instead of monthly. 'I taught her that when she was five years old — I was almost nine. Her dad still hates me for it.'

I tried not to laugh as I imagined Steph running around as a little pocket rocket. 'So you're a journalist?'

'Yeah, I've been a freelance travel writer for about two years now,' he said. 'It pays the bills, sometimes, and when it doesn't, I chalk it up to seeing the world.'

'Cool,' I said, trying not to swoon too obviously at the fact that he was a writer, especially one who navigated the globe for a living. And it didn't take a genius to realise that if Alex's parents were friends with Steph's, they were extremely well-off. No wonder he was so relaxed about whether or not he earned enough to cover his bills.

'It's alright. I've spent a lot of time waiting at airport gates,' he drawled, running his hand through his hair. 'So you write for magazines and websites, huh? I used to know a few people from that world pretty well. Nowadays, most of my talks with editors are via email — there's less bull that way.' His eyes rested on my pyjamas. 'You, ah, seem kind of embryonic to be working already. Are you one of those quirky Mensa kids with an IQ of one-sixty?'

'What? No! I'm still studying ... and I'm not *that* young.' Or that smart.

'Those sharply dressed ducks quacking on your boxers tell me otherwise,' he said, standing up and wandering over to our bookshelf. It was piled high with a messy mixture of Prue's manuals, Steph's glossy coffee-table books and my collection of novels and journalism textbooks. Uttering a low whistle, Alex pulled my copy of *To Kill A Mockingbird* off the shelf. 'Well, look at you go,' he said, noting my name scribbled on the front page and giving me a nod of approval.

I didn't know why, but I felt pleased he was impressed.

He reached for another book — one with a pink, prissy cover. 'Is this yours too?'

I blushed. 'I've had it since I was a little girl,' I said, unsure why I was making excuses. I loved that book and should have said so, but something held me back.

My phone beeped. James was on the way. 'Anyway, I need to get to the library,' I said, standing up.

'The library?' he teased, reaching over to the coffee table and plucking a green apple from the bowl. I hoped Prue didn't notice; she was protective of her fruit. 'Are your weekends always this extreme?'

'Er ... I went go-kart racing once. And I know someone who sky-dives ... well, they want to ...'

'*Almost* extreme by association, huh?' he said.

Quick, Josie, I told myself, act cooler, smarter, edgier, *better*. This guy's a writer. A real writer. He's paid to write while travelling the world. Learn from him. Go against every natural urge right now and *schmooze*. As Alex crunched on his apple, I searched for something to say that would prove I wasn't a duck-PJ-wearing, uptight bumpkin from the suburbs.

'So, um ... I like your tattoo,' I said, pointing to his arm. 'It's very ... colourful ... and big. Must've hurt.'

'You should see the one on my back,' he said, and for a moment I thought he was going to peel off his T-shirt and show me. 'I'm guessing you don't have any?'

No, I didn't. I'd never even considered the idea. Years ago, in the change rooms down by the river, I'd seen a wrinkly old lady with tattoos on her saggy, naked bum, and that was enough to swear me off them forever.

'Well, no, I don't … but I'm thinking about getting one.' Oh, Josie.

'Yeah?' I could tell from the sparkle in his eye that he was interested. 'What design? I know a few tattoo artists if you need their numbers.'

Uh-oh. This lie was off the leash and running away from me too fast to keep up.

'You know, one of the usual picks,' I stammered, trying to think of tattoos I'd seen. 'You know, like a name, or a symbol, or barbed wire, or an animal … Yeah, like a really cool, freaky but beautiful animal. What are they called?' I continued, digging the hole even deeper. 'Like when it's a goat's head with the body of a fish? Or a shark's head with the body of a gorilla? Something like that.'

Alex snorted. 'Did you say barbed wire before?'

'Yeah,' I said, hating myself for sounding so foolish in front of him, and then hating myself for caring what this stranger even thought of me. Embarrassed, I stared at the ground. 'I better go … I'll leave you to break up the fight, yeah? They're as stubborn as each other.'

I was walking towards my bedroom when I heard Alex call my name. I turned, startled that the conversation wasn't over.

'Maybe I could read your work sometime?' he said.

'Why?' I asked, wondering if he was mocking me again.

'Just keen to see the kinds of yarns a girl who wears rubber-duckie PJs, reads Harper Lee and plans on getting a gorilla-shark tatt strings together,' he said. 'I'll show you mine if you show me yours.'

I blushed again. 'I'll think about it. Bye, Alex.'

'See ya, Josie the journo.'

I hurried into my room and shut the door, exhausted from trying to keep up with the conversation. I reminded myself to get the lowdown from Steph later on her relationship with Alex, then shook my head at the sight of my rubber-duckie boxer shorts in the mirror. I dragged them off and walked over to put them in my dirty laundry basket. But with Alex's teasing ringing in my ears, I threw them in the bin next to my desk instead.

I had a quick shower, slipped into a pretty top and skirt, added a slick of lip gloss and hint of mascara, and I was ready for my library date with James. I double-checked my reflection and added an extra coat of lip gloss, just to be sure. We'd both been so flat out with work and study that this was the closest we'd had to a real date in a while, so I didn't want to waste the opportunity, especially when my overactive brain cells had been pumping away at a million miles a minute about taking the next step.

The sound of James honking out on the street caused me to throw my handbag over one shoulder, yell goodbye to Prue and Steph (and awkwardly wave to Alex, who was still lounging on the couch like he owned the place) and hurry out the front door, my wild wavy hair billowing around me in the rush. I raced down the steps and there he was, smiling at me, dimples and all. James. My boyfriend.

I still wasn't tired of calling him that. In fact, I was so excited by the novelty that I was on the slippery slope to becoming an annoying bragger. You know the kind: 'Sorry I can't make your party, I have plans with my *boyfriend*'; 'Which school did you say you went to? Oh yeah, I think my *boyfriend* went there'; 'Yes, I have the time, it's 5.39 pm. Oh, and did I mention I have a *boyfriend*?' I used to want to throw rotten eggs at those smug types, but now I'd joined their sucky little love-in.

James was sitting on his scooter with his helmet hooked under one arm, a spare for me in his other hand. 'Here she is, looking pretty,' he said with a grin and passed me the helmet.

I took it, and he wrapped his arm around my waist and pulled me towards him. We leaned in close, our noses gently bumping, a jumble of whisperings sweetening the air between us. When we were all out of 'Hello', and 'I've missed you', and 'Have you been eating chocolate croissants without me?' (he had), I wrapped my arm around his neck and brought his lips to mine for a soft, tender kiss.

'Maybe we should blow off the library,' he murmured.

I pulled away a little. 'C'mon … you have something due. On your bike!'

James laughed. 'I'm already on my bike — and you are so country.'

'Yes, it's one of my many wonderful qualities,' I said, putting on my helmet. 'I'm happy to have a complete list couriered over. Now, onto my most pressing concern … How I'm going to hop on your scooter in *this* skirt without scaring my neighbours to death.' I'd been so worried about looking good I'd forgotten about practicality.

A minute later, after some yoga-like manoeuvring and almost splitting a seam, I was perched behind James with my arms wrapped tightly around his waist. He revved the motor and we were off, scooting down my tree-lined street. A corner here, a corner there, a sharp left, an easy right, a roundabout, followed by a stretch of brown and grey buildings lined side by side, and we'd arrived.

Eager to claim our spot inside, James parked in a rush, took my hand to help me off the scooter (this time I did flash someone — a rather surprised parking inspector), and we hurried up the steps, through the huge doors and into the library.

Before I knew it, James and I were cuddled up and whispering in a study pod, but despite trying to keep our voices down, we sounded like we were booming out of a loudspeaker in that cavern of quiet. We received a few filthy looks from a man with thick grey hair sprouting out of his nostrils who was struggling to use the photocopier, as well as from an older woman in a floppy white hat who was leafing through the newspaper behind us.

Ignoring their stares and the sign in front of us saying 'No food in the library', James and I crunched through a packet of barbeque-flavoured chips that he'd dubbed his 'study fuel'. He leaned over to kiss me — first on my nose, then on my forehead, before planting one on my lips. I sank into it, enjoying the salty aftertaste and feeling like the happiest girl on the planet.

'Are you only kissing me for the taste?' he said.

'No!' I said, laughing.

He raised an eyebrow.

'Okay, maybe a little,' I admitted, leaning in for another.

'You want chip taste, you got it,' he said, pulling me onto his lap and kissing me again.

'You're a giant cheese ball, you know that?' I said. 'If you were a pizza, you'd be a four-cheese pizza — all gooey and —'

'Delicious?'

I could feel the heat rushing through me, settling on my cheeks. 'How do you get away with all this cheese-balling? I think it's your eyes. They're all wide and puppy-like. Or maybe it's your face. It's kinda cute and —'

'I missed *your* face this week,' James interrupted. 'This course is so hectic, I'd kill for a day of nothing to do.'

'You're supposed to be studying, remember?' I said. 'Maybe I can help you take notes 'cos you've only done about five minutes.'

'Study boring. Kissing fun,' James joked, beating his fists against his chest in his best Tarzan, King of the Jungle impression. It was daggy, but I loved it. 'Tell me more about you, Josie Browning, or should I say Miss Features and Beauty Director?'

I shook my head. 'I'm basically a professional seat-warmer. If Liani needs a butt from *indi* at an event, I'm her butt!'

'It is a pretty nice butt.'

'Only pretty nice?' I said, and James laughed. 'I don't know what I'm doing half the time. I'm like, "Yes, Liani, whatever you say, Liani, sure, I'll schmooze, Liani".' I shrugged. 'I had no idea journalism would involve so much networking. You know the saying "flying by the seat of your pants"? Well, that's me at work, except I feel like my pants have split wide open and I'm careening headfirst towards the ground with no parachute! Thanks to this launch and Sia's pregnancy, I'm *flailing* by the seat of my pants.'

The stupid email I'd sent to the entire industry didn't help either, but I left that part out.

'You paint quite the picture — anyone ever tell you that you could be a writer, J-Bird?' he said, winking. 'I bet you're doing great. You've been killing it for months — why would now be any different?'

He crunched a chip and pulled me in for another salty kiss. Someone cleared their throat behind us. We turned to see the librarian — a haggard woman with a thin mouth that looked like it might have been drawn on — glaring at us.

'Are you quite finished?' she said, her thick eyebrows narrowing so much they met in the middle. 'There are other people here trying to enjoy the library.'

'Ah, nearly. I think we have about ten minutes of making out to go, right, Jose?' James said, while I bit my lip to stop from cracking up.

'Get out,' the librarian snapped. 'This is a public library, not a place for sinning.'

'We'll restrain ourselves, promise,' said James, holding his hands in the air like he was under arrest. 'Look, no sinning to be seen.'

'And the chips?' Her thin lips were now pressed together so tightly it looked like her wrinkly face was swallowing them whole.

'Oh, do you want one?' I asked, completely forgetting food was banned in the library.

'Do I ...? Take your chips and leave,' she hissed.

'We're outta here,' said James, collecting his books before the librarian rallied the other grumps to chase us out with pitchforks. 'C'mon, JB.'

A meagre ten minutes after we'd entered the library, we marched back out through the big doors and burst into laughter on the front steps.

'I didn't know it was possible to get booted from a library!' I said. It felt kinda bad-ass, before I realised how lame it would sound to anyone else. 'What now? You've done *zero* study.'

'Yeah, but how about all that sinning?' he said, taking hold of my hand. 'Here's a plan: we could take my stupid books to the park and study there for a bit?'

'And by "study" you mean ...?'

'You can kiss me with those lips under that tree by the fountain, we'll get ice-cream, have a nap ... and then I'll freak out about not doing any study later this arvo.'

'You've got it *all* thought out.'

He grinned. 'I am a thinker.'

'You're definitely something,' I teased, nuzzling into his chest, the flailing sensation of the past week feeling like a distant memory while I was wrapped in his arms.

8.

The rest of the weekend flew past. James and I took out gold, silver and bronze in the Kissing Olympics and, as predicted, he got no work done Saturday afternoon so needed to go into study lockdown from then on (which apparently involved sending me a stream of texts and prank-calling me in a mix of different voices).

On Sunday, Prue followed her usual routine of hitting the gym, going for lunch with her brother, then heading to the lab, and Steph had picked up an extra shift at the café, so I had the place to myself.

I showered, climbed into a fresh pair of pyjamas, called Mum (no love again), sent Angel a message on Facebook (also no reply), then cosied up on the couch to watch back-to-back romantic comedies. The sink remained piled high with dishes, my bedroom needed cleaning and I was positive nearly all my undies bar one pair were in the dirty laundry, but after a stressful week I needed to reboot my brain with the predictable, mindless gloriousness of rom-coms.

A cool breeze was drifting through our lounge room window, so I rummaged around in the ottoman for something to pull over me. I found a T-shirt of Steph's, Prue's favourite pillowcase and my baby blanket. An image of Alex cocooned in it the previous morning popped into my head. A little weirded out, I stuffed Benji back in the ottoman, and settled for going to get my dressing gown. But I still couldn't shake the thought of Alex; our conversation on writing had permeated my brain. Before you could say 'stalker alert', I'd plugged his name into Google. The screen flooded with links to his work.

I clicked on the first one — an article on his trip through Dubai. I scanned a few lines, then moved on to the next — a passionate, long-form essay on his life-changing experience walking to Machu Picchu in Peru. I read piece after piece, impressed by his writing style and jealous of the exotic places he'd travelled to in such a short time. The Cook Islands, Laos, New Orleans, Barcelona — and to think I'd never even left the country.

Just as I was about to click on his review of a hotel in Monaco, my phone buzzed.

I was expecting it to be James, but instead it was a photo of Sia pointing at her belly with the caption: *The little monster is making me crave ice-cream with BBQ sauce. WTF? Send help. And fried chicken. PS: I have more doc's appointments so will be in on Tuesday. Have fun at the wellness event tomorrow. You'll be great!*

I texted her back — *Step away from the BBQ sauce! Yell if you need me to bring anything around, except gross condiment–dessert combinations. PS: I'll try to do you proud xx* — then snuggled up on the couch, pushed Alex's travel-writing career aside and prepared to get a solid five movies under my (dressing gown's) belt before bedtime. And that I did — well, four and two-thirds, if you don't count the half an hour when I dozed off.

Afterwards, I laid out my outfit for the next day — a cream silk top with a navy skirt — booked a taxi and slipped some gym clothes (as requested on the e-vite) into my bag. I fell asleep that night happy, with square eyes, and a sink full of dirty dishes.

The sound of my phone ringing snapped me awake in fright. I rubbed my bleary eyes, groaning when I saw the time flashing on my bedside clock: 6.23 am. But the phone kept ringing, competing with what sounded like soft rain pattering on the roof.

'Who on earth?' I muttered, ruling out James and Kat, who wore their ability to sleep through anything, on anything, at any time, like a badge of honour.

'Hello?' I mumbled, although I was so sleepy it probably sounded more like 'Shmarlo?'

'Love!' Mum's voice sang down the line, suspiciously full of cheer for so early in the morning. 'Look out your window — how about that sun? Isn't it glorious?'

I yawned. 'Mum, I'm pretty sure it's raining here. And anyway, if I look out my window I'll probably see Mr Petty making breakfast in his tighty-whities.'

'But love, you're missing out. It's orange and pink and gorgeous here! My old counsellor — you know the one — taught me to be grateful and it's paying off. You're crazy if you don't care how beautiful the sky can be, Josephine.'

I rolled my eyes. '*I'm* crazy? You do know what time it is, right? Does this qualify as child abuse?'

'I just felt so terrible that I missed your calls — did I tell you I've joined a book club on Sundays? Anyway, now that I've stopped smoking I have so much energy, so I thought I'd see what you're up to.'

'Other than sleeping?' I said, yawning as I turned on my lamp. 'Hey, you know there's only one week to go until I'm home? And James is coming too.'

'Love, I know, Saturday morning won't come fast enough,' she said, her voice softening. 'It's been too long, and I'm sure he's lovely. Well, he'd have to be better than some of the dimwits chasing your sister. I just wish she spent as much time studying as she did worrying about boys.'

'We can't all be nerdburgers, Mum.'

Mum chuckled. 'Well, that's true. Hey, what do you want to eat for dinner on Saturday night? Such a special occasion calls for a special meal.'

I had to laugh — it looked like I wasn't the only one excited that I'd got off the bench and joined the dating game. 'Mum, don't stress. We can always go out.'

'Does James eat peas? I make a delicious soup, but it's rather pea-heavy.'

I tried not to gag. 'Let's steer clear of anything too, er, pea-heavy.' For everyone's sake.

'Love?'

'Yeah?'

'I need to say something, so it's said, and doesn't need to be said again ... I don't think I'm ready for you and James to share a bed at home ... especially with Kat in the house. She's far more impressionable than she lets on.'

'Mum ...' I said, hoping this wasn't the birds and the bees round two. 'It's all good, whatever you want.' I was eager to end this conversation as soon as humanly possible.

'I'm sure you guys get up to all kinds of things in the city, but —'

'Mum, can you not —'

'Let's keep James on a blow-up mattress for now.'

'I said it's all good.'

'Good,' she said. 'Now, I'll leave you to get ready for work, but get that bony little butt of yours home as soon as you can.'

'Have a fun week,' I said. 'Love you.'

It was only after she'd hung up, and I'd recovered from all the James/bed/mattress talk, that I realised she hadn't said anything about her own love life. Maybe Kat had been stirring me the other night. Or maybe Mum really *didn't* think I could handle it.

Wide awake now, I went into the bathroom to get ready for my second-ever media event. The softly sprinkling rain had built to a crescendo and was pelting against the roof so loudly I worried it might spring a leak. 'Great,' I muttered, relieved I'd already booked a taxi.

As I went through the motions of showering, slipping into my new outfit, blow-drying my hair and applying my make-up, I couldn't stop myself wondering about the morning. What did 'wellness event' even mean? The request for us to pack our workout gear was semi-alarming, considering my idea of exercise meant reaching extra hard for the TV remote. What if I had to run around in front of everyone and they saw my technique was reminiscent of Bambi learning to walk?

I looked in the mirror and, for once, was semi-pleased with my reflection. My hair was behaving, I'd mastered the art of applying eyeliner, and had picked the perfect shade of coral-pink lip gloss to complement my outfit. Something was finally coming up Josie Browning!

It was almost time for my taxi to arrive, so I collected my handbag, gym gear and an umbrella. But minutes later, I still hadn't got a text saying it was on its way. It's fine, I thought, it's just a little late.

I waited some more. Still nothing. I opened the front door and peeked outside, dismayed to see the rain had grown more torrential. The taxi didn't appear. Strike one.

I checked my phone, but there was still no alert. Strike two.

'C'mon, c'mon, c'mon,' I muttered, calling the taxi company. It rang, but a pre-recorded message began to play … and play … and play. Seven minutes later and I was ready to throw my phone down the stairs. Strike three.

I was out of luck — and the event was starting in fifteen minutes.

The weather wasn't letting up, but I had no choice: I teetered down the stairs onto the street in search of a taxi driving past.

The rain pounded against my umbrella as I wrestled it into place to protect my hair, handbag and outfit. The umbrella had different plans: it contorted itself back and forth like a rhythmic gymnast.

Taxis were peppered through the traffic, but none of them were empty. I felt the 'suck it!' mentality emanating from the warm, dry people inside each car as they saw me battling with my umbrella on the sidewalk, my once blow-dried hair now damp and limp.

Finally, a lone empty taxi took pity on me and came to a sudden halt, splashing filthy gutter water all over me. I swore when I realised my cream silk top was now drenched right through. I was on my way to an important work event in a transparent blouse worthy of a *Girls Gone Wild* clip. Oh, happy day.

The taxi stopped in front of the wellness centre. Through its fogged-up window I saw beautiful women stepping out from their cabs and clinging to each other under umbrellas as they tottered inside. They looked gorgeous, perfect, *dry*. No one else was spattered in muddy water. Only me.

I knew that if I entered the wellness centre looking like I did, it would get back to Sia, fast, and I'd be pulled off schmoozing duties. *indi* needed a strong, confident representative — not a klutz who couldn't get to a work function without looking like she'd swum there. I had an idea. It was risky, but I hoped I could pull it off without ending up on the news, in jail or fired.

'Please keep the meter running — I'll be one second,' I said to the driver, and clambered from the front seat into the back, dragging my bag and umbrella with me. 'Um ... would you look at that,' I cried, pointing outside. 'Is that woman even wearing a bra?'

'Where?' the driver said, looking out the window. 'I can't see anything in this weather.'

'Over there to your right. Is that someone famous with her too?'

As the driver craned his neck, I wriggled out of my wet clothes, stuffed them in my bag, and pulled on my workout gear, thankful my distraction was working.

'I think it's that famous guy with the huge muscles who's in that new movie with the big robot,' I went on. 'What's it called …?'

The driver began to turn to look at me. 'Miss —'

'Quick, to your left!' I said, and he looked out the window again as I wriggled into my gym pants, which was difficult in the limited space. 'It's that actress from that show! You know, they spend all day in that bar?'

'No, I don't think that's her,' he said, turning on the radio.

I silently congratulated myself. I'd pulled it off and hadn't flashed anything, not even a single nipple. It was a new record.

I dragged my hair into a tight bun to disguise the frizz, coated on more lip gloss and thanked the cabbie. It was time to learn what a wellness event was. Hopefully it would be more appealing than being served a steaming bowl of broccoli for breakfast and getting my tonsils checked in front of everyone.

Five minutes later, precariously balanced in downward dog position in front of a celebrity yoga teacher, I wasn't sure which was worse. All I seemed to be experiencing was the feeling of blood rushing to my head — greens for brekkie suddenly didn't sound so bad.

'And hold … Keep holding … Don't forget to breathe … Feel the positive energy in the room … A few more breaths to go …' the instructor said in a wispy voice that made me want to beat her over the head with a celery stick.

My ankles cracked as I readjusted my position, pushing my butt up in the air and pressing my heels down one at a time to feel the pull through my calf muscles. This was exercise? I'd got my heart rate higher chasing a Mr Whippy van down the street.

It was while I was bitching to myself upside down, staring through the gap in my legs, that I saw her. Edwina. She wore sleek jet-black designer yoga gear that complemented her sleek jet-black ponytail, which swished over the floor as she tilted further into a perfect downward dog position. Wow, I thought, half-impressed, half-intimidated by the fact the industry's queen bee was here too. Looked like I was rolling in her circle now.

It was in that moment of ego-fuelled self-congratulation that my sticks-for-arms gave out. I slipped with a shriek and a thud, my left knee missing the cushiony yoga mat and connecting with the floor.

Everyone gasped and stared as the teacher rushed to my aid.

'Are you okay?' she asked.

I rubbed my knee, but it was my ego that was more bruised. 'Ah, yeah, I'm fine. Sorry, I, ah, saw a … bee.'

A queen one. I couldn't bring myself to look to see if Edwina had released her infamous smirk.

'A bee?' the teacher said. 'Inside? Well, where is it? We don't want someone getting stung.'

I needed to diffuse this, and fast. 'It flew out the door, probably off on some crazy bee adventure with all its bee buddies, collecting pollen and scoping out flowers and stuff.'

The teacher raised an eyebrow, clearly not used to having awkward weirdo freaks in her class. 'Right … well, be careful because this isn't supposed to be a strenuous class. A few of us will come around now and make adjustments to everyone who needs them.'

She may as well have swathed me in bubble wrap, then labelled me with a 'Fragile' sticker.

'Now return to your mats, please, and let's do some side lunges … and breathe,' she said.

The class obeyed, and I attempted to ignore my aching knee and follow suit, stretching my legs wide and willing my feet to turn out further.

'You know, your posture isn't *that* terrible,' a voice said.

I looked up to see Edwina standing in front of me. 'Excuse me?'

'I fell over in a yoga class once, so don't worry, you're not alone,' she said, lowering her voice and forcing a wry smile as she adjusted my arms and legs. 'Josie, right?'

'Hi,' I managed, trying not to stare at her nose after what the French model had said. 'You're a yoga teacher and even *you* fell over?'

'Not officially, but the teacher and I go way back so I help out sometimes. And yes, I fell while doing a headstand and looked just as ridiculous as you did then. Humiliating, isn't it?'

I was unsure if she was insulting me or empathising with me. 'Ah, yeah.'

'Sorry, I'm sure no one thought you looked *that* ridiculous,' she said. 'You're learning the ropes, after all.'

I was. More than she knew.

Edwina pulled her yoga mat closer to mine. 'Activate your core when you're posing, it makes all the difference.'

'Thanks.'

'Now, everyone move into the next position,' the teacher sang out. 'Thank you, Edwina. Please keep helping out over there as we don't want any more accidents.'

'She thinks I need training wheels,' I whispered.

'Follow what I'm doing,' Edwina said. 'By the way, I love your hair in that wet-look bun. Very chic. So ... how's James going?'

'He's great, pretty busy and ... wait.' I stepped out of the yoga pose and put my hands on my hips. 'You know his name now?'

'Curiosity got the better of me — I reread the email,' Edwina admitted. 'It was sweet. Seriously, your *adorable* little love problem is child's play compared to some of the Mrs-Robinson-style dramas friends of mine have going on. And ... how's Sia's pregnancy going? Is she doing okay?'

I paused, not sure how to respond. 'Um, she's well.'

'Then the rumours *are* true — she is pregnant? I'd noticed she'd gained weight.' Edwina's eyes lit up like I'd given her a diamond-encrusted ring in front of the Eiffel Tower.

'Er ...' Crap. Now I had one more thing to add to my to-do list: work out how to explain to Sia that Queen Bee Edwina had tricked me into giving up her secret.

Edwina smirked. 'Anyway, I know something that will *totally* distract you from the fact that you spilled the beans on Sia. Manis, pedis, massages, blow-dries and fake tans are up next.'

'Seriously? We get free massages?' I asked, before realising what else she'd said. 'Hey, I didn't actually spill the beans, right? You already knew.'

'Josie, relax. People would kill to be you right now and you're *stressing*. With Sia incapacitated, this isn't a bad way for you to spend a morning, is it?'

A montage of me flagging down taxis in the rain, wrestling an unruly umbrella and changing out of my wet clothes in the cab played in my mind, but I still meant every word when I said, 'Not bad, not bad at all.' The toughest decision I had to make in the next few hours was whether I wanted a colourful or French-style manicure.

I just hoped that if Sia was going to kill me, she would do it as quickly as possible.

9.

'You're so tanned — like beach-babe tanned not trash-bag tanned,' Sia said. 'Is that a French mani? Unbelievable! I go away for one day and you've turned into California Barbie.'

'I don't look that different,' I said, rolling my eyes. But even I didn't believe what was coming out of my mouth. Anyone could see I was Josie Browning 2.0 — the version that came with better hair, skin and grooming. Steph had even screamed when I'd got home the previous night because she thought we had a 'super-hot intruder' — her words, not mine.

'Sweetie, your nails usually look like you've painted them wearing a blindfold, no offence,' Sia said.

'Has Harrison been texting you bitchy stuff to say to me or something?' I asked. 'You're a bit snarky this morning.'

'No, I'm not,' she snapped. She perched on the edge of my desk, crossed her arms over her chest and huffed once, twice, three times.

'Whatever you say.' I shrugged. Liani had warned me that Sia's pregnancy hormones were here to stay.

'Four months,' she said. 'I'm four months pregnant already.'

Before I had a chance to reply, Liani had hurried over and swept Sia into a hug. 'Oh darling,' she said.

'I'll have a baby in about five months … a real-life baby,' Sia cried. 'I've spent longer deciding whether to try a new haircut! The doc was so happy for me too, suggesting prams and cribs … it made me sick. Well, even more sick. What am I supposed to do? I've taken this job and … I'm sorry I'm letting you down, Liani. I have no idea what happens next — where's the parenting book titled *I'm Completely Unprepared for Having a Baby Because I Didn't Realise I was Pregnant, I Just Thought I was Fat, Tired and Stressed*, huh? Someone should write that book. I'd buy it.'

I held my breath as she spoke, petrified I'd let out a nervous cough or hiccup.

'You're not letting me down,' Liani said, stroking Sia's hair. 'Put that out of your head right now. We're going to work this out together, okay? In fact, you know what, let's do it. You and me: kitchen.'

Sia looked petrified. 'Now?'

Liani held out her hand to help Sia stand up. 'You're four months, honey. Let's not wait any longer.' She turned to me. 'Josie, can you follow up on those save-the-date emails from last week? Mya and I are dying to hear if we've got a nibble from Maxxy. Might be good to make some calls?'

'On it,' I said. 'Whatever you need.'

As they walked towards the kitchen, I heard Liani telling Sia, 'I'll get you a lolly, sweetie, and we'll talk it out. Research shows that eating lollies brightens your day, and also increases your chances of becoming rich and highly successful. That last bit may or may not be true.'

Based on Liani's theory, I was destined for great things — I'd been powering through the lolly jar on a daily basis.

Back at my desk, I found I'd received quite a few RSVPs for the launch from a mixture of B- and C-grade stars. Now I just needed to convince the A-listers that our launch would be the hottest one around. You can do this, I reminded myself. You're no longer an intern; you're inviting them to an incredible red-carpet event. If anything, they should be calling *you* begging for their names to be put on the door.

Hours — and about a litre of soft drink — later, I'd made serious progress. I'd managed to get forty-nine excited 'Yes' responses; twenty-four counts of 'Maybe, send over the details again'; and six flat-out 'No' replies (one agent told me her client — a star on a much-loved soapie — didn't 'rough it'). I'd also left countless voicemails (each one excruciating); got two wrong numbers and accidentally extended an invite to a 64-year-old florist called Nancy.

To make sure I had my pitch down, I'd saved Darlene Wright, Maxxy's manager, for last. I punched in her number, trying not to be intimidated by her photo on Maxxy's website — she had huge red hair, a huge blue power jacket and huge diamond earrings. Something told me she'd have a huge attitude too. But I didn't get a chance to find out: the phone rang three times, then went to voicemail. Caught off guard, I left a longwinded message about the launch.

I was rereading the spreadsheet when my phone blasted to life, showing an unknown number.

'Er, hello, *indi*, Josie speaking,' I said.

'Darlene here,' said the woman on the other end of the line, before clearing her throat with the grace of a kitchen garbage disposal. 'I had a missed call and voicemail from this number?'

'Hello, Darlene, ah, yes, that was me, Josie Browning,' I said. 'So you heard my voicemail?'

'No.'

'Oh.' I paused, waiting for her to say more. She didn't. 'So ... I was calling to tell you about a fantastic opportunity for Max that —'

'It's Maxxy.'

'Yes, sorry,' I blabbered. 'So, I'm calling from *indi* magazine — well, we're technically a website — and

I wanted to follow up on a save-the-date email I sent through. We're having a launch soon and we'd love Maxxy to perform if she's available.'

'*Bindi*?' Darlene said. 'Never heard of it.'

'Ah, no, it's *indi* … as in "i" for island, "n" for neck, "d" for dagwood dog —'

She cut me off. 'Still never heard of it. I must have lost the email.'

Another eardrum-rattling cough echoed down the line.

'Look, I'm in a rush,' she continued. 'Who else will be there? And, in addition to Maxxy's usual rate, is there also an appearance fee on offer?'

'Um, a lot of fantastic people will be there,' I replied, knowing full well I wasn't answering the question. 'And I'll have to get back to you about the fees —'

'Will hair, make-up and transport be provided too?' Darlene fired back.

'Um …'

'You do know she's based up north now? When is this, anyway?'

That was a question I *did* know the answer to. 'It's not this Saturday, but the next one.'

'So this is a last-minute invite?' Darlene snarled. 'Was Maxxy your second or third choice?'

'No, no, she's top of the list, I can assure you,' I said. 'Let me get all those answers for you and I'll call you straight back.'

'Email's better,' she said, and told me a different address to the one on Maxxy's website.

I lunged for a pen and scribbled it down. 'Well, thanks for your time. I'll be in touch about Max — I mean Maxxy,' I said, but Darlene had already hung up.

Bloody hell. I was completely at a loss how to answer Darlene's questions.

My mobile rang with another unknown number and a little tingle of excitement ran through me. Maybe it was Darlene calling to say Maxxy would be delighted to come after all.

Of course, it wasn't her.

'Josie!' a man's voice boomed. 'It's Professor Fillsmore.'

'Filly, hi! Is everything okay?' Uni hadn't gone back yet, so I wasn't sure why he'd be calling.

'You betcha it is — and what about you? Still loving being a real-life reporter?'

I winced. 'You bet. Living the dream.'

'Great — couldn't be happier for you,' he said. 'I bet you're wondering why I'm calling, hey? Well, your journo class from last year is heading up to the city tomorrow to meet and greet with a few media outlets and we'd love for you to come along.'

Ever the nerdbot, I knew the first-year curriculum from left to right and top to bottom, and was a hundred per cent sure that hadn't been a part of it.

'That's a little last-minute … and we're technically still on holidays.'

'Yeah, it's a bit of a late addition, to be honest … and we sort of forgot to tell you about it,' Filly admitted. 'Sorry! I'll level with you. We got word late last semester that we need to put even more of a focus on prac and networking. The industry's changing and it's the only way to keep up.'

'It sounds good,' I said, 'but with my fulltime job at *indi* I probably have all the practical skills I need for now. If it's okay with you I'll give it a miss and —'

'Sorry, I didn't phrase that properly,' he said. 'Josie, you have to come along, it's a compulsory part of the course.'

'Filly, I understand, but my workload's huge and —'

'I get it,' Filly said, softening his tone. 'Your marks are stellar, you've got a busy job — you're kicking goals. But what's compulsory for the others has to be compulsory for you too. It's got to be completed before semester kicks off. We've already stretched the rules for you about as far as we can.'

'I know,' I said, wishing he wasn't right. 'I guess I'll be there.'

'We're meeting outside the big post office in the city — you know the one?'

'Yeah, I do.' I'd once walked past that post office with my dress tucked into my undies, but Filly didn't need to know that. 'Who are the meet-and-greets with?'

'Still finalising the itinerary, but it's shaping up to be a cracker ... Hang on, do you want to show us around your new workplace? Maybe arrange a writing workshop with your editor?'

I visualised a group of students stampeding into the office as Liani suffered through one of Mya's long-winded phone calls, and Sia had a pregnancy meltdown at her desk. 'You know what ... we're on deadline, so it's all a bit ... you know ... frantic. Maybe one day.' Or never.

'Alrighty. Well, dress to impress and I'll see you at 9 am outside the post office.'

'Bye, Filly.' I hung up, realising I now had to ask Liani for a day off when she needed me most, *and* scrape together a respectable outfit.

An hour later, Liani and Sia emerged from the kitchen — both tear-stained, both exhausted. I mouthed, 'Here if you need anything,' to Sia, and she nodded and returned to her seat.

'Any luck with Maxxy?' Liani asked me.

'I spoke with her manager. How do you feel about paying for hair, make-up and transport?'

'All three? That pushy, self-entitled —'

'She also has gig rates ... and an appearance fee,' I added.

Liani released a string of expletives, which sounded odd coming from her usually polite mouth. 'She's Maxxy, not the queen of England. She's barely been on the scene for five seconds! Besides, if we offer every guest those perks we'll be out of business before we've officially launched the new site. Try to talk some sense into her people.' She swore again, and I wondered if she was crunching numbers in her head. 'Pass me that pad, could you, hon?'

She huffed and scribbled, then huffed and scribbled some more.

'Introducing the new launch rules for everyone,' she said, passing me the pad.

I scanned the list. 'Okay, so no appearance fees ...'

'Unless it's the *only* way to get Maxxy across the line,' Liani added, 'but don't tell her manager that.'

I nodded and kept reading. 'Don't offer hair and make-up — but if they ask, then tackle on a case-by-case basis as it'll depend on how much we want them there. Don't mention transport — but if they ask for transfers or cab charges, say yes. That all sounds easy enough,' I finished. 'I'll email Darlene the details before I leave.'

'Thanks, Jose.'

'Oh, and Liani ... I hate to do this — like, really hate to do this — but I might need a favour tomorrow ...'

Luckily, Liani scored eleven out of ten on the Niceness Scale when I told her about the excursion, although she requested I check my work emails on my phone during the day so the launch-planning tasks didn't get bottle-necked. I knew that I'd be making up the lost hours in my own time; there was too much to do.

It wasn't until I was packing up for the day that Sia popped over for a chat. 'So, um, I'm sorry about before, hon. I'm a walking stress hormone at the moment.'

'It's fine. Take it easy, yeah?'

She dropped her voice to a whisper. 'Can you imagine if I was still working for Rae? She'd have me swing past an event on the way to the maternity ward … Hey, Jose?'

'Yeah?' I yawned, exhausted after another huge day.

'Any idea why Edwina couriered me *this*?' Sia pulled out a basket from beneath her desk. Inside was a fluffy plush puppy and three of the smallest pastel onesies I had ever seen.

'Um … funny story actually,' I said.

'I bet.'

'I am *so* sorry. Edwina bailed me up at the wellness event yesterday and basically had me pinned in the corner, asking me questions.'

Sia shook her head. 'You're going to have to strengthen your defences against those girls. They sniff out stories like Scotland Yard police dogs.'

'I feel terrible —' I started.

'Oh, it's all good,' Sia said. 'I'll be the size of a fridge in a couple of months! Everyone might as well know now.'

I snorted with laughter and she pulled me in for a hug, squeezing me like a rag doll.

'This is a seriously maternal hug,' I teased her. 'You're going to make a great mum, you know that?'

'Tread carefully, Browning.'

'It's true,' I said, pleased to see Sia blushing at my compliment.

I waved goodbye to the team, reminding Liani that I'd only be a call away tomorrow. But first, I had some well-earned Josie-and-James time to catch up on that evening (did I mention I have a boyfriend?) and a wheel of brie cheese to demolish.

Or maybe not.

My eyes widened as Steph sliced off another hunk of brie the size of her fist.

'Dad threw a fit and begged me to move home this afternoon,' she said, shaking her head.

I could feel a rant brewing.

'He reckons he can't handle me working as a waitress, living here in this dump — his words — and then going back overseas to see Tim … He thinks I'm better than all this. You should see the emails I'm getting from him and Mum. They're soaked in guilt and self-loathing. These are the same people who openly cheat on each other, and I'm expected to listen to them? I'll show you the rubbish they're saying …'

James and I exchanged looks as Steph hurried off to her room to collect her phone.

'Didn't she have a shift tonight?' he muttered so Steph couldn't hear.

'It fell through, but they'll buzz if they get busy,' I whispered.

'Right … Hey, you look kinda different. Have you been relaxing on the beach in Hawaii without me?'

I smirked. 'Okay, you know that scene in *The Wizard of Oz* when they primp and preen Dorothy? That was me at work yesterday — there was even a wicked witch!'

'I'll say it again: you get paid to do this stuff?' James laughed. 'Tough life for some, J-Bird!'

'Shuddup!'

'Alright, alright.' He lowered his voice. 'Hey, do Steph's parents *really* have affairs?'

'Have I never told you?' I whispered, remembering the first time Steph had explained her fascinating family dynamic to me. Last I'd heard, her dad had been seeing Rae Swanson, of all people, and her mum was hooking up with the landscape architect. Now that her folks were getting a new en suite installed, Steph was betting money on the plumber joining in on the fun too.

It was strange seeing Steph so fired up. Usually she loved pissing off her dad with her outlandish adventures, but maybe nineteen years of defending her right to be a troublemaker had taken their toll. Or maybe she just really missed Tim. In the past week he'd moved from India to Cambodia to help out in an orphanage for a month and was begging Steph to join him. Only her serious lack of funds — and her frozen credit card — were holding her back. The way she saw it, Tim was looking after beautiful little kids, while she was selling out by serving suits their daily coffee.

'Just because my father sold his soul doesn't mean I should,' Steph said, storming back into the room and waving her phone. 'Here, look at this: *Your mother and I love you* ... blah blah blah ... *but that doesn't stop us feeling disappointed about what you're doing with your life. Move home now and we can prepare a plan for your future.*' She threw her phone on the couch. 'I had a plan with Tim. I *had* it worked out. I was going to pay back every cent from the trip. Besides, I'm nineteen, not fifty! Dad's like a walking superannuation ad with all his preparing and planning.'

'Maybe he just wants to help set you up?' I suggested.

'Please. That's alright for you to say, Little Miss I Have My Life Together and Probably Always Will,' she snapped. 'What would you know?'

Silence hung in the air.

'Steph,' James said, almost as a warning, as I sucked in a breath. Steph had never so much as raised her voice at me before; and while she'd always teased me about being 'wise beyond my years', I could hear a new hardness in her voice.

'I think you've had enough brie,' was all I managed, as I collected the cheese and carried it to the kitchen.

My tear ducts burned from Steph's cutting words. Everything wasn't exactly rosy in the Browning household, but in a sick way she was right. What would I know about an interfering father? Mine cared so little he'd run away. As for having my life together: a few months earlier, Mum had been in hospital and we were struggling to pay the bills. Things were improving, but I was still scraping to afford rent and food.

Even though I hadn't told Steph the whole story about my dad, she knew enough to know she'd crossed a line.

'Josie, I'm sorry,' she said, following me to the kitchen. 'I'm an awful friend. I'm selfish, I'm not worthy of being in your presence, I'm a loser —'

'You're worse than Kat when she's sucking up,' I said. 'You're forgiven! Just ... don't forget who cares about you — and I'm not just talking about me.'

Steph squeezed my hand. 'I'm sorry, babe ... I am. I love you like a little sis, you know that, right?'

'Yeah. And you're like my older sis. Don't worry, not too much older,' I added before she jumped in.

'Anyway, so how *is* Tim, Steph?' James asked, not-so-subtly changing the subject.

'He's loving the orphanage,' she said. 'Says it's the best thing he's ever done. That he's found what he wants to do with his life.'

'What, go on holidays forever?' I asked.

'No,' Steph said, laughing for the first time all evening. 'Work with little kids. Be a primary school teacher.'

'No way!' I said.

She nodded. 'I wasn't so sure either, but then I saw some photos of him … He had this look in his eyes that I've never seen before. Maybe he'll never come home.'

'He will,' I said, knowing that he would have no choice eventually. He wasn't made of money.

'Makes you think, huh?' said James. 'Maybe there's a whole bunch of jobs out there that we don't know we're meant to be doing.'

'Maybe I'm supposed to be a tightrope walker, or a kazoo cleaner, or a heart surgeon — I just haven't worked it out yet … or got over my crazy fear of blood and guts,' Steph said. 'All I know is I'm a waitress 'til I get over to Cambodia. What about you, Jose? Think there's another life out there you're supposed to be living, and you just haven't discovered it yet?'

'Um … maybe,' I said, trying to fit in.

James pulled me onto his lap. 'Yeah, right, JB. You and your computer are a match made in heaven. Trust me, let's all regroup in thirty years and compare — I betcha Josie will be a world-famous editor.'

I grinned. 'And you?'

'Three-time Grammy award-winner, of course. What about you, Steph?'

'Happy sounds good, for a start,' Steph said. 'Anyway it doesn't look like I'm getting the call-up from work so I could make us a stir-fry for dinner?'

I paused. James had reservations for us at a restaurant around the corner. 'Um, it's just that James —'

'Is allergic to ginger,' he interrupted, lying his dimples off. 'But otherwise a stir-fry sounds great. Thanks.'

Steph cheered and hurried into the kitchen.

'What about the restaurant?' I asked James.

He shrugged. 'She needs you. We'll try to catch up just us later this week, plus don't forget we're seeing your family on the weekend. You'll be sick of me by Sunday.'

I wasn't much of a gambler, but I would have bet my pitiful pay cheque he was wrong.

'You're the best,' I said. The words 'I love you' screamed inside my head, but I didn't want to say them with Steph clattering away at the kitchen counter.

He grinned. 'I know, it's exhausting.'

I tossed a pillow at his head. He caught it like a footy player, then threw himself onto the couch. Steph's phone starting ringing beneath him.

'Hey, that's mine,' she called. 'Can you see who —'

But he'd already answered it. 'Mate!' he cheered. 'Guys, Tim's on Skype!'

The three of us crowded around the tiny screen, pulling faces at my cousin. Tim's hair had grown longer since I'd last seen him, and he was sporting a huge smile and a half-arsed attempt at a beard, although it was more skin than hair in most places.

'Ma people!' he yelled, and it was as though he was sitting with us on the couch, like old times.

We all jostled to tell stories, interrupted each other, and met the two tiny Cambodian boys Tim had hooked up on his hip and tugging on the back of his shorts. Then we hatched a crazy plan to smuggle Steph over in some luggage (okay, so it needed finessing). Suddenly I realised how much I'd missed our ragtag little group. We'd been so busy following our own paths the past few months that the magic had slipped a little, and it was amazing to reconnect.

My heart panged as I wondered what Angel was up to, but the sound of Tim singing a Cambodian lullaby — much to the delight of the little boys, who yelled and clapped along, apparently immune to its sleep-inducing properties — snapped me out of it. I had another busy day ahead of me tomorrow, but until then I wanted to soak up every minute with my friends. Maybe sneak the almost-destroyed wheel of brie out of the fridge when Steph wasn't looking too.

Maybe … if 'maybe' meant 'definitely going to happen'.

10.

I woke up the next morning with memories of excursions-gone-wrong imprinted in my brain: throwing up on buses; getting spinach caught in my teeth and no one telling me for the entire day; and being partnered with the class weirdo who rubbed boogers under the seat on the bus.

Sensing my bad mood — yelling at the toaster was the giveaway — Steph loaned me a dress to help me 'impress'. It was sleek and slate-coloured, and I teamed it with a newish pair of peep-toe heels, which, surprise, surprise, hurt my feet. (I was considering becoming a Band-Aid ambassador.) Combined with my fancy blow-dried hair — still holding up from the wellness event — and mani and pedi, I didn't look too bad.

Not even receiving a text from James (*Have a good day, JB xx*) could stop me fretting about the to-do list that I couldn't get to at work today — well, that and facing my classmates for the first time since taking the job at *indi*. I was out of the loop with the class's social scene — who was clocking up the best (and most) internships, who was hooking up, who was breaking up, who had the most followers on Twitter, whose blogs were getting the most hits, and who was hating on me for scoring an industry job so soon.

But after arriving at the post office, it didn't take long to realise I hadn't missed much at all. Everything was as it always had been. Tony and Jeff, two news journo wannabes, were salivating because our first stop was at one of the biggest newspapers in the country.

'People still need news, right?' Tony ranted to Jeff. 'And they need somewhere to get it — and that's where we'll come in. Newspapers, websites, magazines — this industry is far from dead. Hey, Josie!'

'Ah, hey, guys,' I said, surprised they were talking to me. We weren't exactly friends — more like competitors.

'Well, you look like a bit of alright,' Tony blurted out. 'Have you had a haircut or something?'

'Er, thanks … I think,' I said, remembering why we hadn't stayed in contact. 'No, it's the same old hair.'

'You look different,' said Jeff. 'I don't remember you looking this good at uni.'

'I don't remember you being this much of an asshat at uni,' I retorted. 'Oh wait, yes I do.'

'I know what it is, you're taller!' Tony said. 'Are you wearing, like, platforms or something? They're sexy.'

'They're just shoes.' I rolled my eyes, wishing I'd ignored

Filly's instructions to dress to impress and worn flats. I wanted to fit in, hide away, *blend*.

Jeff smacked his lips. 'First to break into the industry, now this "new you", huh?'

'Would you guys grow up? I'm the same old Josie,' I insisted.

But as the boys rabbited on, I couldn't help but wonder if the city and new job were changing me more than I realised.

'This industry is evolving — and evolving fast. If you don't keep up, you'll all get squashed like a daddy-long-legs,' said Rupert, the *City Journal*'s award-winning deputy editor. He was a wrinkled, weathered man who looked like he'd spent a few too many weekends falling asleep in the sun with a drink in hand.

Tony cleared his throat. 'Keep up how, sir?'

Rupert exhaled. 'The fact you have to ask that worries me,' he said. 'I know I'm meant to roll out the "work hard and your dreams will come true" line, but the truth is it's tough, and it's changing, so it's not for the faint of heart. If you're not up for that, you may as well walk out that door right now.'

Silence had never sounded so loud. Filly rubbed his bald head, no doubt wondering whether he should herd us out of the building before Rupert motivated us right into the ground, like a verbal sledgehammer.

Despite his gruff manner, Rupert seemed pleased to have students hanging off his every word. He ushered us through a side door — into the newsroom. It was filled with the buzz of phones ringing, people talking, shouting and laughing and had a fast-paced energy I'd never felt before. Not one of the journalists glanced in our direction until Rupert shouted for them to give us a wave.

As Rupert concluded his presentation, I was horrified to hear my phone buzzing. It was Liani.

'Sorry, it's my editor,' I said as Rupert glared at me, the lines on his crinkled face becoming deeper and defined. 'Do you mind if I —'

'Hang it up or answer it outside,' Rupert said, shooing me away.

'Liani?' I said, rushing out the door. 'I have to be quick, but is everything okay?'

'Sorry to interrupt, hon, just wanted to see if you've heard back from Maxxy's manager yet? I know it's wishful thinking, but I was hoping the email fairies may be looking out for us.'

'Not since I last checked,' I said. 'Do you want me to try her again?'

'You know what, hon, I'll tell Mya we're still working on it and we'll talk tomorrow. You enjoy your day.' She said goodbye and hung up.

'Josie!' Filly bellowed behind me. 'What did I tell you about turning off your phone?'

'Er … don't do it?' I joked.

Our group poured out the door and onto the pathway, laughing as Tony impersonated Rubert's gruff voice. Filly shook his head, but I caught a twinkle in his eye.

'Well, you've blown any chance of ever working at the *City Journal*,' he said to me. 'I'll tell you that for free.'

'You're kidding!'

I didn't even want to work there. But being told that I was blacklisted from one of the country's top publications before I'd even finished my degree wasn't ideal. 'Should I apologise to Rupert again?'

'I think it's best if you don't,' Filly said. 'I, ah, may have told him your name was Mary-Jane. That'll let you off the hook in the future, should you ever slip him your CV. Just put that damn phone on silent before our next meet-and-greet.'

I smiled. 'You got it. Thanks, Filly, you're a real hero.' If heroes were sweaty, tubby and collected fishing rods.

Filly cleared his throat, signalling the soppier portion of our conversation was over. 'Alright, gang … let's keep moving,' he said, gesturing for us to follow him. 'We have another stop and this time, Josie, it's right up your alley.'

'No way,' I murmured, coming to a standstill in front of a magnificent building that housed the biggest and most powerful magazine company in the country. A building that I was all too familiar with.

I'd had some of the best and worst moments of my life because of that building. Well, because of the *people* inside that building. Fine, because of *one* person inside that building: Rae Swanson, queen of the glossies, former editor of *Sash* magazine and current editor of the glamorous and high-end *Marilyn*.

Now Filly wanted me to step into the building. Her building.

'Filly, I'm not feeling so well. I don't think I can go in there,' I said.

I was about as convincing as the times I tried to wag PE in high school.

'C'mon in, guys,' said Filly, ignoring my feeble excuse as he herded us inside. 'The receptionist is taking us on a tour.'

I cringed as the chic and polished people filing into the foyer ogled our odd little group. We may as well have lined up in two rows and held hands, like eager kindergarten students on their way to a petting zoo.

I winced at the blisters threatening to erupt on my heels, but was relieved I looked presentable — not quite glamazon, but I was making progress. I caught a look at my reflection in one of the floor-to-ceiling mirrors that lined the walls of the foyer and realised things had changed since the first time I'd rushed through this building's doors. I didn't have an orange juice stain down the front of my dress, I was wearing nice heels and I'd done my hair — even if the blow-wave was morphing into more 'shaggy bird's nest' than 'shaggy chic' from the humidity. Maybe I was finally slotting into this shiny, sparkly world where everyone looked perfect from the outside.

But still, I worried that Rae might stride through the lift doors any minute and zap me with her icy glare. Did my hair really look okay? Was this nail polish colour the right choice? And last but undeniably not least, could anyone tell I was wearing ill-fitting undies? A quick scan in the mirrors proved my fear correct — my undies were bunching up in all the wrong places.

'Crap,' I muttered.

Naturally, that was also the moment I heard a soft, sweet voice calling my name.

I glanced around, but all I could see was Filly repeatedly checking his watch then rechecking the clock on the wall.

I heard my name again. I turned and saw Edwina standing next to me in skinny-cut pants and a loose white top. Her long dark hair was so shiny it looked like she'd stepped straight off the set of a shampoo commercial.

'Josie Browning, it *is* you!' she said, flicking her mane. 'What are you doing here in my world?'

The way she rolled my surname off her perfect pink little tongue made me feel nauseous with embarrassment.

'Um, hi! I'm here because …'

I trailed off as I gazed around the class group. Tony was scoffing a bag of steaming hot chips; Jeff was scratching the eczema on his inner arm; and Filly was booming out a voicemail message, ending with, 'Just wondering where you are … I'm in the foyer with a herd of rabid kids.' That about summed it up.

Edwina's lashes flickered with impatience as she waited for a reply. But I couldn't tell her why I was here or who I was here with. My two worlds couldn't collide yet — not while I was in charge of schmoozing for *indi*.

I tried again. 'Um, well, I'm here because —'

'I knew it!' she interrupted. 'You're here for *it*, right?'

This conversation needed subtitles or a translator because I had no idea what she was talking about.

She sniffed. 'Fine, make me say it … *Marilyn*.'

Familiar nerves rebooted in my stomach at the mention of Rae's prized magazine. '*Marilyn*? No, not at all.'

Edwina eyed me up and down. 'You're not here for the features writer interview? But you look so great … I almost didn't recognise you.'

Another of her trademark backhanded compliments.

'Look,' I said, 'I'll be honest, I'm here for a —'

'Oh, hi darling, nice to see you too,' Edwina cut in, talking to a girl with short curly hair in an orange dress who was walking towards the lift. Once she was out of earshot, Edwina wrinkled her nose. 'Urgh, that outfit was so cheap.'

'Er, yeah,' I nodded, thinking half my wardrobe was hand-me-ups from Kat, hand-me-downs from Steph or bargain-bin clothes from designers who were otherwise out of my price range.

'What were we saying before she rudely interrupted us?' she said, then went on without waiting for me to answer. 'It's like I said to Rae at my soirée the other day, some people are totally clueless about fashion ... Wait, did I see you at my party? No, of course not ... But I suppose I'll catch you at that resort launch up north next week? I've bought three bikinis already. So naughty!'

'Ah, yeah, that ... I'm so busy with work that I have to miss it,' I mumbled, not wanting to tell her I hadn't been invited. 'Deadlines — you know how it is. Maybe I'll see you at the next one?'

'Maybe ...' Her voice trailed off as she noticed my uni class. 'What the ...? Is it Bring a Freak to Work Day?'

I forced a laugh. 'I know, right? Weirdos.'

'Security are slacking off letting them in here. Anyway, I better run, so kiss, kiss,' she said.

Of course I misread the situation and leaned in for cheek-to-cheek contact. Edwina didn't respond, although her stiffened body posture said it all.

'Hey Josie, who's your friend?' I heard Filly ask behind me.

My stomach churned. Please don't talk about fishing, please don't talk about fishing, I silently begged him.

Edwina raised her eyebrow and turned to shake Filly's hand. 'Hello … I'm Edwina, from *Marilyn* magazine.' Once done, I saw her wipe her hand on the back of her pants — Filly's sweaty paws had struck again.

'You work here?' he boomed at Edwina. 'Are you the receptionist I'm supposed to meet with?'

Edwina pursed her lips. 'No. Are you Josie's … father?'

Filly snorted. 'Please. Do I look old enough to be her father?' He did, but I wasn't going to be the one to tell him. 'I'm Professor Fillsmore — Josie's tutor and lecturer. We're here on an excursion to show the kids the city. In fact, if you work here, perhaps *you* could take us around?'

I didn't know which was worse: Filly revealing I was a student and mentioning the words 'excursion' and 'kids' in the same sentence, or him proposing that Edwina take us on our tour. Any credibility I'd built up with her in the past week was now about to be suffocated by the overwhelming scent of Filly's cologne.

'Ah, no, Filly, we'll wait,' I said, in an attempt to save the situation.

Edwina's eyes widened. 'Hang on … lecturer?' she asked. 'Josie, are you doing your master's or a PhD?'

Filly laughed. 'She's barely started second year.' He may as well have shown Edwina baby pictures of me running under the sprinkler with my undies on my head. 'Anyway, it was great meeting you, Edwina. I have to make another call ... excuse me.'

'You little prodigy,' Edwina said, drawing each word out. 'You haven't even graduated yet? Wait, you're getting paid to work, right? Tell me you're getting paid.'

I nodded.

'Girls are going to scratch your eyes out when they hear about this. I know I would have. I'm kidding!' she added when she noticed my horrified expression.

'What do you mean?' I asked.

'I receive about a hundred emails a day asking me if there's a job at *Marilyn* — and most of those people are graduates. And look at you, waltzing into the industry at your age, in this economic climate. Josie Browning, you are far more fascinating than you first seem.'

I didn't know what I felt more uncomfortable with: her latest backhanded compliment or the way she full-named me.

She cocked her head to one side. 'I have to go, but you should give me your number so we can catch up — we're bumping into each other this much anyway.'

Edwina rattled off her digits. Trying to hide my shock, I added her ten precious numbers into my phone, then hurriedly gave her mine. Liani would have been so proud — I'd schmoozed *and* had the evidence to prove it.

'No doubt I'll see you soon ... prodigy,' said Edwina, before sauntering off with her hips swaying.

Tony appeared by my side, groaning with lust like a horny schoolboy. 'Who was *that*? They sure do breed them nice in the city.'

I elbowed him in the arm, hoping no one had heard.

'Great news, team.' Filly's voice thundered through the foyer as he slid his phone into his pocket. 'Our tour guide is ready. We had a mix-up with the times — my bad. Now, stay on my trail. We're going up to level sixteen.'

I sighed with relief. *Marilyn* magazine was on level four, so I was safe. I stuffed a handful of Tony's chips into my mouth and followed Filly into the lift.

When we got to level sixteen, I quickly ducked into the bathroom. When I came out (wedgie fixed, for now) I looked down the hallway to the right, then the left. I couldn't see my group anywhere. They can't have gone far, I thought, taking a stab and going right.

I teetered past doorway after doorway, my feet aching in my heels. Suddenly I heard voices coming from around the corner, so I powered on, eager to catch Filly and the others.

But when I turned the corner, I realised it wasn't my group. Not even close. Instead of a shabby bunch of students, seven well-dressed, glossy girls and guys stood in a row along a wide stretch of wall leading towards a closed black door. Not everyone was talking — some had their heads buried in their phones or their folders —

but the ones who were sounded nervous. The guy at the front of the line was tapping his foot and staring into space.

I approached a girl at the end of the line closest to me. She looked poised and calm, until I said, 'Hi there,' and she narrowed her eyes, looking suspicious.

'I don't suppose you've seen a group of … um … people go past?' I asked. 'Tall guy with a bald head leading the pack? Probably accidentally trashing the place?'

'Bald? No, can't say I have.' She shrugged. 'Sorry.'

'Thanks anyway.' I pulled out my phone to call Filly in defeat.

The black door opened and a plump woman with blonde hair and thick black specs strutted out, ushering a beautiful girl with a lowered head and drooping shoulders. 'We'll stay in touch,' she told the girl, but her sharp tone suggested otherwise. The girl wiped away tears as she rushed past me.

'I need a drink,' the blonde woman muttered, eyeing the remaining line. I felt her eyes rest on me. 'You there, pacing girl, you're up.'

'Er, me?' I said. 'Sorry, I think there's been some confusion. I'm actually here with —'

'Do I look like I'm in the mood to argue?' the woman said, readjusting her glasses. 'You're standing in the line, correct?'

'Well, technically, I'm standing *near* the line, but —'

'I get that you're nervous, but it's now or never. Put that phone away and come with me.'

And so, fearful of ending up on the wrong side of this surprisingly scary woman, I followed her through the black door, mouthing 'I'm sorry' to the rest of the group, who were drilling me with death stares.

They needn't have worried, because what I discovered on the other side of the door was so petrifying it had the potential to knock me out cold for the rest of the day. Sitting behind a long glass desk with a signature skinny cap in hand was the editor of *Marilyn* magazine herself: Rae Swanson.

'Crap!' I squeaked.

'Indeed,' Rae said dryly. She turned to the woman who'd shown me in. 'Margie, would you give me a moment alone with this candidate, please?'

'Rae, we discussed this, we need to make a joint decision,' the woman retorted.

'I know, and we will,' Rae said. 'I'm asking for a moment, not your credit card details.'

Margie huffed as she stormed past me, slamming the door on her way out. Rae took a slow, deliberate sip of her coffee, then locked her eyes on mine. I tried to take a step towards her, but it felt as though my feet were superglued to the carpet.

'Sit,' Rae said.

As I shuffled towards the table and sat down, the air felt thick, as though I was breathing in sludge.

'Rae, please let me explain before you —'

'I don't remember adding your name to my candidate list,' she said, and I immediately clamped my mouth shut. 'I don't remember calling you up to invite you to this interview. I don't remember thinking that Josie Browning would be a fantastic addition to the *Marilyn* features team. Yet here you are, sitting before me in our corporate meeting room, and I bet Liani doesn't have a clue you're sneaking around behind her back.'

'I swear, I have no idea what you're talking about,' I stammered. 'I'm in the building for a uni excursion. I'm still at *indi* with Liani — I love it. I ... I got separated from my group, that's all. I didn't even know interviews took place up here.'

'Are you trying to prove me wrong for what happened at *Sash*?' Rae asked, leaning forward. 'I rarely give second chances. You say you're not here for an interview, but let's be honest, your appearance suggests otherwise.'

I gulped. 'I swear I'm not. I'm just lost. That's it.'

Rae released a small smirk. 'Lost? You're not here to barge your way into a job?'

I shook my head. 'No. I mean, I respect you and your magazine, but ... no.'

'There's no portfolio tucked in your handbag? No referees you want me to call? No hard sell on why you deserve to work here?'

'No, none of that, sorry.'

Rae paused, then nodded. 'Fine. Send Margie and the next candidate in on your way out.'

'Of course,' I said, standing up.

'You know, Josie, I've been following *indi*. Even read a few of your columns. They've got ... potential.'

'Thanks,' I said. *Potential*. It mightn't have sounded like much, but to me it was like being told Rae was giving me a million dollars. I repressed the urge to throw myself into a body-slide over the glass desk and wrap my arms around her lean frame in gratitude.

'Keep pushing yourself,' she said. 'Based on your email, I can tell you have a lot of passion — more than I probably gave you credit for. Just make sure it comes through in your *indi* writing too.'

My hand rushed to my mouth. 'Wait ... you saw my email?'

Rae shrugged. 'Word travels fast and emails travel faster. You've got a knack for personal essay writing — you should aim to own the genre one day.'

'I'm so embarrassed —'

'Josie, snap out of it,' Rae said in her usual tough-love way. 'You think I haven't been embarrassed? You think

I haven't put myself out of my comfort zone? You think I haven't cared too much about what people think?'

'Um … no?'

She threw her hands in the air. 'Ohhh, of course I did, I'm human — but I learned to put it behind me. If you want to cut it in this industry — and your columns show me that you *do* want that — you're going to have to do the same. Stop worrying about who read that email. You should print it off and get it framed as a reminder to stay authentic.'

I laughed, but quickly realised she wasn't joking. 'Oh. Oh, okay,' I managed, although I couldn't imagine myself doing that.

It was alright for Rae. She already fitted the industry mould with her sophisticated looks and designer wardrobe. Me? I was just a girl from the country with a fading fake tan, good uni marks and a blow-dry.

Rae looked me up and down. 'Josie, sometimes being yourself is harder than being someone else, but it's important to try.'

I lowered my head. 'Thanks, and I truly am sorry for today. I swear this is the last crazy thing you'll ever see or hear of me doing.'

Rae's lips curled upwards, the closest I'd seen to a smile. 'Why make promises you can't keep?'

I scuttled out the door, my heart pounding from adrenaline.

My phone vibrated: Filly. 'Josie, where are you?' he said. 'We've finished the tour and we're back in the foyer, ready to leave. Did you hurt yourself? Are you lost?'

'No, not any more,' I said, looking back towards the black door and the queue of hopefuls lined up outside.

'You scared me.' Filly sighed. 'I forgot to get everyone to sign the insurance papers, then you go missing and —'

'Relax, I'll be right there.'

I weaved through the hallways, hardly registering the floor-to-ceiling-length magazine covers on the walls or the packs of women in power outfits striding past. I silently congratulated myself on surviving another terrifying encounter with Rae. Her words pounded on repeat: *Keep pushing yourself*, *You have a lot of passion* and *Stay authentic*. I may have missed most of the excursion, but I couldn't help thinking I'd received a more important lesson.

Not that I'd tell Filly that.

11.

The next day, catching up with work was as painful as I'd predicted. With only a week and a half to go until the launch, organising was my top priority. But, as the office minion, I was also responsible for all the fun-filled 'pleb' chores, such as printer-fixing. Today, 'The Beast' — christened during a particularly stressful afternoon in my first week at *indi* — beeped like a truck driver with road rage as I pushed its buttons in an attempt to reset it. Meanwhile, Harrison moaned that he couldn't finish his work without his printouts.

'Oi, doll, ignore him,' said Sia, using a notebook to fan her face. 'Sweet lord, I'm like a human hot-water bottle wrapped in a doona in front of a heater at the moment. And did I tell you about the constant farting?'

'Josie, can you pop over for a second?' Liani cried out, thankfully coming to my rescue before Sia had a chance to finish *that* story.

I pulled up a seat next to Liani and tried not to stare at the mess on her desk. Piles of papers threatened to topple onto the keyboard, her favourite coffee cup was accompanied by at least four others, and the desk was dusted with crumbs. Lots and lots of crumbs.

'First things first: what's the word on Maxxy?' Liani asked.

'No luck yet. But we have plenty of other great people locked in.'

Liani sighed. 'Follow up with her manager again and, in the meantime, put some feelers out for a back-up option. We are cutting this way too fine. I want Maxxy, though, I really, really do.'

Funny what happens when you decide to plan a launch in less than three weeks, I wanted to whinge, but held my tongue. I knew Mya was pulling the strings more than Liani would ever admit.

'I'll get on it,' I assured her.

'Thanks. I also wanted to chat about your latest columns.' She paused. 'You know I love your writing, and they're getting good clicks on the site, which is ... good.'

'Good,' I repeated, wondering where she was going with this.

She squirmed in her seat. 'But as good as those stories are — and please don't take this the wrong way — from now on I need them to be *great*.'

'Okay, great.'

I pinched my hand to stop myself repeating more words back to her. The truth was, I wasn't that surprised. After my talk with Rae, I'd reread my columns and could see that, while they were well written, I had some way to go in perfecting my message. Like Rae had said, the columns showed potential, but I could dig deeper. Do more. *Be better.*

'For your next column, pick something juicy, smart and topical to sink those pearly chompers of yours into,' Liani said. 'Something to boost hits, and give us something to dangle in front of new advertisers. Something to give those glossies a run for their money.'

I nodded. 'Okay, topical ... you mean like ... voting?'

Liani stifled a chuckle. 'Sure, it's topical, but it's not hot enough to sell ... not yet anyway.'

'Um, what about dating?' I suggested. 'That's always pretty juicy. Like, how to date with phone apps, or dating with old-school rules in a new-school world ... something like that?'

'That's getting warmer ... we're in the ballpark. Think dating, relationships, guys, love —'

'Sex!' Harrison hollered.

'What?' I blurted out before I could stop myself.

Liani raised her eyebrow. 'Harrison, this is a site for smart, savvy young women — you know we don't do any of that "How to please your guy" rubbish.'

I tried not to look too thrilled by this news. I didn't know how I'd go about writing something like that, considering how confused I was on the whole matter.

'I didn't say it had to be about pleasing your guy — although that sounds like a great read — but I am saying it's the kind of topic that gets hits,' Harrison said.

Liani nodded. 'Okay ... well, we could give it an *indi* spin. Jose, I know you were talking about something similar with Sophie the model the other day. We could *really* explore the topic: who's doing it, what they're doing, where it's happening, how society has changed in its attitudes, if at all — almost like a history lesson.'

'History lesson?' Harrison cringed. 'Li, that is the least sexy thing I have ever heard — and I studied web design.'

'Er, what about the readers who haven't, you know, gone *there* yet?' I said, pretending I was asking for purely work-related reasons. 'Won't a topic like that be excluding them?'

'Josie, that's it, that's perfect! Focus the column on losing your virginity,' Liani said.

I almost choked. 'Excuse me?'

'In a general sense, of course,' she clarified. 'You can cover it all, from knowing when's the right time, to how to handle the pressure of the decision, how opinions are changing — or not — and how you feel about the topic. It'll be relatable to everyone.'

'You want me to comment on how *I* feel?'

'Well, it is an opinion column, right?' she said. 'This is great — it'll be the perfect topic for our demographic. I'm thinking a smart, cool, in-your-face essay — our readers will eat it up and come back for seconds.'

I nodded, struggling to wrap my head around the fact that I was about to write a racy column that would be accessible to the whole world, including Mum and my much-more-experienced boyfriend.

'Jose, I've got to quickly call Mya and grab a coffee, but spin out six hundred words and we'll publish it as soon as it's been edited.'

I shook my head, stunned at how quickly this conversation had unravelled. 'I'm not sure I can do this.'

Liani crossed her arms over her chest. 'Are you a writer for *indi*, Josie?'

I gulped. 'Of course, I —'

'Then you can write it,' Liani said, in a firmer tone than usual.

'Sounds good,' I managed to say, a little shaken by the strength in her voice. 'Sex me up.'

What followed was the longest, most awkward silence of all time, including when Chris Streaker farted in science in Year Nine and blamed it on Mrs Goodie. This was a gazillion times worse because: (a) I was involved; and (b) I'd just said 'Sex me up' to my boss. I could hear Harrison spluttering at his desk.

I closed my notebook. 'I'm going to get started on sex ideas — I mean, *some* ideas.'

I walked back to my desk, trying to ignore Liani's and Harrison's laughter freely rocketing around the walls of *indi* HQ.

I sat down and opened up a new document. The white page stared back at me. Even after all this time, I still didn't know how to win it over — it's not like I could shout it an iced chocolate.

A column on sex and virginity. Why, oh, why, did Harrison have to plant that seed?

'Josie, is it home time yet?' groaned Sia.

I was glad of the distraction. 'I wish. Have you had any more weird cravings?'

'Not unless pumpkin with chocolate sprinkles is weird.'

'Just a tad,' I said. 'Hey, I was meaning to ask you how you're doing? You know, really doing?'

'I'm fine,' she said, then sighed. 'Scott, on the other hand … '

I couldn't help myself. 'How'd he take it?'

Sia paused. 'He's … taking it. Taking it in, taking his time … We'll see if he wants to take it on.'

'I'm sorry.'

'He was shocked, obviously, so it's a lot to think about.' She shrugged. 'It is what it is. Dad's pretty cute though, he's surprised me. He's already put dibs on "Pa", just in case Scott's family have any ideas …' Her voice trailed off. 'Urgh, my life has turned into a clichéd soap-opera pregnancy storyline. Distract me, I'm begging you. What are you working on?'

I pointed to the blank page. 'Nothing at the moment.'

'Go on, tell me before I have to pee again. This little gremlin is using my lady-bits as a watering can.'

I lowered my eyes then mumbled, 'Liani wants a column on ... doing it.'

'You don't have to whisper, she's popped out. Anyway, I've got a corker on that topic.' Sia clapped her hands together. 'My friend was telling me about this new move —'

'Sia ... it's about *virginity*,' I said.

'Easy! Talk about your first time and ... oh.'

'Yep,' I said, relieved she'd caught on.

'Does Liani know? About you, I mean?'

'I don't think so.' The pressure of wondering whether Liani knew or not meant I was one meltdown away from yelling the information at her, then hiding out in an undisclosed location with a lifetime's supply of Hawaiian pizza. 'I feel like a fraud.'

'It's okay,' Sia insisted. 'You've written stories on politics for uni before, yeah? You've never been a politician. Or stories on fashion and you've never been a fashionista — okay, that came out wrong. But you know what I mean, right?'

'I guess.'

'You don't need to reveal your own situation — do some research instead. Talk to people, ask them about *their* first time. Throw in an expert, and some statistics and charts to give it balls.'

'Balls are a good thing?'

'Don't say a word, Harrison,' Sia said, but he'd already lost it and was cracking up again. 'Aren't you learning all this at uni, Josie? Do a call-out online asking for people to share their first-time experiences and go from there.'

'I can ask that sort of stuff?'

'Josie, you're paid to ask pervy questions — that's what makes journalism fun.'

I couldn't believe what Sia was saying. I would have been more comfortable asking people to tap dance for me in their knickers.

'If all else fails, you could always do some empirical research with your boy, eh?' She let out a giggle.

'Ha, yeah.' I forced a laugh, thinking of the lacy lingerie set collecting dust in my chest of drawers.

'Don't look so scared, hon, I'm kidding,' Sia said. 'Anyway, good luck.'

I was one line into a draft call-out — *Looking for case studies to share their first-time story* (something told me 'cherry-popping' wouldn't be appropriate) — when Liani showed up next to my desk.

'So, Mya let me know she isn't sold on the column idea after all,' she said, sipping her coffee.

'Oh?' I tried my best to fake disappointment, which was hard when every part of me wanted to jump in the air and squeal with joy. I wasn't ready to put my virginity under the microscope yet (or ever). 'Hey, what Mya wants, Mya gets. If the idea is not good enough for *indi*, I'll tinker around with something else.'

'Josie, I'm kidding. Mya doesn't like — she *loves* it!' Liani screeched. 'I haven't heard her this excited since we locked in the launch date.'

My jaw dropped.

'Sounds like Mya, the saucy minx, wants to get down on bended knee in front of the idea, then whisk it off on a honeymoon and hand-feed it grapes,' Harrison said, his cheeky face begging for a good slap.

'Um ...' I couldn't talk.

'And that's not all,' Liani went on. 'Mya suggested we run a panel on the night of the launch to cement our place as a social commentator. We still have to work out who'll be up on stage, but isn't that amazing?'

'Actually that is kinda amazing,' Sia said. 'Mya may be a genius after all. Crazy, but a genius.'

'This will be our chance to share our thoughts on the issues that matter, and it'll help encourage advertisers to throw cold hard cash our way ... hopefully.' Liani beamed at us. 'That's enough good news for one afternoon to get us motivated. Let's keep making the magic happen. Now, get cracking on that article, yeah?'

My fate was cemented. There was nothing left to do but stare at my call-out again, with Sia's words ringing in my ears: *You could always do some empirical research ...*

My phone buzzed with a text from James: *Hey, pretty lady, you home tonight? I could pop around and say hi.*

I thought about Sia's joke. My article. My freak-out of virgin-sized proportions. The overpowering urge to tell James how I felt. It was like everything had been building to this moment, and the word 'love' was dancing on the tip of my tongue. The time was now. V-plates be damned.

I fired a quick text back to James before I changed my mind. *Sure am, come around! I think the others are out tonight …*

I'd never been one to play games. My approach with James was more 'Hi, here I am, this is me!' than 'Hey, what's up? I've been busy being awesome without you.'

The phone hummed again and I scanned the text quickly. James was coming over. He didn't know it yet, but it was *on* and I was going to make sure it was perfect.

I just had to remember to shave my legs first.

I wanted James to think I was the hottest specimen he'd ever seen. I slipped into the lacy underwear, then, chickening out at how much skin was exposed, I put my loose T-shirt back over the top. Leaving my skirt crumpled on the bathroom floor, I brushed my teeth and fluffed my hair, then tiptoed down the hall towards my bedroom. I paused when I realised my palms were sweating. Hot specimens didn't have sweaty palms. In fact, in that moment it felt like everything was sweating — even my eyebrows seemed to have sprung a leak.

I turned the door handle and entered the room. James was on the bed fiddling with his phone, oblivious to my plans. Everything was in its place: the vanilla candles lit on the dresser, half-opened blinds for ambience, and soft music playing on my stereo. I slid onto the bed and James rolled onto his side to face me, causing his T-shirt to rise and reveal a smattering of soft hair below his belly button.

'Well, hello sunshine,' he said, noticing I wasn't wearing my skirt. 'Is it no-pants Thursday?'

I weighed up my next move. It was the Perfect Time. He was the Perfect Guy. Tonight was going to be All Kinds of Perfect. I was about to tell the hottest, nicest guy I'd ever met that I loved him. For the first time. *Ever.*

'JB, you're staring right through me,' James continued. 'Everything okay?'

'Um … yeah,' I said, wiping my palms on my T-shirt. 'Wait, that candle's out of place.'

I leaped from the bed and straightened it, then turned back to James, who had a curious expression on his face.

'Looks fine to me,' he said. 'Come here, you look gorgeous.'

'Everything has to be perfect,' I said. 'These candles weren't cheap, you know.'

James sat up. 'Hey, remind me to show you this cool app later that —'

'Damn it, James, I'm trying to seduce you!' I said, voice raised.

He froze. 'Is that what this is? Okay then …'

My T-shirt had slipped off one shoulder during my outburst, revealing the bra strap and a hint of lace. I didn't fix it up. Instead, I put on a breathy voice and sashayed towards him, slowly, deliberately. 'So … James … I bought this for you,' I said, gesturing to the bra.

'You bought me a bra?' he cracked. 'That's sweet, but you know I don't wear them.'

'Would you take this seriously?' I hissed, trying to pull at the strap in an alluring way, but flicking it against my collarbone instead. 'Ow!' I rubbed at the tender skin.

'You're a worry,' he said, pulling me onto the bed with him. 'And I'm serious. Very, very serious.' Yet the grin on his face was anything but.

'Do you understand what I went through to buy this stupid bra? I flashed the sales lady. She was a hundred years old.'

'What's the problem?' James asked. 'I'm sure she's seen loads of naked people — and none as pretty as you.'

'No more candle, bra or sales-lady talk,' I said. 'This is supposed to be special. I'm in the zone.'

'For what?'

'For … for …' I lowered my gaze. I wanted to say the words, but nothing came out.

James didn't force me to explain myself, or push me for more information. His fingers brushed my shoulder as he gently moved aside my T-shirt and lowered his lips to my collarbone where the strap had reddened the skin. He kissed me once, twice, then a third time. 'Better?'

I smiled. 'I'm sorry for being so intense. I ... I ... I've been thinking about you a lot lately.'

'Can't say I blame you,' he teased, pulling me in closer, his arms wrapped tightly around me.

'I keep wondering if you think we're moving too slow ... or too fast ... or are we standing still?'

'You're like the Goldilocks of relationships, huh?' he said, kissing me on the tip of my nose. 'We're just "us". I don't think about where that fits in with anyone else ... do you?'

'No ... yes,' I admitted. 'Every day. Are you still as happy as that day you kissed me on Tim's sofa?'

James cocked his head to one side. 'Does a cheeseburger taste better without a pickle?'

Yes. He got me.

'JB, if anything I'm happier,' he went on. 'You're over-thinking again. Now, what are those lips of yours doing all the way over there, huh?'

I leaned down, my wavy hair falling over his face, and brushed my lips against his. That familiar tingly feeling rushed through my body. He moved in close and kissed me back, before cupping my face in his hands and squishing my mouth into a funny fish expression.

'Admit we're awesome,' he said.

'No,' I giggled through my fishy lips.

'Admit we're awesome or I'll tell Prue who broke her favourite coffee mug.'

'You wouldn't!' I spluttered, laughing at how muffled my voice sounded.

'Wouldn't I?' James raised an eyebrow. His hands moved from my mouth to my stomach, and the flurrying, fast movements of his fingers tickling my bare skin sent jolts of electricity through my body. I writhed and wriggled, gasping with laughter.

'Okay!' I shouted. 'Okay! Wait! Stop!'

James paused, holding his fingers a few centimetres from my body, the threat of tickling still imminent. 'Say it, Jose. Repeat after me ... okay?'

I nodded.

'We.'

'We,' I parroted.

'Are.'

'Are.'

'Awesome.'

'Awful?' I teased.

'Awesome.'

'Oh! Awkward.'

'Awesome, smart-arse.' He rolled his eyes. 'We're awesome.'

Before I knew it, he'd flipped me underneath him so he was looking down at me. For a second I thought he was going to tickle me again, but instead he lowered his lips onto mine. He tasted of orange juice. His lips traced a line from my mouth, to my neck, to my earlobe — and I burst out laughing again.

'You're hopeless!' he said.

'It tickled, that's all.'

He kissed my neck and I felt another laugh hurtling through my body, desperate to get out. I held my breath to restrain it, but it didn't work: the giggle evolved into an air-rattling chuckle and, for an added bonus, concluded with a snort. I groaned and pulled the sheet over my head.

'Hey, I have more candles,' I said. 'I bought them especially —'

'We don't need them,' said James, wriggling under the sheet with me.

It now covered us completely, hiding us away in our own little world and pushing our bodies closer together. For once, I didn't giggle as James kissed me on the small formation of freckles beneath my right eye. They were so light, so pale, that most people didn't even see them — but he did, and called them my Milky Way.

'I love these freckles,' he said, planting another kiss.

'Well, I love these dimples,' I said, my fingers tracing over them. 'And hot dogs, I really, really love hot dogs … with tomato sauce, mustard, onions and cheese.'

James mumbled something, but I didn't catch it.

'And hot chips with gravy, I love them too,' I rambled. 'People who eat plain chips are weird. I mean, no gravy. Insane! And what about those people who wear —'

James cleared his throat. 'Did you hear what I said?'

'About gravy?'

'No …'

'Was it about those people who wear thongs over socks, 'cos I was about to say they're —'

'I love you,' James said.

'— freaks,' I finished, voice trailing off. My eyes widened. 'Wait, what did you say?'

He pulled away a little. 'Um … I said, I love you.'

'And I said, "freaks" … Oh god. I stuffed it up. You said the words! This is amazing … but it isn't how it's supposed to go! Can we rewind?'

Never in a million years did I think James would say it before me.

'Rewind?' James said, running his hand through his mess of brown locks. 'You do realise this is real life? Jose, it's fine, let's forget I said anything. So … Mexican for dinner?'

'No, no, no, repeat those words — those exact words — and I'll say what you need to hear, I promise,' I said. 'It'll be perfect. I feel the same as you do, trust me, every fibre of me feels the same, but I can't say those three words now 'cos it seems like you're kinda grumpy. You've got the same face as when I accidentally scratched your scooter last month. I need to wait until you look happy again … unless, maybe you could face away from me while I say it?'

Now it was James's turn to snort. 'You're mad.'

'I feel the same,' I said again. 'I have for ages. But when it comes to those three words, I want the first time I ever say them to be —'

'Perfect. You mentioned that. Romance movies have a lot to answer for.'

'You *are* angry.'

'No, I'm hungry.'

'I'm sorry, I'm sorry, I'm sorry, I'm sorry,' I murmured, wriggling down on the bed and feeling James pull me in close. I rested my head on his chest, enjoying the feeling of him stroking my hair.

'Look, JB, let's just leave it for a bit, yeah?' he said. 'I've got my assessment and class lunch tomorrow, then I'm meeting your family — why don't we deal with one thing at a time? I don't want to do anything you're not ready for, and I know this is a big deal.'

James was right. This was a big deal. A huge deal. A Mount-Kilimanjaro-sized deal. Despite how much I'd been thinking about saying the words, and taking the next step with James, it turned out I wasn't ready to rush it after all, especially not for the sake of an article.

12.

The places where *indi* readers were hooking up sure were out there: pool tables, parents' beds, even a department-store change room. I filed the email replies to my call-out in a folder on my computer, reminded once again that I was the last virgin on earth. (Well, except for my great-aunt Bertie, a wrinkly old woman who'd never married and farted while she knitted in her rocking chair — surely she'd never got it on with anyone?)

I giggled as I read an email from a young woman who left her half-naked boyfriend stranded at a party when she realised she was too nervous to go through with it.

Luckily, the reader had a great boyfriend who understood it was a big deal and they agreed to wait, but the final line in her story rang on repeat in my mind: *How do you know if you're ready yet?* She was asking the wrong girl. That same question had been bugging me and I still didn't know the answer. Thankfully James was being super cool about it. Sometimes I wondered what I'd done in a former life to score such an awesome boyfriend. He'd even sent me a cute text that morning to let me know he was thinking of me. No surprises: I'd been thinking of him too.

Liani cleared her throat. 'Hey, can I grab everyone for a meeting?'

'Now?' I said, thinking about all the emails I still had to sift through.

'Bring your bags — we're going for a short walk.'

Harrison, Sia and I swapped looks as we followed Liani out the door. She and Harrison set a cracking pace, with Sia and me huffing along behind.

'C'mon, slowpokes,' Harrison said. Clearly his daily cardio sessions at the gym were paying off.

'What's the rush?' I whispered to Sia.

'I haven't seen her this excited for ages,' she replied. She stopped for a moment to catch her breath, but Liani kept charging ahead. 'Hold up, Liani!' she called.

Liani turned and rushed back to us. 'Sorry, girls. We're nearly there.'

Sia frowned. 'As in, around the corner or another fifteen minutes to go?'

Liani linked arms with her for a few metres or so. 'As in ... we're here!'

I didn't know what we were meant to be looking at. The surrounding buildings weren't spectacular; there was a kebab shop nearby with flashing neon lighting, and a spruiker trying to sell cheap shoes across the road. But Liani was about to prove that looks can be deceiving.

'Follow me,' she said, leading us into a dull brown building and up a stairwell.

'Couldn't you have chosen somewhere with a lift?' whined Sia, wiping sweat from her cheek.

'It's broken, but will be fixed soon,' Liani said. 'Nearly there, I promise.'

We hauled ourselves up three flights of stairs and at the top came to a large grey door.

'Do we go in there?' I asked.

'We do,' Liani announced, barely containing her excitement. 'Here's the key, open it.'

I did as she said, turned the handle and gasped. Behind the door was the largest renovated warehouse space I'd ever seen. Light radiated through the floor-to-ceiling windows, and the room was filled with exquisite white furniture and large framed mirrors. There were a number of large, closed doors nestled in the walls and I couldn't help fantasising about what mysteries lay behind each of them.

Harrison was looking at himself in the enormous mirrors, and Sia had propped herself up against the pretty pink cushions piled on the couch nearby. I sat down next to her, but before I could sink back into the softness, Liani called out, 'Over here!'

She waved to us from the other end of the warehouse, where she stood on a small stage surrounded by white chairs. I helped Sia up from the couch — it was so soft it had swallowed her butt whole, she whispered — and we headed over to Liani and took a seat.

'We're not lugging these chairs anywhere, are we?' Sia piped up.

'Humour me for a second,' said Liani. 'Imagine it's early evening, flowers cover every table, tea lights fill the room ...' I stifled a giggle at her singsong, storytelling voice. 'There are laughing, chatting people everywhere — familiar faces from magazines, radio, film, music, sport, politics ... This is the perfect setting for a —'

'Surprise wedding?' Harrison joked.

'Quiet, Harrison,' Liani said. 'I called in some favours — alright, *a lot* of favours — and am thrilled to say we'll be throwing our launch party here next week!'

'Do you think we'll have enough guests to fill this space? We're kinda nobodies,' Sia blurted out. 'Wait, that came out wrong. Baby-brain!'

'Sia, I thought you credited yourself as a scene-stealer,' said Liani. 'If we're doing this launch — which we are — then we're doing it right. An incredible venue like this makes a statement. It lets everyone know we've arrived and we're going to make a real difference in people's — especially young women's — lives. They need *indi*. They need us. They need you. You're all role models now.'

'Even me?' I asked, wondering if there was an awesome group of girls with serious role-model credentials sitting behind me.

'Yes, Josie, you too,' said Liani. 'Mya and I have a clear vision for *indi* and it's up to us to deliver it to the country — hell, to the world!'

Sia's eyes had glazed over and I couldn't tell if she was overwhelmed with excitement, falling asleep or holding in one of her aforementioned farts. Maybe all three.

'I'm going to lie back on the couch for a while,' she murmured.

'Would you go home already?' Liani said.

Sia shook her head, paused, then nodded. After an overly emotional apology, and a quick kiss on the cheek for each of us, she was out the door.

'This all sounds amazing,' I said, trying to make up for Sia's less-than-ideal reaction. (Besides, the straight-A student/goodie-two-shoes/ego-stroking side of me was flattered by Liani's spiel about me being a role model.)

'I'm glad you think so,' said Liani. 'We'll be the talk of the town!'

She walked down the steps from the stage and pulled a chair over to a nearby table, rummaged in her handbag and pulled out notebooks, pens, textas and Post-it notes.

'What, no butcher's paper?' Harrison asked, winking.

Liani rolled her eyes. 'Alright, so I want to pick your brains about how we can design the room on the night, then we'll move on to catering and entertainment. This needs to be a party people talk about for years.'

Two hours later, with the Launch Brainstorm Session To End All Launch Brainstorm Sessions completed, I had a to-do list that rivalled *War and Peace* (translation: freaking long). Back at the office, the afternoon flew past in a whirl of emails, calls and voicemails. With still no word from Darlene about Maxxy, Liani had asked me to secure a girl rock act called The Blue Dames as a back-up, although none of us were that excited by them. Sure, they could sing, but they didn't have the same media pull as Maxxy. I felt like I'd let Liani and the *indi* team down.

The only consolation was knowing I'd be home with Mum, Kat and James in a few hours. Mum had sent me an excited text earlier that day: *One more sleep to go!* It had taken every shred of my willpower not to reveal that James and I would be home that night instead.

Steph sat on my bed, watching as I filled a suitcase with beauty products and books.

'That's a lot of stuff for a weekend,' she said. 'You're not moving out, are you?'

'Kat puts in her orders for the freebies I get at work,' I explained, stuffing a pair of strappy sandals and my toiletries bag into the suitcase. 'Go on, help yourself from that box in the corner.'

'Is that a CC cream?' Steph squealed.

'You're as bad as Kat. Take it.'

'Uh, yeah!' Steph snatched it from the box. 'This is amazing and, like, the only brand that doesn't test on animals. And I totally can't afford beauty products right now …'

'Well, it's yours.'

'You rock my frock,' she said, giving me a hug. 'Man, I am pumped for this road trip — it's going to be epic! The perfect distraction. I heard from Alex — he's on the way over with the car. Where's James? I thought he was getting here an hour ago? If we leave in the next ten we can drop you at your mum's by eight.'

I paused, unsure how to tell Steph that I hadn't heard from James since that first text of the day. Normally that wouldn't have been a problem, but today was different. He was meeting my family. Part of me couldn't help thinking it had something to do with my freak-out the previous night. Maybe James had replayed what'd happened and changed his mind about wanting to be with me. He'd been so patient, but perhaps he'd grown sick of waiting. Why else would he go MIA the day after we'd fizzled between the sheets?

'Um, I'm not sure if James is going to make it,' I said.

'Yeah? Why not? Better offer, eh?' She giggled, elbowing me in the side.

'Maybe,' I said, zipping up my suitcase and fighting back the tears stinging my eyes and threatening to slide down my cheeks.

'Oh, you're serious,' she said. 'What's happened? If he's running late we can wait. There's no rush.'

'He's not answering his phone and I don't know what to do. I know he was hanging with his music mates today, but I don't have any of their numbers.'

'Maybe he's caught in traffic,' Steph said. 'Although that'll make leaving the city a real bitch for us too.'

'He could call then … Why isn't he calling me back? I think he's pissed off with me. Urgh, let's give it a few minutes, okay? At least until Alex gets here.'

I flopped backwards on the bed and glared at my phone, willing it to ring or beep with a new message. Something to show I hadn't been abandoned, or he wasn't lying in a gutter somewhere.

Suddenly the phone burst into life.

'James? Where are you?' I could hear people cheering in the background.

He sounded slurry, not like himself at all. 'Imma sooo silly, baby … Can you get me water for the trip tomorrow?'

'James, we're leaving now, tonight, remember? Where are you?'

'The water, I need the water … Hey, a poodle!' He erupted into giggles. 'Can we get a poodle tomorrow at your mum's?'

'No, it's tonight. We're leaving right now —'

'I wanna name the poodle "Josie" after the most beautiful girl I ever —' The phone cut out.

'He hung up on me,' I told Steph, 'and I'm pretty sure he's wasted. Oh, and apparently he wants to name a poodle after me.'

I could tell she was trying not to laugh at the last part.

I called James back, only this time it went to voicemail. I tried once more. Nothing. The minutes dragged on, each more stubborn than the next, until Steph got the call to say Alex was downstairs.

'J, we can wait,' she said. 'If you two have had a fight then, honestly, sort it out first —'

'No, it's fine,' I said, pulling myself off the bed and collecting my suitcase. 'This has been planned for ages. Besides, he's ignoring my calls and ... I don't want him to meet my family like *this*. I never thought I'd say it, but I think we should leave without him.'

'Really?'

'Yeah, I want to surprise my family. I'm going to need a freaking good excuse for why he's bailed though,' I added. 'Kat already thinks I have an imaginary boyfriend.'

'Maybe he can meet you there tomorrow?'

Maybe.

James and I technically hadn't fought, but something told me the next time we spoke, that would all change. Our first fight was brewing and I got the feeling it was going to be a corker. Perfect James suddenly didn't seem so perfect after all.

* * *

Steph fell asleep in the front passenger seat fifteen minutes into the car trip. Her head lolled from side to side, until she slumped backwards and let out an almighty snore. So much for our epic road trip going down in history.

Alex, who was driving, barely flinched. 'That may be her new record for staying awake,' he said, fiddling with the rear-view mirror. 'Last time she was out in six minutes.'

'Hopeless,' I said from the back seat, suddenly feeling as though Alex was chauffeuring me. 'I thought she wanted to make this road trip a party.'

'I think she peaked last night. What did you guys get up to? Take those rubber ducks out for another spin?'

I stiffened. 'Very funny.'

'Who's been pulling at your pigtails?' He laughed, then turned up the radio. 'Rock music cool with you?'

'Sure, why not,' I murmured. I didn't like rock; it reminded me of my father.

A quick peep at my phone showed there was still no word from James. I wished I could debrief with Steph, but not even Alex's singing (which sounded fantastic, though I wouldn't tell him that) or the thumping beat of KISS could wake her. I played with the empty lolly wrappers in the car door pocket, ripping them into pieces until they were scraps the size of dots.

The raging bass line filled the silence in the car. I was happy to let it swell and throb around me, even though my eardrums were threatening to burst at any minute. When a power ballad started up, Alex scanned the stations. I picked at my fingernails, staring out the window.

'You seem bored,' Alex said. 'I'll make you a deal: you can pick the radio station if you can guess … my middle name. I'll even give you a clue. It starts with —'

'John.'

He grinned. 'Whoa. How'd you know?'

I held up a black wallet. 'Your licence is on the back seat.'

'Well played, zygote, well played.'

'So, John, huh?'

He shrugged. 'Mum's obsessed with Elton. No biggie.'

I laughed. 'Well, that's settled then — pop, please.'

Alex fiddled until he found a station blasting candy-sweet Top 40 goodness. 'Your wish is my command.'

Steph woke up, bleary-eyed and muttering, 'Turn this rubbish off.' She slammed the volume down and squeezed her eyes closed tight again.

'Sorry, Jose, outvoted,' said Alex. He yawned and stretched his arms out in front of him one at a time, flexing his triceps.

I couldn't tell if he was doing it deliberately or not. Either way, I noticed how toned his arms were. It was hard not to with him flaunting them like that.

'Confession: I haven't read any of your stuff yet,' he said.

I felt a twinge of embarrassment. Alex didn't need to know I'd already drooled over his enviable online writing portfolio. 'You still want to do that?'

'Well, yeah. You're a writer. You need readers.'

'Um, it's probably not your thing.'

'I get it. You're scared. Writing's like cutting out your heart and splattering it on the page.'

I reddened. 'Well, I wouldn't go that far … and I'm not scared.'

'Hey, rejection isn't easy — I know. An editor once told me he'd never publish me, not even if *I* paid *him*. I heard about one guy who kept all his rejection letters on spikes above his desk to motivate him. I'm thinking about doing the same.'

'Stephen King, right?' I couldn't believe Alex had heard that story.

'You know about that?'

'Yeah, I love it. Getting rejected still hurts though.'

'It's brutal, but you gotta take the good with the bad. I've been rejected a ton of times,' he said, 'but I've also been to some islands in the South Pacific, America, parts of Asia, even South Africa for a week.'

'I still can't believe it's for work.'

'Yeah, you get flown somewhere to road test all the features. Like, say it's a spa resort, you *literally* get paid to have spas for a week.'

'Sounds like the life,' I said, remembering the few hours I spent at the wellness event.

'You wait,' he said. 'One day you're fetching some diva's mail; the next you're going on a free trip and every other person in the office hates your guts. It'll happen, and when it does, send me a postcard telling me I was right. Not that you'll even care because you'll be beach-side sipping on a raspberry cocktail.'

Before I had a chance to reply, Alex had pulled the car off the road near a patch of trees.

'Bathroom break!' he said.

'What? We're, like, five minutes from Mum's place.'

Alex pointed at his tatts. 'Yeah, and I bet your mum'll want a guy like me barging into her house.'

I had to agree, although I was sure Kat wouldn't mind.

'It's fine, I've got the roadie whiz down to a fine art,' he went on.

'Ew.'

'Ew?' he teased. 'I either pee out there or in here.'

I shuddered and pointed outside. I watched Alex run down a grassy bank and walk up to a tree. He turned to give me a little wave. Embarrassed, I pulled out my phone and stared at the screen, scrolling and swiping to busy myself.

'Get a good look?' he asked when he got back in the car.

'Nope, I, um, I can't see that far without my glasses,' I stammered. He didn't need to know I had perfect vision.

'Next stop, your mama's,' he said and shook Steph, who groaned. 'Wake up, we're nearly at Josie's.'

'What? But we just left,' she murmured, yawning, then looking at her watch. 'Is that the time? Shit, I totally flaked. I bet the car ride was stupid-boring without me.'

Alex caught my eye in the rear-view mirror. 'We did alright.'

'Yeah, it was, ah ... Hey, slow down!' I said, realising we'd turned onto my street. 'It's the house up here on the right ... the one with the broken gate ... Hang on, it's fixed. Um, stop here, that's fine, thanks.'

I'd been hassling Mum to get the gate fixed for months. She must be feeling better if she was attending to jobs like that. The lights were on and Mum's car was in the front driveway — she was home for my surprise. I imagined the tears of joy that would run down her face when she opened the front door, and I wondered how many daughter brownie-points this would earn me. Hopefully, arriving boyfriend-free wouldn't detract any. I still hadn't thought of a good excuse for why James wasn't with me.

'Thanks for the lift, guys,' I said, blowing kisses to a still-yawning Steph. I climbed out of the car, dragging my suitcase with me.

'Anytime,' Alex said, resting his arm along the window. 'You need a lift home too?'

I swallowed at the sight of the naked woman woven into his sleeve tattoo. 'I'll get the train on Sunday ... but thanks.'

'Righto, have fun in your old playpen,' he said and grinned. 'Let's get outta here, Smelly Socks!'

Before I had a chance to conjure a witty retort, the car sped off, leaving faint tyre marks on the road. I smiled all the way up the driveway, but within 3.9 seconds was feeling guilty for perving on Alex's arms and wondering what he looked like with his shirt off.

I was about to send James a *You're hot* text to appease my guilt when I remembered. I was mad at him. Furious, even. Tonight was about surprising Mum and Kat — it always was — and it was going to be some of my finest work. Not even James's epic boyfriend fail could ruin this weekend for me.

13.

I opened the door and barged into the lounge room shouting 'Surprise!' at the top of my lungs. I expected Mum to be startled. I imagined she'd cry, 'You're the best daughter in the world and I can hardly handle life without you here!' before showering me with all my favourite treats — fresh sheets, chocolates by the boxload and a marathon gasbag session. Instead, she gave a warrior-style yell that set the neighbours' dogs barking, and spilled a glass of red wine down the front of her dress.

The jazz music, low lighting and jasmine-scented candles should have clued me in to the situation, but in all my excitement I missed the signs and lurched towards her with the enthusiasm of a baby giraffe.

'It's me, Mum!' I shrieked. 'I'm here early! I'm surprising you!' *Aren't I amazing?*

'Love, you scared the willies out of me,' she said, shaking her head. 'Give me a minute to catch up, my heart's racing.'

As Mum dabbed at the red wine stain with a serviette, I had a chance to soak in the scene in front of me. The first thing I noticed was Mum's hair: her usually wild mane was pulled into a polished up-do. No wilting daisies tucked behind her ear. No clothes pegs clipping her hair together. Not even a stray wispy bit had escaped.

The second thing I noticed was the man in the room. A man with a receding hairline, shiny faux-leather jacket and shaving nicks on his chin. He'd rushed to Mum's side to dab at the stain with a tea towel, and was asking if she was alright.

'Don't worry, Rodgie, it's okay,' she said, touching his shoulder.

Rodgie? Now it was my turn to be surprised. Who was this guy and why was my mum touching him?

'Um … Mum … so hey!' I said, bouncing on my heels. 'Hi. Hello. Surprise and … all that.'

'Come here, love, give me a kiss,' she said, pulling me in for a hug.

She smelled different — she was wearing a new perfume that I didn't recognise, and there were no sneaky wafts of cigarette smoke. I'd pestered her to shake the habit for months, but I still felt thrown.

'You feel tiny, love,' she said. 'Have you been eating enough? Now, before I forget, this is my new friend, Rodgie.'

'Ah, hi …' I mumbled, nearly choking on my tongue.

'Hello, Josie,' he said. 'I'm Rodger. It's great to meet you — your mum's told me all about you.'

We shook hands, but I couldn't come up with anything civil to say. I was thinking 'Wish I could say the same', but I managed to hold it in.

I turned to Mum. 'Um … so, about James …'

'Yes, where is that boy of yours?' she said, looking around. 'He's not waiting outside, is he?'

'No, um, well, the thing is … some study came up, and it all got a bit crazy-busy, so … um … he couldn't make it in the end … but he says sorry. Yeah, he's, ah, really sorry.'

He mightn't have said sorry yet, but he was going to be. Especially because I still hadn't heard from him.

'Poo,' Mum said. 'Well, lucky I hadn't blown up the air mattress yet.'

I sighed. 'I said he's sorry.'

'No need to get narky, love. I'll meet him another time.'

'Yeah, of course,' I said, doing my best to keep it together. 'Hey, where's Kat? Maybe we could make pancakes? Or you could bust out the banjo and we could muck around with some songs. Want me to put the kettle on?'

'Your sister's staying at a friend's, love … and we're heading out too,' Mum said. 'If I'd known you were coming, then I wouldn't have made plans. But Rodgie's reserved a table at that gorgeous little Italian restaurant on the main street …'

'If I'd told you I was coming, it wouldn't have been a surprise, would it?' I said, feeling my face flush.

This *definitely* wasn't part of the plan. Crime shows, a cuppa and the couch were Mum's go-to Friday fixes. I had no idea who this social cyborg was who'd replaced my mother.

'Rodgie, could you give me and Josie a sec? I'll change my dress — red-wine chic wasn't the look I was going for.'

Rodger was only too happy to take up Mum's offer. He nodded to me, said, 'See you next time,' and left, slamming the front door behind him. That was a relief: he mustn't have been on the scene long enough to know the front door needed to be closed gently, so it didn't shake the house to its foundations.

'Now, love, I'm sorry to leave you, but we've had this planned all week,' Mum said, waving me to follow her into her bedroom. She yanked another dress — a floaty green number that brought out her eyes — off the hanger. 'It is good to see your little face. Sometimes I want you to stop growing up so fast, but then I see what a magnificent woman you're becoming and —'

'Mum ...' I paused, wondering how to stop my lips trembling. Between the stress of work and James, I felt like a ticking time bomb of emotion.

'Anyway, will you be okay tonight?' she asked. 'There's leftover beef strog in the fridge if you fancy it — I know it's your favourite.'

No, you don't know that, I thought sulkily, because it wasn't my favourite. It was my father's.

'Mum, we've been over this. I can't stand ... Okay, um ... great,' I said, accepting defeat. I didn't want to upset her. 'You know, this works out even better 'cos now I can relax and catch up on some work.'

'And call that boy of yours?'

'Ah, yeah,' I said. Not that he was likely to answer.

'Good on you, love,' Mum said, opening the linen closet and thrusting a set of sheets into my hands. 'Make yourself comfy — this is still your home too.'

'Thanks,' I said. 'You should probably go. Your friend is waiting.' I couldn't bring myself to say 'Rodgie'.

'You're right, I'd better run,' she said, touching up her lipstick. 'Kat's back in the morning, so we'll have our big day tomorrow, yeah?'

'Yeah ... Hey, Mum?' I began as I followed her into the lounge room, a million thoughts smashing around in my head. Please don't date someone else. Please don't leave me alone tonight. Please tell me it's not over with James.

She spun around to look at me, her dress swishing around her knees. 'Yes, love?'

But I couldn't say any of it. 'You look beautiful.'

'Oh, shush, love,' she said, glowing like a teenager on her first date. 'So, Rodger ... he's something, huh?'

'Yeah, he's ... he's ...'

'I'm sorry I haven't said anything until now ... I thought you might be a little funny about it, but you've proved me wrong,' she said, thankfully unable to mind-read my crazy anti-Rodgie thoughts. I felt a sharp pang of guilt. 'He's lovely though, even fixed the gate the other day — he's brilliant with his hands.'

Every fibre of my being hoped she was still talking about the gate.

Mum pecked me on the cheek. 'Love ya — you're a treasure for surprising me.' She rubbed at the fresh lipstick stain on my cheek, before closing the door behind her.

I swallowed, still shocked that Mum had blown off my surprise for a date with a dude who wore faux leather. He probably picked lint out of his belly button, and had a pet bird who made snarky comments too.

To erase any thought of their date, I turned off the music and blew out the candles. I popped my train ticket on the fridge using my favourite magnet — my lame way of marking my territory. Then, for nostalgia's sake, I explored each room of the house. After her recent rough patch, Mum had returned to her domestic-goddess status with a vengeance. The toilet had a pile of new magazines nestled next to it, and the bathroom sparkled. A quick look in Kat's room proved that some things never changed: there were clothes strewn everywhere, posters clogging the walls, and the air was thick with perfume, fake tan, incense and cigarette smoke. Subtle, Kat.

I reached my old bedroom, which I'd left just as it was because Prue had offered me a furnished room in the terrace. All I'd needed to take with me were a few suitcases and my laptop. I turned the handle and entered my room. Except it wasn't my room at all. Gone was the single bed with its lilac doona cover, the posters on the walls, the photos of Angel and me grinning like idiots. My chest of drawers, the corner desk piled high with dusty books and bedside table with its broken handle were also missing.

Instead, the treadmill that used to stand in the garage collecting dust took up one corner, and the ironing board stood in the other. The treadmill blocked the little measurement chart Mum and Dad had drawn on the wall to mark how tall I was growing. The rest of the room was bare, except for a pair of white roller-skates by the door, which were too big to fit either me or Kat, and a photo of the three of us on the wall. I recognised the picture: Dad had been in it before Mum cropped him out — squeezed in next to Kat and wearing an oversized cowboy hat to make us laugh. I wondered how many other pictures Mum had doctored.

There was no doubt about it: my room was gone. Mum had told me this was still my home, but it suddenly felt like a stranger's house. I didn't even have a bed.

Kat's bed wasn't an option, as it was invisible under a heap of clothes, and I couldn't be bothered blowing up the air mattress, so I settled for the living-room couch. It was small, so I curled up like an echidna to make myself fit.

By ten thirty I was starting to drift off, but I tried to force myself to stay awake 'til Mum got home. Somehow, she'd become the fun one, while I was tut-tutting with my beady eyes glued to the clock on the wall. With no James or Angel to call, time moved at a glacial pace. Eventually I stopped straining for the sound of a car pulling up in the driveway and fell asleep.

The jangling of keys woke me. I opened one eye: it was 12.03 am. I heard the clicking of heels on the tiles — just one set of shoes. Phew.

Within seconds Mum was hovering above me, smelling of perfume. 'Love, why didn't you turn it into a fold-out?'

Crap. I'd forgotten the crusty old couch opened out into a crusty old bed.

'Just mixing things up,' I said. 'How was your date?'

'It wasn't *really* a date, love. It was more like two people catching up for dinner, wine and conversation.'

'That's a date,' I insisted. 'You were on a date. You're dating.'

'I suppose I am,' she said. 'Well, my date was ... very pleasant. Let's leave it at that.'

I didn't want to know more, yet at the same time I did. But there was something else on my mind.

'Mum ... where's all my stuff?'

She paused. 'Oh, that. Well ... my counsellor told me a change is as good as a holiday and, since I can't afford one of those, Rodgie and Kat helped me create a little haven for myself by packing up the spare room.'

Typical Kat, conveniently leaving that out of our phone conversations.

'You mean *my* room,' I said.

Mum sighed and sat down next to me on the couch. 'Yes. Your room. I'm sorry for not telling you, but I figured with your exciting new life in the city you'd be fine to let go of a few childhood knick-knacks. Everything's in storage in the garage — we can go through it tomorrow if you want. But now you need some sleep. Do you want me to help you turn this couch into a bed?'

I nodded, enjoying her fussing over me as we set up the fold-out. Once I was curled up in the makeshift bed, Mum kissed me on the forehead, smoothed down the blankets and turned out the light.

'It's great to have you home, love,' she whispered into the darkness before leaving the room.

I didn't say a word. I couldn't. If I told the truth — that home didn't feel like it existed any more — then there would be no turning back.

Kat came back to the house earlier than planned to avoid the 'weird muesli' at her friend's place. As she and I crunched through our bowls of Weet-Bix, Mum pottered around the kitchen humming, even wiggling her hips a little. She smiled to herself as she buttered her toast, gliding her knife back and forth. I'd never seen her like this. Maybe there was more to this dating business than she was letting on. But I didn't get a chance to corner her about it — because Kat cornered me first.

'Where's James? Did he chicken out or something?' she asked. 'I knew he wasn't real!'

'He's busy, Kat. People get busy.' I wondered how convincing I was, especially as I was furious with him. 'He says hi, and hopes to see you soon.'

The truth was, after twenty-four hours with no word apart from some drunken poodle-related ramblings, I wasn't sure if he wanted to see *me* soon.

'Busy?' Kat scoffed. 'Isn't he studying *music*? All he'd do is sit around smoking. Sounds real busy.'

'Music production — he wants to be a producer. And he doesn't smoke ... unlike some people,' I muttered under my breath. 'He's crazy-busy. That's it. We both are.'

'Unless he's blowing you off,' said Kat, her teeth caked with Weet-Bix.

'Kat,' warned Mum.

'Fine,' she said, 'but it sounds like a blow-off to me.'

I knew she was trying to rile me up, but her words still stung. Kat had thrown my worst fear a life vest and now it was bobbing on the surface of my mind, impossible to ignore.

'Anyway, Josie love, how's work going?' Mum asked, pulling up a seat next to me. 'You've barely said a peep about it. I hope they're not working you to the bone — you are looking a bit skinny. You know what, I'm going to get you some toast.'

'Mum, I'm fine,' I said.

'I've heard stories about these start-ups — all underpaid and overworked. Go on, here's a banana too.'

I took it. 'I told you to stop watching those crappy news programs. Can we fast-forward this conversation? Everything's great.' Mum seemed so happy, so light, I didn't want to burden her with my stresses. 'I'm living the dream and I couldn't be happier. Living with Steph rocks. There's the big launch coming up at work and it's pretty full-on, but didn't you see all the free stuff I brought you guys? You won't need to buy shampoo for a year.'

I pointed to the suitcase, hoping the freebies would shut Kat up and please Mum, who'd been struggling to manage household expenses since Dad ran off.

'Love, it sounds so glamorous,' Mum said. 'My daughter running a website in the big city … I'm chuffed. Really chuffed.'

'Er, thanks, Mum.' I let her have that one, even though I was far from running the website. She just looked so proud.

'And James? How's that going?' she asked.

I paused. 'You'd like him. He's a good guy.' Usually.

'This is all way too vanilla,' announced Kat. 'I'll be in my room if anything interesting happens.' She walked off, ponytail flicking behind her.

'Nice to see you too, and you're welcome for the beauty products,' I muttered.

'Love, I think Harry broke up with her, and she misses you, you know,' said Mum. 'We also had to get her a maths tutor, so she's not too happy with me either. Give her some time to warm up.'

Who was Harry? Last time I'd spoken to her she was talking about someone named Matty. And no, I didn't know Kat needed tutoring or missed me. She was more likely to tell me I had a booger up my nose or a chipped nail.

'Well, what about you, Mum?' I asked. 'Are you alright here alone? And what's with those roller-skates?'

'I'm not alone,' she said, her voice sharper than usual. 'I'm happy. I'm *finally* feeling happy.'

'I know, but only a few months ago you were crying a lot, and the bills weren't getting paid and —'

'Do you see tears?' Mum asked, peering at me over her coffee cup. 'I'm back at the library, I have new friends, I'm learning to roller-skate and I have food on the table. And I'm dating and it's nice.'

'I'm glad you think that,' I began, 'but —'

Mum cut me off. 'I had a lovely day planned for us, but if you'd rather sit here and dissect everything that's wrong with my life, go right ahead.'

'Mum, that's not what I was doing! I don't want to ... I don't want to see you get hurt again.'

'Save your worrying for something else, love. I'm a big girl. Now, let's get this day happening.'

So I did what Mum told me and locked my worry deep down inside.

Once the three of us were showered, dressed and made-up (Kat raiding the box of beauty goodies without a word of thanks), Mum drove us to the park. We sat on the grass, ignoring the growing breeze, eating passionfruit, caramel and chocolate macarons and making daisy chains.

'This is what you had planned for Josie and James? Daisy chains?' Kat quizzed Mum, who laughed.

'I might have made a few adjustments this morning,' she said.

'Jose, any luck getting me an invite?' Kat said, lowering her daisy chain onto my head. 'The launch is next week, right?'

'Kat, don't start, you know that's impossible,' I said, readjusting the flowers as they slipped down over my brows.

'Seriously?' she said. 'Doesn't sound like you have much pull there at all.'

'Enough you two,' Mum said. 'Kat, you're not going anywhere next week. Now, shopping?'

Kat's eyes lit up, until she realised Mum meant window-shopping — and antique window-shopping at that. We trailed behind her while she ogled yet another old wooden chest or dusty ceramic vase.

'So … are you okay after your break-up with Harry?' I asked Kat.

'Who? Oh, him. We were together for, like, five seconds. I'll get over it, but he ruined my no-dumps run.' She shrugged in typical Kat fashion. 'And what about you and James? Are you okay after the break-up?'

I stopped walking. 'Excuse me?'

She lowered her voice so Mum wouldn't hear. 'You heard me.'

'Who told you that?'

'No one. But he's not here and you're acting weird. Well, weirder than usual.'

'Am not. And we haven't broken up.'

'You don't have to hide stuff from me, I'm not a kid. Don't forget who was home with Mum during all her episodes —'

'He's busy. Now, cut it out.'

Kat's eyes narrowed to piercing slits. 'Keep lying to me and yourself then, but it doesn't suit you,' she said, then hurried after Mum.

I stood there in shock, the wind whipping my dress around my thighs, my hair lashing my face, as I tried to register what the hell had happened.

Click, click! Click, click! Mum was snapping her fingers in front of my face, bringing me back to reality. 'Let's move it,' she said. 'The weather's turning, and we've got lunch, a trip to the cinema, pottery and dinner to go.'

'Pottery?'

She winked. 'Just wanted to see if you were listening. C'mon, love, let's catch up with your sister.'

Mum's hand folded around mine and I let her pull me along the street as I tried to ignore the stinging in my eyes. I wasn't sure if it was from the wind, or the fact that James still hadn't contacted me.

Sunday began as a blur. After a fitful sleep, I dragged myself out of bed midmorning to the sound of bacon sizzling in the kitchen and rain pelting down outside. Before I had a chance to load up my plate, Kat had already pecked me on the cheek and rushed out the door to spend the day at a friend's place — shooting me a cheeky 'Say hi to James from me' before slamming the door behind her. So much for spending more time together. Not that it really mattered. Faster than you could have said, 'There's no place like home', it was time to say goodbye and get the train back to the city.

Mum's eyes were red as she drove me to the station, but by the time we'd pulled into the car park she'd composed herself. I felt the familiar pangs of guilt, loneliness and sadness charge through my body, settling in my stomach to taunt me all the way home. Little white lies such as 'Yeah, I can *totally* afford to buy groceries this week', 'Don't worry, James is meeting me at the train station' and 'Working at *indi*'s not stressful at all' were still scalding my lips as I boarded the train and waved goodbye. It was like déja vu from my first solo trip to the city and, once again, I was fighting back tears. Things were changing, and I was being left behind.

I lumped my suitcase onto the seat next to me and stared out the window as we passed paddock after paddock, the gumtrees slanting on the hills like hobbling old men. I checked my phone. Still nothing. James sure was good at going off the radar. I considered calling him, then decided the risk of me stuttering something absurd was too great. It didn't take long before staring progressed into *glaring* out the window. Irritation at an all-time high, I caved, texting him to tell him not to worry about messaging or calling me back *ever* 'cos I didn't want to hear from him. Half an hour later there was still no reply, which was a total headache because I couldn't tell if he hadn't replied because he didn't want to or because I'd told him not to. I was in the middle of my first real relationship crisis.

Two more texts and no replies later, as I was on the verge of a mini meltdown, someone tapped on my shoulder. I spun around, hoping it wasn't the creepy guy who'd commented on my 'enchanting legs' when I got on the train. It wasn't him, or the scrawny woman from a few seats back clipping her toenails, or even the little kids who'd been fighting over a set of colourful blocks. Instead, Kat was on the seat behind me, a small suitcase on one side of her and a colourful tote on the other.

I was so stunned I forgot to blast her about why this was: (a) a terrible mistake; (b) going to get her grounded for longer than when she'd wagged school to make out with a boy at the local pitch-and-putt; (c) not ideal considering I had a launch to organise; and (d) the last thing I could handle right now when I'd self-sabotaged my relationship by morphing into a psycho text stalker.

'How long 'til we get to yours?' she said. 'And what should we get for dinner? I was thinking Indian could be nice, or even Thai —'

'Kat, what are you doing here?' I asked, trying, but failing, to keep a calm tone. 'You can't come to my place! And how did you even know which train to get?'

I slid into the seat opposite her so we were facing each other and I was travelling backwards. I got motion sickness, but there was no time to feel queasy. I suddenly had more responsibility on my hands than which microwave-dinner-for-one to heat up that night.

'Your ticket was on the fridge, dummy,' she said. 'And everything's fine. Mum thinks I'm staying at a mate's.'

'For the rest of the week?' I said. 'Kat, I have a job, and deadlines, and housemates, and you have school and … *school*. Mum's going to flip!'

Kat sighed. 'I have it all worked out. I'll hang at yours tonight, then I'll come to your office tomorrow and help with —'

'Are you freaking nuts? You can't bludge at my work all day. This is the real world.'

'Fine,' she said, sitting up straighter. 'Keep pushing me away then.'

'I'm not. If anything, you ignored me for half of the weekend and —'

'I saw through your crap,' Kat interrupted. 'All those lies you were spinning about your perfect life in the city. Mum may have been too caught up to notice, but I wasn't. Whatever, I'll leave you alone.'

She hoisted her bag over one shoulder and the tote over the other, stormed down the carriage stairs and waited in front of the door. A few moments later, the train pulled in at a dingy, deserted station. The doors opened. Sheets of rain struck the concrete, and Kat leaped from the carriage onto the platform.

Swearing, I dragged my suitcase to the doorway. 'Kat!' I yelled, my voice drowned out by the storm. 'Come back!'

But she'd already disappeared around a corner in a huff. I glanced up at the timetable — I had less than one minute to decide whether to stay on the train or jump onto the platform and follow Kat to god knows where.

I jumped.

My suitcase crashed down next to me as I stumbled onto the wet pavement. Rain saturated my outfit, bag and hair, which now clung to my face in thick, wet strands. But I barely noticed. I needed to find Kat.

First, I checked the girls' bathrooms — nothing. Then the boys' — still nothing, except a rather surprised guy zipping up at the urinal. The other platforms — nothing. The ticket booths — nothing. I hurried out onto the street, dragging my suitcase behind me, ignoring the rain running down my dress and seeping into my shoes. And then I saw her. Kat was crouched in front of a vending machine, searching her bag for coins.

'Soft drink rots your teeth,' I said. Even I knew it was a crap attempt to lighten the mood.

Kat shrugged, shoved some coins into the machine, pressed the necessary buttons, and watched the can drop. She opened it, causing it to fizz and spill everywhere. She marched off into the rain, drinking from the can like it was a potion to cure her less-than-perfect day.

'Kat, wait!' I cried. 'What's the real problem here? That I said you couldn't come to the city?'

She kept walking.

'I don't have time for this,' I said. 'If you could speed this up to the point where you tell me what's wrong so we can make up and get you on the train, that would be fantastic. I'm pretty sure I saw a dude with no teeth and enormous pink gums *leering* at us.'

Kat spun around, almost smacking my cheek with her ponytail. 'Why can't you tell me the truth?' she demanded.

'The truth? The truth is, I'm feeling pretty annoyed.'

'No,' she almost growled. 'The truth about how unhappy you are. Life isn't perfect, yet you pretend it's all roses and rainbows every time we talk.'

Guilt washed over me for lying to her. I hadn't wanted to; I just didn't want to give the family another reason to worry. 'Kat, I'm your older sister. It's not your job to look out for me.'

'After everything that we've been through ...' she murmured, then her voice grew fiercer. 'Just admit you're freaking out about work! And tell me what the hell's happened between you and James ... if he's even your boyfriend any more.'

I swallowed. 'You're right. Work's hectic. You know the launch is next Saturday — well, I have a lot riding on it.'

Kat crossed her arms over her chest. 'And James?'

'You're too young for this stuff. We just had a fight. That's it.'

'Tell me or I'm bailing again,' Kat threatened.

I knew that tone. I didn't want to mess with it.

'Fine ... he's blowing me off,' I admitted. 'I have no idea what's happened, if I've done something, if we're over. It's unlike him. Well, at least I thought it was.'

'Shit. I thought you guys were super loved-up, like, repulsively so?'

'Yeah, well, me too, but I ... well, we ... *wehaven't-saidIloveyouordoneit* yet so ...' The words rolled out in a rush.

'Sorry, I missed that.'

'We haven't said "I love you" or done it yet, okay?' I raised my voice. 'We haven't! We haven't! We haven't!'

'Shout a bit louder, I don't think Mum heard you back at home,' Kat said.

'You're a little pain in the arse. Forget I said anything.'

I grabbed her arm and dragged her back to the platform. As angry as I was, I didn't want to leave her alone with just some graffiti-covered garbage cans for company. She protested a little, but mostly hurried to keep up.

'I can do my own thing, find my own way,' she said. 'You're not my boss.'

'You're right,' I said. 'I'm not getting paid to deal with this. But Mum'll kill me if she finds out I left you here alone. You know how she's terrified of weirdos on the train.'

I looked up at the timetable. We'd missed the next train to Mum's by two minutes and now had a half an hour wait.

'You happy now?' I said, and kicked my suitcase, doing a good job of replicating a toddler's tantrum.

'Jose, calm down,' Kat said. 'I meant what I said before. It sucks that things have turned crappy with James. I don't know what's really happened between you, but you can talk to me. This isn't kindie — your best friend isn't a banana any more.'

But I was too wound up to laugh. 'You never stop, do —'

'Jose ... I thought I was helping.'

I plopped onto my suitcase, staring at the timetable. 'I'll call Mum, tell her you're okay.'

'No, don't. *Please.* She'll ground me for life. I promise to be the best friend you've ever had, more than that stupid overripe banana ever was. Jose? Can you please not say anything to her? Please? Can you do that for me?'

Turned out I could, despite the whole banana dig.

Kat and I didn't speak much on the train. We got a cab to Mum's, and I asked the driver to park around the corner. Kat stared at me, wondering whether I was going to race her to the front door and dob her in.

'I'll say goodbye — again — here,' I said.

'Oh ... thanks for being cool about this,' she said, giving me a quick hug. 'I'm sorry about James ... and I really did like the make-up.'

'I know. Keep an eye on Mum for me, yeah?'

I waved goodbye and directed the taxi driver back to the station. Once I was collapsed on the train again, I closed my eyes, my mind melting into a swirling mess of dreams.

When I woke up I had three missed calls from James.

I buried my phone in my handbag, suddenly not ready to talk to him yet.

14.

The first thing I heard when I walked into the office the next morning was Liani calling my name. It was only 7.16 am and I'd thought I'd be alone.

'Josie, you have a visitor,' she said.

Weird, I never had visitors. Not unless the printer technician counted. I turned to see James standing next to Liani. His hair was shaggier than ever and his eyes were glassy, like he hadn't slept for days.

'What are you doing here?' I asked, only too aware that Liani's eyes were practically piercing the side of my head. 'You look … kinda terrible.' As angry as I was with James, at least I knew he was alive and not hitchhiking his way across the country in a motorbike sidecar.

'I was worried,' he said. 'I needed to see you, but you weren't answering your phone yesterday.'

Liani had slipped back to her desk, but I knew she was in prime eavesdropping mode.

'*I* wasn't answering my phone?' I said. 'That's rich.'

'Morning, squids!' Harrison announced as he walked in. He quickly sized up my expression and James's dishevelled appearance. 'Why, hello.'

'What are you doing here?' I hadn't seen Harrison in the office this early since … ever.

'I work here,' he said with a grin, and continued over to his desk. 'Launch countdown, baby, lots to do this week. How was the big family meet-and-greet, lovebirds?'

'Um … got postponed, sort of,' I said.

'Curiouser and curiouser,' Harrison said.

'About Friday …' James tried again, almost whispering.

I snatched his hand and dragged him to the other side of the office. 'You mean when you got wasted and blew off meeting my mum and sister?' I said, folding my arms across my chest. 'And you wanted to name a *poodle* after me? That Friday?'

'Yeah.' He hung his head. 'Jose, I'm so sorry. Some of the guys invited me out for a drink after the class lunch — you know, to blow off some steam after all the hours we've been pulling. One thing led to another, I was matching them drink for drink and … I stuffed up. You know that's not me.'

'Sure, I get it.' I shrugged, not getting it. Not one little bit. 'Look, I can't talk about this here. Maybe you should go.'

'No, Jose, listen,' he pleaded. 'I'm sorry. I wanted to call you all weekend, but I lost my phone.'

I raised an eyebrow. 'You could have borrowed someone else's ... Or gone on someone's Facebook?'

'Jose, I went to your place later on Friday night, but you weren't there,' he said.

'Funny that. I was with my family. So your phone ...'

'I got it back. They found it in the garden at the pub yesterday afternoon. I called you as soon as I could, but you didn't answer.' James looked down at his toes. 'Let me make this up to you. I'll take you out tonight, it'll be super romantic and you'll forget I ever screwed up. What do you think, JB?'

'I don't know ... I have plans,' I lied, hiding the fact that I loved it when he called me that.

'You do?' He sounded surprised. Too surprised for someone who was supposed to be winning me over.

'Yep,' I said. 'Big plans. Can't break 'em. Maybe next time. And ... and don't call me JB.'

James was startled by my reaction, but he wasn't taking no for an answer. 'Can I come with you?'

'Well ...' I didn't know what to say. This was my first real couple fight, and I'd never quite understood how these things were supposed to play out. If he was nice to me for a second longer, I was going to forget we were in the middle of a tiff and shout him dinner.

'Sorry, she's coming out with me!' announced Harrison, appearing behind us with his hands on his hips. 'Right,

Josie? Don't go bailing on me now. I've been looking forward to dancing for days.'

I turned to James. 'Yeah, I have … dancing. Sorry.'

'Right … well … I'll call you, I guess. Have fun.' He pecked me on the cheek and walked away.

'High-five, miss,' said Harrison once James had left the office. We slapped our palms together. 'That boy of yours looks like a total bum, but I can tell he's seriously good-looking beneath all the grime. Dimples and everything. Anyway, you played hard to get for once and he learned his lesson. You should be proud of yourself.'

'Yeah.' I'd stood my ground, played it cool, kept him on his toes — done the complete opposite of what I usually would've done. So, why did I feel so guilty?

'Where are we going dancing tonight?' I asked Harrison.

'Pipsqueak, no. I was your "out", part of your evil-genius plan. I already have a date tonight — a very hot date.'

Of course he did. So while Harrison was off sipping sangria with a gorgeous guy, I'd be at home alone or working late again. Perhaps I wasn't such an evil genius after all.

'All okay?' Liani called out to me from her desk, proving there was no escape from prying ears or eyes in this office.

'Uh, yep, he, ah … James forgot his keys so … yeah,' I fibbed, although I was pretty sure she'd heard most of the conversation. 'Anyway ... busy, busy! Lots of launch planning, and I have that article to go live today too.'

I'd cobbled together a column that focused on sex and virginity from a social point of view rather than my personal experiences (or lack thereof). It was meant to be an opinion piece, but I'd let the statistics and case-study anecdotes do the talking so I didn't have to reveal my own secret. I wasn't sure whether it was a cop-out or a smart move.

'Sounds like you have it all under control,' Liani said.

Even I had to admit I was getting awfully good at this faking-it business.

Maybe too good.

The next day, after endless chasing of Maxxy's manager, Darlene, to no avail, I called her again and she finally answered her phone.

'Josie Browning,' I said, flustered to get a real person after so many voicemails. 'B-r-o-w-n — yes, we spoke the other day and I've been emailing you for ... Yes, I sent through the details ... I'd be more than happy to resend ... It's a fantastic opportunity for Maxxy and ... Are you sure there's not a way we can organise it? I'd love to show her around and we can discuss the fee again ... Well, think it over. Thanks, Darlene,' I managed to splutter out before hanging up the phone in a huff.

'That went well,' Harrison called out from his desk. 'Lost the main event?'

'I haven't lost her,' I said. 'I just haven't *caught* her yet.'

He smirked. 'Sounds promising. Well, I'm here if you need a human shield when you break the news to Liani.'

'I'm sure she'll understand.' At least, I hoped she would. She was nice, it couldn't be too bad. I'd tried, I'd failed. People didn't always succeed … right?

'You sure about that?' Harrison said, scooting his chair closer to my desk. He lowered his voice. 'You know what comes with being an editor? Pressure and wrath. A whole lotta wrath.'

'*Wrath?*' I scoffed. 'Way to be melodramatic.'

Harrison threw his hands up in the air, proving my point. 'I'm just saying, she's a long way away from holding your hand at *Sash*.'

I couldn't imagine anything close to wrath escaping from Liani's mouth. I'd only heard her raise her voice once, when her husband forgot to buy nappies. But I'd seen the wrath Rae Swanson could unleash on people. That was the stuff of nightmares.

Harrison crossed his legs. 'No need to get your bloomers in a twist. My advice? Give up on Maxxy. You're going around in circles.'

'I'm not giving up — I won't,' I said, taking the bait. 'And bloomers? Who are you? My nanna?'

'Glad you're not giving up. You passed my test,' he said. 'I've been meaning to ask, how's everything with Mr Scrumptious?'

I paused. James wasn't a topic I wanted to discuss right now. 'Everything's ... great.'

'I've heard toddlers lie better than you.'

Luckily, a phone call came to my rescue and I snatched it up before Harrison could interrogate me any further.

'*indi* magazine, Josie speaking,' I rattled off, crossing my fingers it was Darlene calling to change her mind. It wasn't. But it was still good news.

'Brilliant, I'll put him down,' I said. 'And a plus one? Perfect.' I hung up the phone. 'Stevie Q's coming — you know the guy who hosts that funny panel show.'

'Good work, he has amazing calves. Still, he's no Maxxy ...'

I had to give Harrison credit where it was due: his bitchiness deserved some kind of award.

'Stevie Q also has great shoulders,' I said as I updated my guest list, trying not to stare at Maxxy's name in the 'Pending' column.

While Harrison launched into a blow-by-blow account of Stevie Q's best features, I tuned out. He doesn't know Liani like I do, I told myself. She's one of the good ones. I could tell her anything, anytime ... couldn't I?

'You two are whispering together like a couple of schoolgirls,' said Sia, no longer able to block us out. 'What am I missing out on? Other than soft cheeses?'

I checked to make sure Liani wasn't within earshot. 'I'm on a mission,' I whispered.

'That sounds naughty,' Sia said. 'I like it.'

'A pin-down-Maxxy mission.'

'And?'

I sighed. 'Nothing so far. Her manager hung up on me, plus I've tried Twitter, Facebook, her website ... nothing. Darlene's like a big annoying moat around Maxxy — she won't let me in! I'm so desperate I'm thinking of looking her family up in the phone book ...'

Harrison snorted. 'Do phone books even exist any more?'

'I know, it's a terrible idea.' I held my head in my hands. 'I wonder where Maxxy does her groceries? Maybe I could casually swing past her in the dairy aisle.'

'That's an awfully expensive plane ride up north to accost her by the butter and yoghurt,' Sia reminded me.

'I'll keep thinking,' I conceded. 'Oh, and don't either of you breathe a word of this to Liani yet. I want to make sure I've exhausted every avenue before I tell her I've failed.'

'Wouldn't dare,' Harrison said. 'She'd shoot the messenger and I'm far too pretty to die this young.'

Half an hour later, I still had a big fat load of nothing seasoned with a light sprinkling of zilch. I had officially run out of options — there was nothing email-chasing or Twitter-stalking could do for me now. I needed a miracle.

And since the chances of that happening were one in a million (probably even lower when it came to my unluckiness in life), I resigned myself to the fact it was time to tell Liani. I would face the wrath, and I would be ready for my punishment.

As I approached Liani, her landline started ringing. Saved by the phone again.

'Jose, let me get that,' she said. 'Mya? Hi. No, my mobile's in my handbag and ... We what? When? Yes, Sia got the save-the-date teaser, but we didn't RSVP with her being so unwell, and it's so close to the launch and ... Oh, it's for advertising, really? Mya, I'm already so understaffed and the launch is only days away ... Maybe we could send a freelancer?' There was a pause. 'No, I understand the pressure we're under to get sponsors. People can work remotely, but with the launch coming up ... I guess I have no choice then. Look, I'll talk to her and we'll go from there, okay?'

Liani hung up the phone. 'Bum! Josie, how quickly could you pack a suitcase?'

'Why?'

'I need you to go on a media junket up north, and help us build some more relationships for advertising purposes. The location's at a new luxury resort — Lavish.'

Media junket? Up north? Luxury resort? Based on those variables I was pretty sure I could pack my suitcase in five minutes flat. Maybe even four.

'Of course,' I said, trying to sound calm and grown-up. 'When?'

'The flight leaves tomorrow morning.'

I gulped. 'What about the launch prep? I don't want to slow anything down.'

Liani swallowed. 'It's fine. Keep checking your emails on your phone, and Sia, Harrison and I will cover everything from this end. Now, Mya doesn't know the details so she's asked the organiser to email you directly. I imagine you'll get it any second now — she wields a certain influence in that scene.'

I walked back to my desk. Before I got there, Harrison and Sia pounced on me.

'Liani's letting you go to Lavish?' squeaked Sia. 'Oh god, I am green with envy! They asked me, but I've been feeling so off that Liani and I decided it wasn't worth it.'

'Mya needs someone there for advertising, something about building relationships,' I explained, hoping Sia wasn't annoyed with me. 'So, is Lavish meant to be nice? They must have a lot of money to potentially spend with us if Liani's happy for me to drop everything and go.'

'Lot of money? Nice?' Sia shook her head. 'Oh, honey.'

'Nice is the smoked salmon bagel I had for lunch,' Harrison quipped. 'Lavish is just that — lavish, over the top, decked out. It has everything.'

'Six pools!' Sia gushed.

'Eight,' corrected Harrison. 'Plus the beach, three day spas, a bowling alley, a nightclub and a mini roller-coaster.'

'You're joking!'

'Yeah, there's no roller-coaster ... but there's a merry-go-round!' he said.

'Oh, and it's *more than* five stars,' Sia swooned. 'It's, like, rated six out of five.'

I raised an eyebrow. 'Is that even possible?'

'I swear,' she said.

I still wasn't convinced. I'd heard her swear to things before, and at least 79.4 of them hadn't been true.

'Now, Miss Browning, you're going to have to fire up your finest packing efforts,' Harrison said. 'Frankly, I'm not sure you're cut out for it.'

'I'm eighteen, guys, I have packed before,' I said, conveniently leaving out the fact Mum had packed my lunch box until I was seventeen and a half.

'Look, there's packing a suitcase, then there's *packing a suitcase for a media launch*,' stressed Harrison. 'Forget all your usual travel comfort gear. I bet you're the type who likes a neck pillow when travelling, right? Ballet flats to keep your tootsies comfy?'

'No.' Yes.

'Leave them at home,' he said, narrowing his eyes. 'This trip is about glamour, even when you're poolside sipping on cocktails. You'll need stylish dresses too — not those prissy numbers you wear.'

'Hey!'

But Harrison was taking charge. 'What else, what else ...? Flowing kaftans, high heels — duh, take at least three pairs, six if you can. Plenty of accessories, your hair straightener, diffuser, make-up, make-up, make-up, and a super-cute tailored blazer. Oh, and fill the rest of your bag with bikinis.'

'Seriously?'

'Eight pools, eight bikinis.'

'Makes sense to me,' Sia said. 'I can't believe I'm missing this!' She rubbed her belly. 'I hate you, beautiful alien baby! So, about the packing, Jose — does that all sound pretty clear?'

'Yeah, crystal,' I said. 'Just one problem: I don't own half — okay, most — of those things. I have one bikini, one full-piece, two pairs of heels, a few nice dresses that *may* make it past your prissy radar, and I don't even know what a kaftan is.'

'Houston, we have a poorly dressed problem,' said Harrison. 'Sia, do you have any gems in the fashion cupboard that the little miss can borrow? Maybe something left from Sophie's shoot the other day? There were some great pieces.'

'Liani's already couriered everything back,' Sia said. 'I know! Jose, you can borrow my clothes.'

'She's much smaller than you, Sia,' Harrison started, then stopped himself. 'I mean, she doesn't have your voluptuous womanly curves. No offence, Josie.'

I did my best to hide a smile. 'None taken.'

'It'll work, trust me,' Sia insisted, Harrison's blunder

slipping past her. 'Jose, come to mine tonight and we'll pack together.'

'Yeah? That would be awesome, thanks heaps.'

'Unless you're hanging with James?' Sia said. 'Sorry, I forget other people have lives.'

'Um ... let's stick with your plan,' I said.

Sia had suffered through months of me mooning over James nonstop, so she knew something was up. 'I wonder if you'll get your first press pass,' she cooed, kindly changing the subject.

As she and Harrison moved on to debating which swimsuits were appropriate for Lavish's eight pools, I took stock of my favourite notebooks to pack, tossing up between the white one with rainbow butterflies or the blue one with yellow suns. I decided to take both. More is more, Sia often told me.

'You get the email yet?' Liani called out. 'The timing could not be worse for this.'

'Opening it up now, then I need to talk to you about something,' I called back, dreading the moment when I'd have to tell Liani I'd failed my pin-down-Maxxy mission. I clicked on the itinerary attached to the email, and that's when I saw it.

A name.

A name so powerful, so needed, so miraculous, I forgot how to think more than a few words at a time. It felt like ice was freezing over my brain, trapping everything inside like frost over a car windscreen on a winter's morning.

'Er ... Liani?' I managed, gliding in shock to her desk, convinced I'd imagined the whole thing out of desperation.

'Yes? What's the verdict? This junket looking like a bigger waste of time than a cooking-show TV marathon?' Liani said, not looking up as she click-clacked on her computer.

'Her. It's her.' The ice hadn't defrosted from my brain.

'Her who?'

'Lavish is going to be dinner performing at the launch of Maxxy,' I spluttered, then cleared my throat. 'Wait, I mean Maxxy is going to be performing at a dinner at the Lavish launch! Did I say that properly? I forget how to speak.'

'You're kidding!' Liani said, her voice hitting a shrillness reminiscent of Kat when she heard one of her favourite celebs was releasing a pop album.

'I'm not, I swear I'm not ... at least, I think I'm not,' I said, rushing back to my desk to reread the email. 'Yep, *Maxxy will be making a special guest appearance ...* blah blah blah ... *great opportunity to meet one of the country's hottest young singers* ... Oh crap, the RSVP was a week ago!'

'It's fine,' Liani assured me. 'Lavish want us there so they're making an exception. Like I said, Mya's influential. Jose, send the RSVP, tie up any loose ends on our launch, then prep for this event. This is our chance to secure Maxxy and a potential advertiser, so I want you to give it *everything*. You've got this. We're going to launch with frigging Maxxy singing her little heart out, I can feel it!'

Liani began humming Maxxy's newest song, which I took as my signal to get back to work.

This was it. My final chance. And I had so much to organise before tomorrow.

As promised, Sia helped me pack my suitcase — if 'helping' meant being a bossy-boots-control-freak and devouring a packet of cream-filled biscuits. We went through her wardrobe and tossed in everything and anything we thought might come in handy. In the end, my suitcase overflowed with stunning designer clothes that, as Harrison had predicted, were too big.

'It's all good,' Sia said, throwing six belts into the case. 'Wear these and the dresses won't look like sacks.'

Her life advice didn't end there.

'Okay, I've waited long enough for you to tell me ... What did James do that's left you sulking?' she added.

'What? Nothing. I ... He did nothing.'

'Is that why he came to work looking like a hot hobo and you didn't mention it?'

Damn Harrison.

'Fine ... I didn't want to make a big deal of it, but he kinda got drunk, disappeared and blew off my family,' I said. 'I don't even know if I'm mad any more, it's too exhausting. I just want everything to go back to normal.'

My phone beeped with an *I miss you* text from James.

'Speaking of which ...' I muttered, and went to reply.

Sia snatched the phone from my hands and tossed it on the bed. 'After what he did, make him sweat,' she said.

Looked like I was the only person in the city who wasn't so keen on playing mind games.

'In light of all this boy drama, I want to say this trip to Lavish is about *you*, so I think it's important that you ...' She paused.

'Take notes?' I asked. 'Fire off lots of questions? Pitch story ideas?'

'No,' she said. 'No, no, no. Oh, dear naive Josie, none of those are *that* necessary.'

'This is a press junket. Shouldn't I be acting like a member of the press?'

Sia tutted. 'Oh, that's cute. You still think this trip is about work, don't you?'

'Well, yeah. We need advertisers. And Maxxy's going to be there. It's why Liani's finally happy for me to go.'

'Yeah, of course, on the top level, the superficial level, it's for work — but beneath all the small talk and rubbing shoulders this is a holiday. Think of the pools! The spas! The potentially hot waiters! Two nights, fully paid, away from the office to do as you please. Away from your life as you know it.'

A temporary break from my life did sound nice, even though I didn't want to rub it in Sia's face.

'When you're at Lavish, don't you dare hide away in your room,' Sia added. 'I want you sunbaking, swimming and relaxing. You hear me, girl?'

Her eyes twinkled and I knew she was encouraging me to have a good time despite the drama with James. I nodded. She didn't need to convince me. I'd never been so ready to hop on a plane and fly away from all my problems.

Next stop, paradise.

15.

I dragged my suitcase off the carousel and weaved my way through the airport. Life up north already felt different — my foundation and bronzer had all but sweated off, and everywhere I looked, girls were wearing cut-off denim shorts. I scanned the crowd for my driver. Men of all shapes and sizes (many with beards of all shapes and sizes) held up signs with names on them. *Kate*, nope. *Tom*, no. *Lawn Bowls Legends*, nuh-uh. *Jackie*, close but not quite ... *Miss Josephine Browning* — jackpot.

I said hello to the driver, who took my suitcase.

'That's okay, I can wheel it,' I said, feeling guilty. But he insisted and led me to the car: a black limo. 'This car? Really?' I squealed and hugged him.

He flinched, but I didn't care. Sia was right: this was shaping up to be a holiday I would remember forever.

Moments later I was lounging on the limo's back seat as we cruised down streets lined with palm trees. I had the window down and was enjoying the fresh sea air blowing on my face.

'Have you tried the cheeses and orange juice, Miss Browning?' the driver asked. 'I can recommend the vintage cheddar.'

I released another high-pitched squeal. 'There's *cheese* back here? How much does it cost?'

'It's complimentary, miss. As are the organic dark-chocolate-covered almonds.'

I bit my lip to stop myself squealing again. The driver looked like he had a girl-squealing threshold and I was sure I'd already crossed it. I was so excited; I could feel the sand between my toes and smell sea salt in my hair already.

We drove for at least twenty minutes, passing high-rise apartments looking over kilometres of white sand and rolling crystal-blue waves. The limo turned down a winding path towards the resort. I pressed my nose against the window and gasped at the view: manicured gardens sprinkled with flowers of every colour were wrapped around the most beautiful building I'd ever seen. It had towering walls, and an open-plan foyer with white marble pillars and tiles.

Ours was the only car in the driveway. I'd been expecting to see other journalists, but I figured they were still on the way. A valet rushed forwards to open the limo door and collect my luggage. He gestured for me to follow him to the entrance. As I walked behind him, I fiddled with the belt holding up my dress and wrinkled my nose at my ballet flats. I'd promised Sia that I'd change into heels before arriving so I looked the part of a glamorous writer.

'Could you please stop for a second, I need something from my suitcase,' I said.

I unzipped the bag and felt around for the strappy taupe pair of heels that, according to Sia, were 'understated, classic and chic'. I found them nestled in a corner and yanked them out. 'Or were these the ones to go with the poolside outfit and kaftan?' I mumbled. Wait, there was a list! Sia had written it for me so I'd remember what went with what. By now, my suitcase was wide open, with skirts, bras, undies and bikinis scattered all around me on the concrete.

The valet looked perturbed. 'If you're not careful —'

'One sec,' I said, pulling cards, receipts and little scraps of paper out of my wallet. 'One sec ... one sec ... I got it! Strappy taupe heels for resort arrival. Nailed it. Now, what were you saying?'

He cleared his throat, and I looked up to see a woman in a tight-fitting corporate dress and patent leather stilettos smiling down at me. Her strawberry-blonde hair fell into loose beach-kissed curls and her face was dusted with freckles.

'You must be Josephine,' she said, thrusting a manicured hand out for me to shake. 'Hi, I'm Penny, the communications manager here.'

Of course I'm Josephine. No one else would be crazy enough to introduce herself with her bras and undies littered around her.

'Yes, hi, I'm Josephine ... er, Josie,' I babbled. 'Sorry, I was —'

'Packing?' Penny quipped.

'Something like that,' I said, as I stuffed everything back into the suitcase.

'You missed one,' Penny said, pointing to a blue and black polka-dot bra on the ground. The valet coughed.

'Oh!' I snatched it up.

'I'm going to have to whisk you away now, Josie,' Penny said. 'You're one of the last to arrive so we need to get you settled in before the fun really starts.'

'I am?' I asked, paranoia setting in. Everyone was already inside, probably braiding each other's hair and becoming best friends.

'Yes, due to your last-minute RSVP, this was the earliest flight we could get you on. But you're here now! You have your own room with a spa, king-size bed and complimentary room service, so please do make the most of the facilities,' she said. 'We want you to enjoy the full Lavish experience.'

Penny linked her freckled arm through mine, excused the valet, took my suitcase handle in her other hand, and led me towards the enormous open-plan foyer, which was now a hub of activity. Staff scurried to and fro, helping people with luggage, checking them in, giving directions. We walked through the foyer, past signs for restaurants, bars, pools and spas, and out onto a winding footpath lined with lush green trees and flowers of peach and yellow.

'Shall I take my luggage?' I said. 'That must be getting heavy.'

'Pierre is bringing the cart around,' said Penny.

Moments later, a handsome bellboy with gelled black hair appeared next to us in what looked like a golf buggy. 'Your bags, miss?' His accent was a mix of Australian and French.

'Ah, thanks,' I said, as Pierre loaded my suitcase onto the buggy and gestured for me to sit next to it.

'Pierre will drop you off at The Princess Suite so you can freshen up, then he'll return to drive you over to join the rest of the group,' Penny said.

Princess Suite? I was beginning to think I should have packed a ball gown and diamond tiara.

'I'll leave you here, so make yourself comfortable. Think of Lavish as your home sweet home.'

I thanked her and clung to the golf buggy as Pierre sped along the path. A sharp left, a sharp right, another sharp left, and we were there. Pierre carried my luggage to the front step, opened the door and nodded for me to walk inside.

I gasped. To my left was a spa bath the size of a small family pool. To my right, a huge couch faced a TV that could have rivalled the screen at our local cinema complex. Heart-shaped chocolates sat in a bowl on the dining table. I tore the wrapper off one and took a bite.

'That's organic raw dark chocolate,' Pierre said, as the rich flavour filled my mouth. 'Now, the phone's there so you can call for anything — room service, fresh towels, day-spa treatments … extra chocolates. I will be back soon to take you to meet the others.'

He gave a small bow. Unsure what to do, I said thanks and curtsied. Fool.

Once Pierre left, I took another chocolate, kicked off my heels and ran into the bedroom. I squealed at the king-size bed — it looked as big as a football field — then flopped onto the mattress. The soft bedding enveloped me like a fluffy marshmallow. Home sweet home, I thought, Penny's words ringing in my ears.

The buggy came to a halt in front of one of the resort's many eateries. Pierre pointed at the entrance. 'Try the caviar, it's delicious,' he said, as he drove off.

I climbed the steps to the café and opened the door. About twenty glossy-haired beauties turned to face me, but I was so nervous, all I saw was a sea of shiny tresses and pouting lips in shades of red, coral and pink.

Penny rushed over, wrapped an arm around me and steered me towards the group. 'Everyone, this is Josie, the features director at *indi* magazine.'

'Ah, I'm the features writer,' I stammered. 'Junior, actually, and we're a website ... and we're launching properly soon ... but ... hi, everyone.'

Note to self: work on *indi* elevator pitch.

Most of the women were too preoccupied with eyeing my outfit to say hello. Some nodded in approval, especially at the taupe heels. I only had about six more costume changes to survive; more if you counted poolside looks. Staring at the floor, I moved towards an empty seat at the back of the room.

'Over here,' someone called out.

I turned and was surprised to see Edwina waving me over. Everyone else eyeballed me, curious about who I must be if the queen bee herself was accepting me.

'Hey,' I said, relieved to see a familiar face, even if Edwina intimidated me as much as Rae Swanson did — okay, *almost* as much.

Edwina shooed a girl out of the seat next to her, then gestured for me to take her spot. I went to apologise to the girl, but she'd already rushed off in the direction of the bathrooms, looking close to bursting into tears. I'd been upgraded to sit with the cool kids. The only question was whether I could pull it off.

Penny was telling us about the resort's health program, but Edwina wasn't interested. 'This girl is a prodigy,' she whispered to the other women at our table. Their eyes widened in interest. 'She's only, like, sixteen, and she's practically the editor at *indi*. I mean, it's only a start-up, but still.'

'Um, I'm not the editor, and I'm eighteen,' I said. Although I did like the sound of 'Josie the prodigious editor'.

'Close enough. Hey, what room are you in?' asked Edwina.

'Ah, The Princess Suite.'

'Fab, I'm in The Queen Suite, just nearby. We're almost room-mates.'

'Everyone, listen up!' Penny announced. 'We *were* going to start off with one of our exclusive health seminars, but we thought we'd postpone that for today and let you all enjoy some time by the pool, on the beach, at the spa, or in your suite.'

I remembered Sia's words about having a holiday. Maybe this *was* less about work than I'd realised.

'Beach?' asked Edwina, although her tone made it more of a statement.

I didn't know anyone else at the retreat, and most of the other girls looked about as approachable as cheetahs on the hunt, so I agreed.

After a quick detour to my suite to slip into my first swimwear outfit — a cobalt-blue bikini and colourful kaftan — I found my way to the private beach. The water was sparkling, the air was warm and salty, and the staff at the nearby open-air bar, like Pierre, were friendly and attentive. It was a perfect sunny day — the kind you dream about when you say 'I need a holiday'. I was there, I was in it, I was living the dream. I should have felt great. I'd ditched my usual baggy, saggy swimmers and was wearing an incredibly flattering bikini loaned by Sia (luckily it fitted me better than the dresses — she'd bought it in the hope of 'slimming down for summer'). And it wasn't like I had horrible green scales on my body, yet I was completely terrified. The reason was simple: I was surrounded by girls in bikinis — polka-dot, string, Brazilian-cut, neon, classic black bikinis — all swaggering around like they were on a runway at Fashion Week.

I ended up on a sun lounge sandwiched between Edwina, who was sipping a diet lemonade and reading a magazine, and her friend Paulina, *Marilyn*'s beauty and health editor. As I lay there, I wondered if anyone had ever felt this uncomfortable in their own skin before. Was my stomach poking out too much? Had I shaved my knees properly? Maybe I should have worn a one-piece? How crazy-small did my boobs look in this bikini? It was exhausting.

The sun was scorching so I reached for my sunscreen, wondering if I'd be the odd one out — like when Mum made me and Kat wear fluoro orange rashies at the local pool. But Edwina stuck out her palm for some SPF — apparently sun safety was cool.

'You sure you're not a beauty editor?' Edwina said, still managing to look graceful as she rubbed sunscreen onto her face and arms.

I blushed. As someone who'd only recently learned how to do her hair in styles other than 'ponytail' and 'wearing down' (okay, not really a style) it felt good to hear that from her.

'Use it whenever you want,' I said, happy to be useful. 'Should we go for a swim?'

'Swimming?' Paulina cringed. 'My hair took me an hour to do.'

She had a blonde pixie cut. Liani's son Dylan had more hair.

'Maybe later,' Edwina said. A quick look at the line of tanned, slender bodies stretched out on either side of us made me realise she meant 'Maybe never'. Everyone was too busy preening, posing and taking selfies from the comfort of their sun lounges. I was the only one willing to get dunked beneath the waves and ruin my hair and make-up. I had a lot to learn about this world.

'The people I'm following online are all boring,' Paulina sighed, staring at her phone screen. 'Can't someone put up an interesting post for once?'

'I know. Everyone's so busy trying to stand out, they're all blending in,' Edwina added. 'It's too dull for words.'

'Speaking of what *wasn't* dull,' Paulina said, sitting up straight, 'E, did you see that hilariously sad email from the girl trying to pop her cherry? I can't remember the details, but one of the guys in the office got it from a friend of a friend and it was so funny. I feel like we should post it online — it would totally go viral. It's gotta be made up though. It has to be.'

'I didn't know you were such a cold-hearted *beyatch*, Paulie,' Edwina said in a fake sickly-sweet voice.

Paulina raised an eyebrow. 'Excuse me?'

'Personally I thought it was adorable.' Edwina sniffed. 'Anyway, it's old news. I've read about fifty things that would go viral before that email. Let's talk about something interesting ... like which Lavish staff member you'll have picked up by the end of the junket.'

The mention of hot guys was enough to distract Paulina and she and Edwina compared notes on the staff, while I took in the fact that Edwina had just saved my arse.

After what felt like hours of talking about guys (thankfully Edwina didn't ask me about James), my stomach started to growl. I knew that if I resisted it any longer there was a 93.5 per cent chance of me turning hangry (hungry *and* angry — a dangerous combination).

'Anyone peckish?' I asked. 'I could get us some food from the bar, like ... um ...' I stopped, wondering what type of food these girls ate. Diamond-speckled mangoes? Chia-seed pudding with platinum sprinkles? 'You know what, I'll grab some menus,' I said, excusing myself.

The guy at the bar (number four on Paulina's Hot Guys Of Lavish list) gestured for me to pull up a stool. I was speed-reading the menu options — scarily healthy items like 'wheatgrass double shot', 'purple antioxidant smoothie' and 'zucchini spaghetti' — when I heard a male voice drawl, 'Hey, it's you.'

I swivelled on the stool to see Alex standing there. 'Hey, and it's you!'

He wore board shorts and not much else. I didn't know where to look, although his toned chest and abs were hard to ignore. My towel and kaftan were over at the sun lounge, so I crossed my legs and folded my arms across my stomach.

'So … you're here too,' I continued, once again proving that small talk wasn't my specialty.

He grinned. 'It would appear so, Josie the journo. I checked in about twenty minutes ago — I slept through my alarm and missed the first flight.' He reached for the menu and accidentally brushed my arm. I flinched, but he didn't seem to notice. 'Hey, have you seen any real food? Everything here's a little green for my taste.'

'Um …' My eyes scanned the options again, taking in the words 'orange detox delight' and 'rejuvenating radish bowl'. 'Doesn't look like it.'

'I would kill for a meat pie,' he said. 'I should have known I'd need to smuggle in my own supplies. How'd you score this junket anyway? I didn't think you got to do fun things?'

'Turns out my boss Liani needed someone here to "make friends" with them for potential advertising. We need all the financial support we can get.'

'And they picked you to come … nice. I'm doing a travel story for the *City Journal*.'

'No way,' I said. 'I had an excur— er, a work trip there once.'

'Cool. I'm sure I'll be too delirious from all the yoga, saunas and meditation to get it written though. Hey, are you going to the group dinner and drinks thing tonight?'

'I'll be there,' I said. 'And not just for the rabbit food. Between you and me, I *really* need to persuade Maxxy to perform at our launch on Saturday. Liani wants her there, like, freaking desperately, and apparently I'm the gal to seal the deal.'

'Maxxy?' he asked. 'You mean that little poplet getting around the media circuit?'

I laughed. 'I suppose that's her.'

'Look at this party for two,' a voice piped up. We turned to see Edwina standing behind us, hands on hips, body and bikini proud. I wondered how long she'd been standing there. 'Josie, I thought you might need some help with the food.'

'Er, thanks,' I said. 'I haven't ordered yet. Ah, this is —'

'Alex,' she said, blatantly avoiding eye contact with him.

'Oh, right. You two know each other?'

'You could say that,' Alex said.

Edwina's eyes narrowed. 'And how are you two acquainted?'

'I live with his friend,' I said at the same time as Alex said, 'We're friends.'

'Which is it?' Edwina pressed.

I noticed the atmosphere had turned icy, despite the warm rays of sunshine.

'You know what, I'm actually not that hungry any more,' I said, as my stomach rumbled again. 'I might head back to the beach.'

'I'll join you,' Edwina said, linking her arm through mine. 'The view down there is much better.'

'See you tonight, Jose,' Alex said.

'Yeah, bye,' I stammered, conscious that Edwina was glaring at him.

He winked at me, before ordering a wheatgrass double shot 'and a bucket — just in case'.

'We only went out for about a second but that guy makes my blood boil,' Edwina hissed when we were out of earshot.

'Oh ... he's just a friend of a friend, basically a stranger,' I said. 'Do you need to talk or —'

'I don't want to go into it, he's not worth it,' she said, taking dainty steps across the fiery sand. 'Tell me about you and that James guy from your email. Are you two loved up yet?'

I paused. 'Not quite.'

She gave a mock gasp. 'Trouble in paradise?'

I forced a smile. 'It's fine. I have other things to worry about.'

'Like Maxxy?'

She had overheard me. 'Yeah, like Maxxy.'

'Well, I got the save-the-date for the launch, so it's in the diary. Saturday, right?'

'You're coming?'

My nerves multiplied as I imagined Edwina judging my handiwork on the night.

'Of course I'll be there, Miss *indi* editor prodigy. I know, I know, you're not the editor ... but it's nice to imagine, right? I'm sure it's only a matter of time.' She elbowed me before we took our positions on the sun lounges.

'What food did you order?' Paulina said, admiring her well-defined cheekbones in her phone screen.

'Nothing because guess who was up at the bar flirting with our friend here? *Alex*,' Edwina said.

'No!' Paulina said, lowering her phone. 'That greasy sack of lies is here? You poor thing.'

'He *really* wasn't flirting,' I insisted. Not that either of them listened.

'This industry is way too small,' said Paulina, screwing up her nose. 'How was he, E? Tell me he's stacked on weight. Tell me he's a porker.'

Edwina sighed. 'Don't ask.'

'Damn, he looked that good, huh?'

'Next question,' she said, slipping on her sunglasses.

The three of us fell silent, listening to the lapping of the waves. My mind drifted to daydreaming about the launch on Saturday. Maxxy would be there, of course, and Liani would shower me with praise and chocolate-coated treats. James and I would say 'I love you' without it ending in disaster (and he'd organise a parade down the main street in our honour — complete with enormous balloon replicas of ourselves). Even Mya would be choppered in to shake my hand and thank me for my loyal service to *indi*.

Edwina was right: some things were nice to imagine.

16.

I sat on the bed in my suite, replying to a stream of emails from *indi* HQ. It had been a tough afternoon — if tough meant completely indulgent. I'd soaked in a bubble bath full of rose petals, fallen asleep on the enormous bed, then taken my time getting ready for the dinner later that night. The blue dress, slim silver belt, statement cuff and cream high heels from Sia's list of outfit suggestions looked great, but I was racked with guilt. I'd ignored another text from James — *How long are you going to give me the silent treatment?* — because I didn't know how to reply. Not yet. Not with a high-pressure dinner only minutes away.

Suck it up, I told myself, pushing down my nerves. Despite what Sia said, this wasn't supposed to be fun — it was work. No one else was here to represent *indi*.

But before I threw myself back into the media crowd, I needed to hear a familiar voice. I punched Mum's number into my phone, but it rang out and went to her voicemail. Moments later, a text came through: *Sorry,*

love, at the movies with Rodgie. Call you later. Kisses!
I tried not to shudder at the mention of Rodger.

Next up, Steph. I caught her in the middle of a shift at the café and could hear her boss screaming at her to hang up the phone. 'Oops,' she giggled. 'Better run. You're sooo coming back with a tan. Say hi to Alex from me!'

Last on my list was Kat.

'Talk fast, sis,' she said, as bossy as ever. 'I'm hanging with Philippe so you've got the ad break to say what you need to say. How's everything with James?'

'Wait, who's Philippe?'

'You're wasting time, Jose. Quick, that cute toilet paper ad is on and you know they always play it before the show starts again.'

I sighed. 'Well, I'm up here on the north coast, and everything's still crazy with James, and Alex is here, as well as this girl who —'

'Alex?' she said. 'Is he hot? Tell him I said hi. Hey, did you know Mum wants to start reiki? Ah, man, the show's back on, Jose. Call me in the next ad break, I want to hear the rest.' She hung up.

I was about to draft an *I miss you* email to Angel when there was a knock on the door.

'Josie?' I heard Penny call. 'You're missing all the fun!'

A chorus of voices chimed in over her — it sounded like she'd collected half the media pack on her way.

'One second!' I cried out, slicking on a coating of lip gloss.

My phone beeped with a text from Kat: *Sorry I couldn't talk properly. Soon, I promise! xx*

It was nice to see this softer side from my sister, but she'd have to wait. I popped the phone in my handbag and opened the door to greet Penny and a handful of journalists with a nervous smile plastered across my face.

'Sorry, my editor rang,' I lied.

Even I was impressed with my fib. The old me would have stammered something unbelievable like 'Sorry, I'm an award-winning fashion designer and I was putting the final touches on this couture dress.'

'Completely understand,' Penny said. 'Follow me, girls — we have a big night ahead!'

I clip-clopped along, listening to Penny chatter about the resort and the special appearance by Maxxy that night. It was the reminder I needed to stay on my A-game.

Penny led us up a large staircase and into an extravagant dining hall. There was a two-metre-tall chocolate fountain in the corner ('For decorative purposes only,' said Penny, which sounded like torture to me), a buffet of healthy food (steamed vegetables as far as the eye could see), and waiters in white tuxedos nodding, bowing and taking orders from the resort's clientele.

We walked through the resaurant and entered a private, more intimate area that had been set up especially for us.

Vases of pink blooms and candles dotted every table, giving the room a soft, romantic look. I noticed Edwina sitting on the other side of the room.

Oblivious to the dramatics earlier this afternoon, Penny sat me across from Alex, fussing as she placed a serviette on my lap. Once she'd trotted off, I looked at the people either side of me. One of them was Paulina, who said hi, and the other was a girl I didn't know, whose name was Jade. I introduced myself and asked what she did.

'Beauty freelancing.' Her mouth was pursed so tight she barely moved her lips.

'That sounds interesting,' I said, trying my best to schmooze.

'It is,' she said, and returned to chasing her food around the plate with her fork.

I took a bite of the entrée: a lone scallop perched on a bed of wilted spinach. It tasted fresh and light, a far cry from the greasy noodles and cheap takeaway to which my palate had grown accustomed.

Alex kicked my foot under the table.

'Ow!' I cried out.

He grinned.

'What are you doing?' I whispered.

'I'm bored ... and how *insane* is everyone here?'

'Just shhhhh,' I hissed, conscious that Edwina or her friends might be looking over or listening.

'Is he bothering you again?' asked Paulina, shooting Alex a dirty look.

I swallowed. 'No, we were talking about … um …'

'Palm trees, we were talking about palm trees,' said Alex, trying not to laugh at his own ridiculousness.

I wished I could wipe the silly smirk off his face with my serviette.

'Palm trees?' Paulina repeated. 'What about them?'

Alex shrugged. 'You know … there's heaps of them here … and they're so tall … and green.'

'I don't get it,' she huffed. 'You're even stranger than I thought.'

'Thank you,' he said as Paulina rolled her eyes.

'Everyone, may I have your attention please,' Penny announced into a microphone. 'As promised, we've arranged for a *very* special guest to perform for you this evening. This will be a regular part of the Lavish experience — entertainers who live and breathe the same healthy living values as our guests.'

'How's this for a healthy living value?' whispered Alex, offering me a jelly snake. 'Called in a favour.'

'Put that away.'

'Your loss,' he said, chomping into the lolly.

'I'm thrilled to announce our first guest,' said Penny. 'The unbelievable, chart-topping superstar … Maxxy!'

Everyone clapped as two girls with long wavy hair walked into the room, each with an acoustic guitar over her shoulder. They perched on a pair of stools, their tiny frames smaller than their guitars.

Maxxy cleared her throat. 'Hey, everyone. I'm Maxxy, and this is my good friend Mirabella, who'll be joining me on guitar and backing vocals.'

Edwina caught my eye and gave me a thumbs up.

I nodded, nerves bubbling in my belly.

'Let's get straight into it,' Maxxy said. 'Here's a song I wrote about feeling out of place from time to time — it's called "Square Peg".'

She began singing and I was instantly swept away by the soft huskiness of her voice.

'You love this poppy, folky rubbish, don't you?' whispered Alex from across the table.

I glared at him. 'Can you be quiet for, like, one second?'

Alex mightn't have cared whether he made a good impression, or if he got a great story, but I did. I was a newbie, and I didn't want to get booted to the loser corner. But he was right about the music: I did love it.

I turned to tell him that, but he'd left his seat. I glanced around, but he wasn't at the bar, or headed for the bathroom, or even irritating Edwina over at her table. And then I spotted him chatting with Penny in the corner. What was he up to?

I wasn't the only curious one: I saw Edwina staring at him. For two people who'd dated, they were total opposites. She was so prim and polished, while Alex was cool and laidback with an attitude that screamed 'You only live once'. It wouldn't have surprised me if he had those words tattooed on his body somewhere.

Paulina tapped me on the shoulder, snapping me out of my nosy thoughts, and I spun around, nervous that she might ask me something about Alex.

'Ah, hi,' I said. 'Having a good time? We're having a great time. Wait … did I say we? I meant *I'm* having a good time. Just me. Not Alex and me. Not that you asked that … or mentioned him … or that we spend that much time together! Well, we did one road trip, and he has come to my place … not to see me. He's friends with my housemate, although he *saw* me, of course, when he was there, he's not blind … obviously.'

Okay, definitely nervous. But I needn't have worried.

'Can you pass the sparkling water, Joey?' she said.

I'd spent hours with this woman and she *still* didn't know my name? Even worse, she thought it was Joey.

Jade leaned over. 'That's your name? Like the kangaroo? Cute.'

'Er …' I said, passing Paulina the bottle, 'it's actually Josie.'

Paulina sipped her water. 'That's not what it says on the seating chart by the bar.'

Great. For a second I contemplated running with the name. Joey Browning sounded fun — like the type of girl who'd cliff jump, dye her hair orange and ride a Segway, just 'cos it was a Tuesday.

Maybe Joey could be my fresh start. Maybe she could be my future.

Or maybe not. Orange wasn't really my colour.

I stared at my empty plate, listening to the shallow small talk around me. One girl was complaining that her portion sizes were too small, another that hers were too big. A girl behind me was whining because their last junket resort had two spa baths in each room, not just one, while another was bitching about her friend who got her boobs done in Thailand. The kicker was the girl whinging about the downsides of all the extravagant freebies: 'You mean I'll have to skip my sleep-in if I want to go for a ride in the hot-air balloon? Forget it.' Boo freaking hoo.

It could have been the fact these girls were the most stuck-up people I'd ever shared breathing space with, or maybe my blood sugar was running low from the lack of sweet treats, but I had the urge to smear the butter that sat untouched on our table all over Paulina's face. And Jade's. And every other person there who looked at me like I was a piece of dog poo on the bottom of their overpriced patent leather heels.

'Excuse me,' I said, walking away to the bar. No one so much as glanced at me.

I was ordering a lemon squash — well, a mineral water with fresh lemon as they didn't serve real soft drinks —

when I noticed the chalkboard seating chart. There it was in perfect cursive lettering: *Joey Browning*. It was official: Josie Browning really was a nobody.

Alex's gravelly voice suddenly filled the room, snapping me and the rest of the guests to attention. While I'd been daydreaming, he had taken a seat on stage with the girls, Maxxy's guitar now slung over his shoulder.

'Hey there, I'm Alex,' he said, running his hand through his shaggy hair. 'My new friend Maxxy here has kindly agreed to let me play with her tonight for a laugh, so, ah, let's kick things up a notch.'

He launched into a song and, unbelievably, both girls did backing vocals for him. He was blissed out, eyes closed, and for a second I forgot this was the same pot-stirring journo who didn't seem to care about anything.

'What the …' I muttered, noticing Edwina mouthing something similar.

Here I was stressing about how to get close to Maxxy, and Alex had just strolled right up and charmed his way into *performing* with her. Plus, not only was he wearing the brooding musician stamp well, but it turned out he could be authentic when he wanted to be. I could see how Edwina — and apparently every other glassy-eyed girl in the room — might fall for him, despite his ability to frustrate anyone with a pulse.

When Alex finished, everyone clapped — except Edwina, who sipped her drink with a sour expression on her face.

Maxxy and Mirabella even planted a kiss on Alex's cheek. He made schmoozing look as easy as tying his shoelaces.

'Thanks for that little surprise, Alex!' Penny said, fanning herself with a piece of paper. 'We're going to take a short break, but don't worry, Maxxy and Mirabella will be back with more soon. Now, enjoy your mains — I'm hearing good things about the fish!'

Everyone clapped, then returned to redoing their lipstick, giggling and competing with one another about the next amazing event they'd been invited to. Everyone except me. I was too busy scribbling out 'Joey Browning' on the chalkboard.

I stood up from the bar, ready to return to my seat for dinner, but was interrupted by a throaty chuckle. 'Alone at a bar again? Should I be worried?'

I turned to see Alex behind me. But this time, he wasn't flying solo. Maxxy stood next to him.

'Ah, hi,' I said, relieved I didn't splutter my drink over her in shock.

'Is that lemon squash?' Maxxy asked, taking the stool next to me. 'I'll grab one too, thanks,' she said to the barman.

'You're Maxxy,' I blurted out.

Oops. She knew she was Maxxy, Alex knew she was Maxxy, the slice of lemon in my drink knew she was Maxxy. But my faux pas didn't seem to bother her.

'That I am,' she said, then lowered her voice to a whisper. 'My real name's Miriam, but don't tell anyone.'

'Oh my ... you told me a secret,' I said, wondering how to turn on the filter that would stop me saying every thought out loud. 'I swear I won't tell anyone. I'm Josie.'

'It's not really Miriam, is it?' asked Alex, as blunt as ever. 'Sounds like an overweight mum who helps out at the school canteen.'

'That reaction is why my manager changed it. Never bothered me though.' Maxxy shrugged. 'Anyway, you sounded great up there, Alex, but next time give a girl some warning!' She clipped him lightly around the ear like they'd been mates forever. 'We could have worked you into the set even more. The other journos seemed to love it, you ladies' man, you.'

I couldn't believe it. Despite her rude manager, Maxxy was cool, nice *and* funny. Not only did I want to invite her to the launch, I kind of wanted to be her new best friend too. Although Alex seemed to have muscled his way into that role with ease.

I cleared my throat and attempted to channel Sia's charisma or Liani's warmth. 'Maxxy, I wanted to ask you something,' I began.

'Yeah, anything. Oh, except what inspires me. If I have to answer that question again, my eyes might roll right out of my head.'

I laughed. And then got nervous to the point where my tongue may as well have been made of jelly. 'No, I was actually wondering ... well, there's this thing ... an event-type thing ... where there'll be people ... yep, lots of those ... and um, food, of course, and drinks,' I rambled, gesturing to my lemon squash and trying to ignore Alex's WTF expression. 'Well, I was wondering, hoping even, to the point of desperation, in fact, if ... um ...'

'Yes?' Maxxy probed.

'If ... if ...' I noticed Edwina was standing mere metres away at the bar and my last drop of bravery vanished. My throat went dry. 'If ... if ... if you ... You know what, never mind.'

I felt like firing myself from *indi* on the spot and sending myself home. Some people conducted open-heart surgery; others sent criminals to jail, fought fires, or researched cures for cancer. All I'd had to do was ask a question and I'd chickened out.

I tried again, fighting through the nerves. 'Actually, I did want to talk to you about the event-type thing ... It's a launch for our online magazine, *indi* ...'

'*indi*? What's it about?' asked Maxxy, who was scrunching up her nose as she sipped on her faux lemon squash.

'I can show you on my phone,' I said, but Alex had already opened up the *indi* website on his iPad and passed it over to her.

'Steph sent me the link so I have it bookmarked now,' he said, winking at me.

'Er, thanks,' I stammered, trying to stay on point and not freak out that he'd finally read my writing. 'Um, so our website's packed with great stuff for young women. Fun stuff, inspiring stuff, informative stuff ...' Stop saying 'stuff', woman. I cleared my throat to refocus. 'Anyway, we're celebrating our official launch with a red-carpet event. It'll be pretty swanky, I think, and we'd love you to be there.'

'Oh! Well, the site looks beautiful,' Maxxy said, still scrolling on Alex's iPad. 'When's the launch?'

My stomach tightened with anticipation. 'Um ... I know it's last minute, but it's this Saturday and we'd actually love you to perform as our special guest.'

'Tight turnaround ... but I'm vibing on the feel of your website. Confirm with my manager, yeah? You'd have her details, right?'

I did. Not that they'd come in handy.

But before I could explain, Edwina appeared next to us.

'Hi guys, how *are* we?' she said, in the most cheerful voice I'd ever heard from her.

I saw Alex roll his eyes, but miraculously he held his tongue.

'Maxxy, you were a true goddess up there,' Edwina gushed, turning her back on Alex. 'Jose, I'm going to steal away this little superstar for a second. We'll be right back, I promise. Business calls — you know how it is.'

Before I could reply, she'd whisked Maxxy away.

I sighed. 'She's like a hurricane in heels — and she *knows* how important this is to me. Look at her over there, chatting up Maxxy. Have I blown it? I think I've blown it.'

'Maybe, maybe not.' He shrugged. 'Maxxy sounded into it. Edwina's probably just doing her usual sucking-up routine. Look, she and Paulina are prepping their duck-face poses for a selfie with Maxxy — check out the puffed-up lips.'

I had to laugh. 'You're right. Darlene's been playing hard to get, but now Maxxy's keen, it's gotta be a sure thing! I can't believe I pulled it off.'

'Yeah, you did! Now, let's celebrate. Penny mentioned something about fish for dinner, so hopefully it's deep-fried.'

'In our dreams,' I said, and took a final peek at Edwina and Maxxy, who were swapping stories as though they were the closest friends in the world. I still had a lot to learn about charming people.

As Alex and I approached our table, I could see Jade and a few of the other girls in a huddle as they picked at their dinners.

'She looks so out of place,' Jade said, as the others tittered. 'I want to pat her on the head every time she opens her mouth and say, "Oh honey, no, just no." And how about those big, baggy dresses she's always wearing? Call me snarky, but she doesn't belong here.'

Another girl who I hadn't met nodded. 'How did she even score an invite? *indi*'s a start-up with a shitty budget, so she's no one special, unless you think being Edwina's latest plaything is something special.'

I froze. They were talking about me.

Worse. They were ripping me to shreds.

I spun on my heel and fled from the restaurant.

17.

Alex thundered behind me, yelling for me to wait up, but I didn't. If I stopped, I knew I'd break down.

I arrived at my suite, breathless and panting.

Alex caught up with me and sat down on the step with his arms folded over his chest. 'They're awful people, don't believe a word of it. You belong here as much as anyone.'

I slipped off my heels and stared at the floor. 'I'm fine. I'm just ... I'm not feeling so great ... Tell Penny I've gone to bed sick ... that my stomach hurts.'

'Don't let them ruin this for you. Come back to the party,' he urged, taking my hand.

I let go as quickly as if I'd touched my finger to a hotplate.

'Well, now I've seen everything,' a voice snarled behind me.

I turned to see Edwina and Paulina glaring at us.

Paulina pursed her lips into her usual fish pout. 'Getting in while she's young, Alex? You know she's only fifteen?'

'Eighteen actually,' I said. 'And he wasn't trying to get anywhere.'

Edwina put her hands on her hips. 'Alex, you were about to walk into her suite — I saw it with my own eyes.'

'That's not even close to true. Ignore her, Jose,' he said.

'Ignore me?' Edwina raised an eyebrow. 'She'd be a fool to do that and she knows it. This is a small industry and I know *everyone*. You haven't changed a bit, Alex. You're an arrogant, slimy ... You know what, forget it. But Josie, I expected more from you. For a prodigy you're not that smart.'

'Edwina, let me explain!' I said, but she and Paulina had already stormed off.

'Charming as always,' Alex called after them.

'I'm screwed,' I muttered. 'My career's screwed.'

He scoffed. 'Why do you care about Edwina?'

'I just do, alright? I care. What did you do to her? You turned her into a monster!'

'Nothing! We dated. We broke up. We moved on. It was over a year ago. And for the record, she's perfectly capable of being a monster without my help.'

I paused, taking it in. Maybe he'd hit on her friend and never apologised. Maybe he'd written something scathing about her in one of his articles. Or, based on the way she was attacking him, maybe he'd broken her heart. Like Sophie said, a crappy break-up could change someone.

'What happened between you guys?'

'Were you just here? She's shallow and conceited, and I don't waste time on either. The worst part is she thinks she's a saint.' He stood up. 'Look, we've missed the mains, but let's see what rabbit food they're offering for dessert.'

'I'm going to bed.' I reached into my handbag and fumbled around in the dark for the key to the suite.

'I guess I'll get back to the party then ... Will you be alright?'

'Sure, except for the whole Edwina-thinks-I'm-trying-to-hook-up-with-her-ex drama,' I said. 'Thanks for following me though ... I bet I looked like a real idiot running through that restaurant.'

'Well, if you did, then I did too. And thanks for the thanks ... I *have* been sweet, haven't I? Tell your friends — the hot ones. Rest up, Josie the journo.' He gave me a little salute and sauntered off in the direction of the restaurant.

'You're not *that* sweet,' I called out into the darkness. But the only reply was the sound of a kookaburra laughing in the trees.

The next morning, I rushed into the dining hall after sending the perfect — if I did say so myself — email to Darlene about Maxxy's interest in the launch. A quick look at the clock on the wall showed it was 8.38 am. I was eight minutes late to breakfast, but there was no one else there — not even Penny. Maybe I had the wrong restaurant?

I took myself for a short walk around the resort, weaving through the maze of paths, but didn't pass anyone except for a few gardeners who said hello as they trimmed the surrounding greenery. Stomach purring, I returned to the dining hall. Still no one had arrived. I heard a man's voice yelling from kitchen and walked towards it. The chef and two apprentices were arguing.

'Excuse me, do you happen to know where all the media guests are?' I asked.

The trio hushed and swapped dark looks.

'We're supposed to be having a breakfast banquet,' I went on.

'I'm sorry, it's been cancelled,' the chef said.

He plopped some ready-made scrambled eggs and smoked salmon onto a plate and thrust it into my hands. 'You wanted breakfast … please, eat up.'

I thanked them. Sure, my stomach was about to be happy, but that didn't answer the question of where everyone was — or where I was supposed to be.

Unsure, I followed the path to the pool and sat down on one of the sun lounges. No one was there either — it was eerie, like it was the end of the world and I was one of the last people left.

I was lifting a spoonful of scrambled eggs to my mouth when a voice piped up behind me. 'You're brave to eat that. Brave … or stupid.'

'Excuse me?' I lowered the spoon and turned to see Paulina.

She pursed her lips. 'Are you too lost in your Alex love-bubble to know what's going on? Everyone's sick — like, really sick. Throwing up, dizzy, white as a ghost … you name it.'

'No way,' I said, ignoring her comment about me and Alex. 'Are you alright?'

'I think so, it took me down early,' she said, shaking her head. 'They're pretty sure it was the fish last night.'

The fish that Alex, Maxxy and I had missed out on because we'd been too busy gasbagging at the bar. Unless they'd eaten some later, while I was tucked up in bed.

'That's awful,' I said, pushing away the scrambled eggs and salmon.

'Even Penny's sick,' Paulina said. 'She sent a group text to everyone to come to the pool and await further instructions if they're feeling up for it. So far there's only me … and you.'

No wonder I was out of the loop. I'd accidentally left my phone on silent in my handbag so hadn't heard it beep. Better rescue it from the suite before I miss anything else, I thought.

Over Paulina's shoulder, I saw a fair-haired woman walking towards us, but it was hard to make out who she was with the sun beaming down. As she moved closer, I could see it was Penny. There was a guy with her — and it didn't take long to realise it was Alex, dressed in his board shorts and carrying a towel.

'Well, look who it is … your little *friend*,' Paulina muttered to me. 'Enjoy yourself last night?'

'You know what, I've had it,' I snapped. 'I have a boyfriend. Called James. Who I love. Yeah, he doesn't know that yet, and he's not perfect, but … look, you want to be a good sidekick to Edwina? Then tell her *that*. I slept alone last night.'

Paulina's jaw had dropped. 'Joey, I —'

'It's Josie,' I said, taking a step towards her. 'You know that's my name. Or are *you* that stupid?'

'Fine, I'll leave it … Josie,' Paulina said, talking as though she had a bad taste in her mouth.

Luckily, Penny and Alex reached us before she could call my bad-girl bluff; the adrenaline had almost worn off.

'Morning, guys,' Alex said. 'Everyone feeling okay?'

'I'm good,' I said, before remembering I was supposed to have been sick when I left the dinner. 'Er, my stomach's better and headache's a bit less, so … yeah. How are you both?'

Penny shook her head. 'Not good.' Her skin was a dull grey and she had black bags beneath her eyes. Even her lips seemed to have lost their usual colour. 'We've had to cancel all the group seminars. But I want you to have a wonderful time here, so if you're up for it please make the most of our facilities.'

I had to admire her: she was oozing every last scrap of professionalism when I was sure she would have preferred to be kneeling over a toilet bowl.

'Personally I'd like to go home,' Paulina said. 'Can I get my flight changed?'

'Don't be like that!' Alex said, gesturing around us. 'You want to leave paradise?'

'Honestly? Yes,' she spat.

'I understand,' Penny said, somehow keeping her cool. 'Due to the circumstances, we've brought everyone's flights forward to this evening.'

Alex shrugged. 'Well, that still gives us the day, so I vote we do something fun. Any ideas?'

'Forget it,' said Paulina. 'I've got another wave coming. I'll be in my suite.' She clutched her stomach and bolted away.

Penny swallowed, and I couldn't tell if she was about to say something or throw up all over us. 'You know what ... I think I'm going down again,' she mumbled, grimacing. 'There's a great little café on the other side of the resort if you want food. Just put it on our tab. In the meantime, try to enjoy yourselves before we catch up tonight — there are pools, spas, the beach, a bowling alley, a merry-go-round, a maze, and a pitch-and-putt course. Think of this as your very own playground.' She clasped her hand over her mouth and ran off in the direction of the suites.

'Did she say bowling alley?' Alex said. 'Up for it?'

'Stop looking so happy,' I said, slapping him on the shoulder.

'Don't you realise what's happened?'

'Yeah! Everyone's violently ill,' I said. 'This is so bad — Lavish will probably make the news for all the wrong reasons. I've barely had time to schmooze for Liani and I don't even know if Maxxy's okay. The launch is only a few days away — what if she's not well enough to perform?'

'You're worried about *Maxxy*?' Alex laughed. 'Jose, relax, we've got a day off! It's a holiday and we're getting paid. Follow me: I'll turn this day around for both of us, you'll see.'

18.

Strike! The word flashed up on the screen for the third time in a row. Alex high-fived me and I cheered. All the years of sipping slushies with Kat at the local bowling alley were paying off.

'Those pins are copping it. Angry about last night, much?' Alex asked, selecting a hot-pink bowling ball.

'Hands off *my* lucky ball.'

'Maybe it'll be lucky for me too.'

We watched the ball shoot down the lane, then veer suddenly to the left, only knocking over one pin.

I laughed and reached for another ball — a bright yellow one with red flames on either side — and that's when I saw her. I ducked down behind the seat. 'Oh! Oh crap!'

'What?' he said, sipping on his cherry cola (he'd bribed a bellboy for one).

'It's her. Look, it's her.'

'Her being ...?' Alex turned to see who I was freaking out over.

Maxxy. She was politely signing a pair of bowling shoes and a pale blue ball for the manager.

'Sweet, at least we know she's not sick,' he said. 'You can relax now.'

'Should I try to lure her over here?' I asked.

'Lure?' Alex laughed. 'Cut the creepiness. She's a normal chick — surprisingly down to earth. Go up to her like you would anyone else.'

'She's famous, not normal.'

'Yeah, she is, and the sooner you realise that, the better you'll be at your job. Stop putting the Maxxys and Edwinas of the world up on these inaccessible pedestals. They fart, burp and wee as much as the next person.'

I snorted. 'Ew.' But I didn't need to be a whiz-kid to know he was right — well, about the pedestals anyway. (I could hardly imagine Edwina clearing her throat loudly, let alone the other stuff.) But I couldn't shake the fact that Maxxy was in one social circle and I was in another. She was respected and recognised around the country for her music; I was lucky to remember to squeeze in a shower on a particularly sleepy Sunday. We had as much in common as a snowman and a frog.

But none of that mattered because I had a job to do. I needed to take the emotion out of it. I needed to earn my spot at *indi*.

'I'm not scared,' I told myself. 'I'm a professional. A professional writer. A professional writer from the city who's —'

'Josie. You're trying to convince the wrong person.'

'*Fine*. I'll do it.'

Boom-boom, boom-boom ... my heartbeat quickened as I walked towards her. She was already on her way out the door, waving goodbye to the manager. My arms ached and I looked down to see I was still clutching the bowling ball. I searched for something, anything, to say to attract her attention. 'Hello' didn't seem enough. My eyes took in the vending machine, the pool table, the lanes, the bumper bars —

'Bumpers!' I blurted out.

Maxxy turned to see me standing there like a loon, clinging to the bowling ball, which seemed to be growing heavier by the millisecond. 'What? Oh, hey ... it's Josie, right? From last night?'

'Yeah. You remembered.'

'Gold star to me,' she said. 'Were you saying something about bumpers?'

I had no idea what I was saying. No idea at all. 'Er, I wanted to see if you were keen for a game ... with or without bumpers?'

'Right now?'

'Yeah, with us.' I pointed to Alex, who gave a wave. I held my breath; could I pull this off?

'Sure, why not. I've got time for a quick one before my flight,' she said, and walked with me towards the lane. 'By the way, I read some of your stuff last night after the gig. The story on virginity? Very smart take on the subject. I flicked it to a friend who totally related.'

'She did?' I couldn't hide my shock. I'd never had a celebrity compliment my writing before. Well, except for Billy from Greed, but he'd had other intentions.

'She did.' Maxxy smiled.

I was starting to realise there may be more of a thriving population on Planet V than I'd thought. I gulped. 'Actually, speaking of *indi*, I wanted to talk to you about Saturday ...'

'Did Darlene lock in the details?'

'Um, she hasn't yet.'

'She's your gal. Trust me, she sorts out all my media requests,' Maxxy said. Before I had a chance to continue, she'd moved on. 'Alex, my main man!'

'Maxx-ay!' he hollered. 'Help! Save me from Josie. I've never had my arse kicked so hard by someone so small.'

'I'm not *that* small,' I said.

Maxxy looked at the screen, taking in the scores. 'You're smashing him! Looks like he might need the bumpers.'

Alex passed Maxxy a bowling ball. 'That's it, you're playing with me. Hey, where's Mirabella? We could play in pairs.'

'Poor thing's gone home sick, texted me something about bad fish,' she said. 'Lucky I'm vegan.'

'This place isn't so lavish after all, is it?' Alex joked. 'Jose, you're up.'

I walked to the lane and swung the ball. *Six*. Alex cheered. Typical: I was back to being average the moment the pop star stepped onto my turf. We played on, and somehow I managed to beat them. (The fact that Alex consistently scored three or less helped swing things my way.)

Maxxy snapped a selfie of the three of us pulling silly faces while holding our bowling balls. She uploaded it to her Instagram page with the hashtag *#mybowlingbiznitches*. I was sure Kat would confirm this as my highest life achievement to date.

'Another game, m'lady?' Alex asked Maxxy.

'Sorry, guys, it's been fun, but I better finish packing. Josie, I'll see you soon, though … Saturday, right? Thanks for the game.' She gave us a quick hug and walked out of the bowling alley.

'Five, four, three …' I muttered.

Alex furrowed his brow. 'What are you doing?'

'Two … one,' I said, and let out a huge yelp of glee. 'I did it! It's official! Maxxy loves *indi*! Liani loves Maxxy! Therefore Liani is going to love me! I schmoozed! I freaking schmoozed!'

Alex laughed. 'Yeah, you did.'

'I have to tell her,' I said, and whipped out my phone to send Liani a one-liner email: *Maxxy loves indi and is keen for the launch. Losing it!*

'Well, Miss Schmoozer, the only thing that could top what you're feeling right now is a ride on that merry-go-round,' Alex said. 'Let's go find it.'

'It's not a merry-go-round, but I think it'll do nicely,' Alex said, too surprised at what lay in front of us to play it cool for once.

We'd got completely lost in our search for the merry-go-round after detouring to take a 'shortcut' through the maze (which, of course, only got us more lost). And at its centre was one of the most breathtaking things I'd ever seen: a hexagon-shaped pool surrounded by palm trees, lush green plants and colourful flowers. It was private, enclosed, serene and mysterious, the kind of place where I imagined hundreds of secrets being told.

Alex looked at me. 'What do you say?'

I sat down on a sun lounge and placed my phone next to me. 'You want to go in? If I can find my way out of this maze, I'll go and get my —'

'Your what?' He laughed, scooping me up and carrying me towards the water. 'Your what?'

'Stop, I don't have my swimmers on!' I screeched, but Alex didn't listen. He threw me into the pool and I plunged beneath the water.

Floundering around, I burst through the surface gasping for air and splashing droplets everywhere. Today's outfit — a tropical playsuit, courtesy of Sia once again — was now sopping wet and clinging to every curve of my body. I folded my arms across my chest.

'Is it nice in?' said Alex, who'd stripped off his T-shirt to reveal his muscular torso. He sat on the edge of the pool, splashing his toes in the water.

'What's the matter with you?' I coughed. 'Do you take anything seriously?'

Alex splashed me. 'Sure.'

'Like what?' I said. 'This trip's meant to be for work, and now Edwina hates me, the other girls are spreading rumours about me — about *us* — and people are sick, and you're laughing it all off.'

'I'd rather laugh than whinge,' he said. 'Look ... I take things seriously. I do. But this drama with Edwina and her army of mag hags? It's not my scene ... and I'm not sure it's yours either.'

'This is my job — this is all I can do — so it has to be my scene,' I muttered, shivering as goosebumps erupted on my arms, across my chest and down my legs.

'Yeah, that's my problem too,' he nodded. 'Hang on, are you cold? How is that even possible? I'll get you my towel.'

'No, I'm fine,' I replied, plunging below the water again.

'Alright then,' he said, and lowered himself into the pool, running his fingers through the water.

'What?' I asked, trying to decode the expression on his face.

'Nothing. It's just … girls don't usually act like this towards me.'

My eyebrows shot up. 'I'm not acting like *anything* towards you!'

'Exactly,' he said, grinning.

'Are you used to girls ogling the tattoo on your bicep or —'

'You noticed my bicep?'

I shook my head. 'Does Steph know how annoying you are?'

'Steph's like my sister — everything I do annoys her. But that's not what I meant before. Sure, you're not *throwing* yourself at me —'

'I know that.'

'But you're sending vibes, so it's confusing.'

'No, I'm not.'

'Oh yeah, your vibes are coming at me left, right and centre,' he said. 'Look, there's one now!'

I splashed water at him. 'I am in complete and utter control of my vibes, thank you, and I have it on good authority that not one is being sent your way.'

'Yep, there goes another,' he said. 'You're cute when you're angry.'

'I'm not angry. Or cute.'

'Searching for compliments?'

'You are the most frustrating person I've ever met, and I like most people!' I blurted out. 'You know those annoying types who everyone gives up on? Well, I don't. But you are on a whole other level of frustrating. I'm here, surrounded by merry-go-rounds and mazes, trying to do a good job and you're ruining it. You're a great writer — you should know better!'

'Nice speech. You think I'm great?' Alex took a step closer.

'I didn't mean it.'

'Oh, *really*?' he said, so close now I could see the water clinging to his long, dark eyelashes. 'I think you're talented too. Josie, I ...'

But he didn't finish his sentence. He was too preoccupied with lowering his lips to mine.

For a split second, I couldn't think about anything other than the fact Alex's lips were smooshed up against my own. It was the flash *after* the split second that stung me. All I could taste was chlorine. All I could see was James.

'Stop ... you can't, we can't,' I said, pulling away.

'You didn't like it?'

I took a step backwards. 'Don't ask me that.'

'Why not?' he said, stepping towards me to close the gap. 'I liked kissing you. Although it was over a little too fast.'

'Alex ... I have a boyfriend,' I said, pressing my hands against his chest to form a barrier between us. I felt a stabbing pain in my stomach as guilt threatened to overwhelm me.

'You're kidding? Well, now I feel like a tosser.'

We bobbed in the water in silence, listening to the soft breeze whistling through the palm trees.

'Ah man, I'm sorry. Is he the guy who was supposed to come on the road trip with us?' he asked.

'Yeah ... It's been a complicated few weeks,' I said, tears stinging my eyes. 'I'm sorry ... things have been kinda crazy ... but I love him.'

Alex burst out laughing.

I splashed water in his face. 'What are you, a sociopath?'

'No!' he said, splashing back. 'I've just never kissed a girl and had her confess her passionate love for someone else before.'

I let a small chuckle slip out, but stopped myself the moment I remembered the kiss. The feeling of his warm mouth against mine. The touch of his fingertips on my upper back. The taste of cherry cola from our trip to the bowling alley. Alex had initiated it, the whole thing had lasted less than two seconds and didn't mean a thing to me, but there was nothing I could do to erase it. No reboot or undo button to press. It was a messy blob on my life, on my relationship, and I had no idea what to do about it.

Getting out of this romantic pool sounded like a good first step.

'I can't be here with you, alone,' I said. 'I'm going back to my room.'

'Jose, let's talk about this.'

'What's to say? I'm the worst person in the world. I'm going to go drown myself in that giant spa in my suite.'

I pulled myself from the water (luckily no one else was around to witness my wobbling upper arms, which had the strength of a bowl of jelly) and wrapped myself in Alex's beach towel.

'For the record, I don't want to be using your towel,' I said, placing myself down on the sun lounge. 'It feels sort of wrong considering the circumstances, but —'

'Stop worrying,' he said. 'I misread the signs, that's all. It was just a kiss! People brush body parts all the time and it means nothing. Think about it: two hands shaking, patting someone on the back, cheek-to-cheek kisses.'

'What are you saying?'

'I'm saying, don't let this two-second *nothing* ruin *everything*. I've gone further with my 93-year-old grandma's bingo caller than you — she tried to slip in her tongue when she greeted me at the Christmas party last year!'

'Oh god!' I said, failing to shake the visual. 'Well, you say it means nothing ... but what do we do now? Are you going to tell Steph?'

'About what?' he said, pulling himself from the pool with ease. 'No idea what you're talking about.'

'Alex, you can't kiss me and then —'

'We're friends. That's it. Stop trying to crack onto me. I know you're a dirty little perve, but no means no.'

I punched him on the arm. 'You're a little ... Look, I don't want things to be weird,' I said, my voice cracking. 'For my career, for Steph ... especially for me and James.'

'I'm the king of the friend zone and I'm fine with that,' he said.

I didn't know whether it was his gentle tone or the quick way he'd apologised when I'd mentioned James earlier, but I believed him.

But I had another concern. 'I can't have Edwina thinking there's anything going on here. It can't be awkward. It just can't.'

Alex shrugged. 'We broke up ages ago — we don't mean anything to each other.'

'Get real,' I said, rolling my eyes. 'Don't you mean you broke up with her, and she doesn't mean anything to you?'

He looked at the ground. 'I'm not sure. Maybe. It wasn't working, we had nothing in common besides ... you know, so I ended things. People break up every day. I didn't want to lead her on, and it wasn't love or anything.'

Yeah, for him.

'Besides, she's got nothing beneath that gorgeous face — no kindness, no heart. I couldn't be with someone like that. She plays people and I'm pretty sure she's a full-blown evil supervillain these days.'

I smiled. 'Yeah, she's full-on.'

'If "full-on" means "total bitch".'

'Yep, definitely one of those,' I admitted, thinking of Edwina's countless backhanded compliments and snarky remarks; she hadn't earned queen-bee status without mastering how to sting people. 'Anyway,' I continued, 'let's stop wasting our time talking about her. I want to focus on my job and the launch, that's it. Nothing else matters right now. Especially not Edwina.'

'Good thinking … friend.' He grinned.

'Well, *friend*, have you seen my phone?' I said. 'I want to see if Darlene's emailed yet.'

'Yeah, no worries,' he said. 'No idea where your phone's gone though.'

'I had it with me …' I muttered, standing up and looking around. 'You know, before you lobbed me into the pool. Unless it's in the water and —'

'Ah, here we go!' Alex said, fishing it off my sun lounge. 'You were sitting on it.' His eyes widened as he stared at the screen. 'Something tells me you're not meant to be calling Edwina?'

No, I wasn't. But apparently I was in the middle of a conversation with her.

'Hang it up!' I shrieked. 'Oh no, what were we talking about?'

Alex ignored me and held the phone to his ear. 'Edwina?' He waited for a second — a second that felt long enough to run a few laps around an oval — and repeated her name, before hanging up. 'Yeah, so I'm pretty sure we've left her a whopping long phone message.'

'Shit!'

'If it makes you feel better I once butt-dialled my dentist while I was … Never mind.'

'She's going to kill me. *Kill me!* Maybe even bring me back to life just so she can kill me again! We need to delete that message!'

'I vote we play dumb,' Alex said. 'She probably never checks her voicemail anyway. I have about twenty-six new messages on mine.'

I sighed.

'Besides, the phone was under your butt — our conversation was probably muffled. I betcha it's a whole lot of static.'

The idea was comforting. 'Yeah? You think so?'

'I do.'

'You're lying to make me feel better, aren't you?'

He grinned. 'I am. And it's not our only problem.'

I pulled the towel even tighter around me. 'What do you mean?'

'I have no idea how to get us out of this frigging maze.'

I groaned and put my head in my hands. So much for Alex turning things around for us today.

19.

After Alex and I escaped from the maze, I spent the rest of the afternoon alone sorting out launch details for Liani. There was still no word from Darlene, but I wasn't too worried. Between Maxxy's excitement about *indi* and my induction onto her Instagram page, things were looking good.

I packed up and, teetering in another pair of Sia's heels, dragged my suitcase to the VIP room in Lavish's most exclusive bar and restaurant. There was supposed to be an unlimited seafood buffet on offer, but no one could stomach that after last night's food-poisoning disaster, so Penny had called in a truckload of bread, crackers and gourmet dips.

When I entered the VIP room, the first things I noticed were the low lighting and the even lower mood. Alex, who was sipping from a coconut at the bar, shot me a quick peace sign, but I kept my distance. Penny, still looking sickly, was talking to a journalist; and two girls sat together at another table, not saying much. It was only when I got closer that I realised it was Edwina and Paulina. Their hair was dishevelled and they weren't wearing make-up — unless you counted the mascara smears beneath their eyes. Neither of them, not even Edwina, was in heels. I was considering swapping into flats when Edwina waved me over.

'Josie, we need to talk,' she said. 'I won't bite. Promise.'

'Um … okay.'

I tottered to her table, convinced I was walking into a trap. *We need to talk* was code for 'Hold onto your knickers, I'm about to deliver some seriously crappy news'. Edwina knew about the voicemail, she knew about the kiss, she knew everything. I considered falling at her feet to confess my sins, but by the time I'd reached her and Paulina I'd wimped out. Even when she was sick, she was intimidating as hell. I swallowed, scared to hear my fate. What would become of me? Trial by magazine editor? A lifetime in career purgatory?

'Let's cut through the BS,' Edwina said. 'Josie, I'm … I'm sorry I ranted at you last night.'

'Let me explain,' I began, then froze. *She* was sorry? 'What?'

'Don't push your luck,' she said. 'I've said it. I overreacted about Alex and I regret it. He's a splinter that gets under my skin, you know? One minute we were together, the next I was alone and he was dating a fashion student. I was young and dumb. Anyway, boring boring

boring. I've spoken with Paulie and I now believe there's nothing going on between you two. That's the end. Let's never talk of this again.'

I should have been relieved, but I'd never felt more two-faced. I considered telling her everything, then thought of my own situation, the consequences, my relationship with James. So, I went against my natural instincts and didn't say a word.

'Um ... thanks?' I managed instead.

Maybe I wasn't that far removed from all the backstabbing after all. Maybe I'd been faking it so hard I'd become as bad as everyone else.

'Fabulous,' Edwina said, nibbling on a cracker. 'Well, that's settled. Now, onto more important things. How'd you go with Maxxy?'

'She's keen to do the launch this Saturday. I just need to firm up the details.'

'Good on you! I knew you could pull it off ... prodigy.' She gave me a small smile. 'Well, in my world, it looks like Maxxy's manager has agreed to let her do a cover shoot with *Marilyn* for an upcoming issue. Isn't that amazing? That's our little secret though.'

'Yeah, of course ... You've heard from her manager?' I said, trying not to freak out. 'Congrats. When's the shoot?'

'Probably not for a month or so, plenty of time to plan.'

I picked at a piece of crusty bread, listening to Paulina whine to Edwina that she'd been so ill she hadn't picked up any of the gorgeous waiters. Eventually, other people hauled their sickly, sorry selves and their suitcases into the dining hall. One girl even carried a bucket in her spare hand.

Penny made a rambling apology to us all. She'd planned on surprising us with an extreme skydiving experience (the mere mention of which made one particularly green-looking beauty editor throw up in the pot plant next to her), but due to the outbreak of illness they were sending us home with a voucher to spend on a fancy meal in the city instead. Penny seemed so desperate to not have this turn into a full-blown disaster that it wouldn't have surprised me if we'd all received an envelope filled with cash.

For the return trip to the airport, we were herded into a sleek black shuttle bus — I even managed to score a seat to myself. Everyone else was slowly perking up: the beauty bloggers were writing on their laptops, Alex was texting someone — probably one of his many girl 'friends' — and a writer with flame-red hair was applying eye shadow for the third time in twenty minutes. I was close to staging an intervention as she looked like she had two black eyes. A handful of women were laughing and talking on the back seat, Edwina's voice trilling among them.

I put in my earphones, but everything that had gone down at Lavish played louder in my head than the music. I'd been so mad at James for screwing up our weekend away, yet the drama with Alex forced me to realise I was far from perfect too. All I wanted was to forgive and forget — or time travel back to when James and I were making out in the library. With the laws of physics working against me, I settled for the next best option: texting James to let him know I'd be home later tonight: *Leaving on a jet plane, let's talk tomorrow xx*. That would buy me twenty-four hours to work out how to handle the whole 'Alex kissed me, but it didn't mean anything — no, really, it didn't' scenario. I hadn't kept anything from James before. Would I tell him about this, or wouldn't I?

Then Edwina tapped me on the shoulder, snapping me out of my thoughts.

'Hey, what's up?' I asked, taking out an earphone.

Her face had deepened to a burnt red, but she didn't say a word, simply slid into the seat next to me, yanked my earphones out of my iPod and jammed them into her phone.

'Edwina …'

'Listen,' she said, as she handed me her phone. 'Just listen.'

And so I did, hating every second of my snivelling, nasal voice. That damn voicemail.

'Yeah, she's full-on,' I heard myself say in the message.

'If "full-on" means "total bitch",' Alex's voice chuckled down the line.

I cringed, knowing what was coming next. 'Yep, definitely one of those.'

It felt like every eye on the bus was staring at us. I looked around and realised they were, and doing a shoddy job of hiding it.

'Did Alex put you up to this?' hissed Edwina, her voice low so no one could hear but me. 'You know, I've heard stories about you, rumours about the kinds of things you *really* got up to at *Sash* when you thought everyone else's backs were turned, but I thought, Really? This young girl? This former intern who's been in the industry for five seconds? No. She couldn't. She wouldn't.'

'They're liars, and I can explain this,' I insisted. 'It's not as bad as it sounds.'

She rolled her eyes. 'I know you're trying to make a fool of me in front of everyone. And the lies you keep telling — have you no self-respect?'

I wanted to stand up for myself, but I felt as though her words had physically winded me, like I'd been punched in the stomach.

'No one — especially not a bratty little nothing like you — gets away with talking about me like this,' spat Edwina. 'You're *done*.'

As she returned to the back seat, I heard whispering from Paulina and the others, but I didn't dare turn around. Instead I curled up in a ball and squeezed my eyes shut, counting down the minutes until I was home in bed.

* * *

At the airport back home, I raced out to the taxi rank in the hope of avoiding bumping into Edwina, Paulina or Alex again.

They were nowhere to be seen, but I still hurried into the queue before my luck disappeared. I pulled out my phone and scrolled through the numbers, wondering who I could reach out to — Mum had transformed into the voicemail queen and the chances of Kat snubbing me for a reality-show repeat were high.

I passed Liani's name — also not an option — and stopped on Sia's. My finger hovered over the call button, trembling. What could I even say to her? Something like, 'Hey, Sia, so you know how Liani wanted me to make everyone fall in love with me and *indi*? Well, I did the complete opposite and I'm now enemies with the most feared features editor in the city. Oh, and her ex busted a move on me in a pool.' Yeah, not ideal. I stuffed my phone into my handbag, defeated.

One air-freshener-doused taxi ride later, I dragged my suitcase to the front door and let myself into the house. I was looking forward to taking myself straight to bed with a peanut butter and honey sandwich, but I heard the unmistakable sound of people talking in the lounge room. With three of us living here, there were always people over. But this time I recognised a familiar voice in the mix.

I peeked my head into the room.

Steph, who was lying on the couch, noticed me first. 'Josie, you're back! Get in here, we're playing cards. Well, two of us are ...'

Prue was napping in the armchair, her textbook open on her lap and her nose whistling like Great-Aunt Bertie's. It took me all of 0.8 seconds to trace the familiar voice to James, who was splayed on our faded blue beanbag.

'Hey,' I said, shocked. So much for having twenty-four hours to work out my next move.

'Josie,' he stammered, seeming nervous for the first time in ... well, ever. 'Ah, hi. I got your message.'

'And he brought you flowers,' said Steph, pointing to a large measuring jug filled with daisies. 'We don't have a fancy vase, sorry.'

'Wow, thank you,' I said. I'd never been given flowers before, but I couldn't savour the moment, not with everything swirling in my brain (not to mention Steph's ridiculous Cheshire-Cat-like grin). 'Um ... wanna talk for a sec?' I said to James.

'Yeah,' he said, so I took his hand and pulled him up.

Steph wolf-whistled as we left the room and I retaliated with a flash of my rude finger. Prue woke with a start at the noise, then got into an argument with Steph about not respecting her quiet time. That was all James and I needed to hurry into my bedroom.

We sat on the bed, leaving a gap between us, as though it was the first time we'd ever been alone together. As though our bodies had forgotten how to be with each other. The space separating us couldn't have been more than thirty centimetres, but it felt like we were on different continents.

'So … hey,' I began.

'You already said that.'

'Sorry.'

This conversation was more awkward than the night we'd first met and I'd accused him of being a burglar.

'I, ah, brought you chocolates,' he said, 'but Steph and Prue have already eaten half the box.'

'Of course they have.'

Hating the awkwardness, I wriggled around and sat with my legs crossed. James shifted into the same position. Our knees grazed yet it felt like we were barely touching.

'So, I screwed up and I need you to forgive me,' he began. 'I miss you.'

I lowered my head. I didn't want him to see me cry, but an ambitious tear broke through.

James wiped it away. 'JB … I don't know what else to say.' He inched closer and tilted my chin upwards. 'Let's book in another weekend to go see your family, yeah? I know I'm not the perfect guy you're always saying I am, but —'

'You're pretty close,' I mumbled. 'And I'm not perfect either.'

James pulled me towards him. His eyes had never looked so clear and blue. I could only imagine how red mine were.

'*You're* pretty close,' he said. 'Don't forget that.'

His lips brushed mine, but just as I was about to let myself sink into the kiss, I remembered what I'd done. I had a choice to make. A choice that would affect everything from this moment on.

'There's something I need to tell you,' I said.

He pulled back a little. 'Yeah? Like you've swapped to a new brand of shampoo? Or, like, you're quitting writing to travel the world?'

'Um … somewhere in the middle … or maybe somewhere else entirely,' I said. 'I don't know how to put this, so I'm just going to say it … James, I … Okay, let me set some context first, especially after everything you've been through before. And can we get under the sheets? I want to get under the sheets.'

'Alright …'

We clambered beneath the sheets and pulled them up around our bodies.

'You know when someone shakes your hand, but you didn't necessarily know it was going to happen until they've already reached out, and done it?' I said.

James chuckled. 'Not really.'

'Or, like, if a stranger pats you on the back. It's one-sided, you know? You didn't want it, or ask for it, but it happened anyway, even though it didn't mean anything.'

'Why would a stranger pat you on the back?' James asked.

'Okay … let's try another angle. Air kisses in the media are —'

'Jose, say what you're trying to say.'

'Someone kissed me.'

'What?'

Having my secret hanging in the air between us was almost too much to bear. All I wanted to do was pull James's lips to mine and forget it ever happened. But instead I said, 'Someone kissed me. On the lips. At Lavish.'

'Wait … *what*?'

'But it didn't mean anything!' I rushed on. 'He's just a nice guy who kissed me when we were alone in the pool and —'

'You were alone in a pool with a nice guy?'

I tucked a loose curl behind my ear. 'That came out wrong. We're friends who —'

'Kiss, apparently.'

'I'm sorry.'

'Is this because I stuffed up on Friday? Some kind of payback?'

'No! I wanted to be honest with you.'

'I need some air.' James climbed out of bed and stretched his arms above his head.

'Great, let's get some air — and maybe a burger — and talk this out,' I said.

'No, *I* need some air,' he clarified. 'I need ... a break from this.'

'A break?' I whispered, feeling a lump swelling inside my throat. 'But you said those three words to me. That meant something. You said them the other day!'

'I know I did. But you didn't. And then you kissed someone else.'

'He kissed me,' I cried.

'I think we should forget I said anything the other day.'

'James, please —'

'I came here feeling sick to my stomach about losing you,' he said. 'Little did I know you've been having *great* adventures with some other guy. I need some time. Just don't call me for a bit, okay?' He walked out of my bedroom, slamming the door behind him.

'James!' I jumped off the bed with the sheet still wrapped around me, shuffled towards the door and threw it open. 'James! Please, come back! I love you! There, I said it! I love you so much! I don't need perfect, I just need you!'

But he wasn't waiting for me in the hallway, ready to declare his love for me. There was only me, cocooned in the sheet with the words 'I love you' hanging in the air. It felt like someone's hand was squeezing my heart over and over again.

I shuffled back into my room, slammed the door and flopped onto the bed, still wrapped in the sheet. Moments later I heard soft knocking at the door.

'James?' I said.

The door creaked open and Steph poked her head in. 'Are you okay?' she asked. 'Prue saw James storm out ...' She sat down next to me on the bed. 'Did you tell him to bugger off after what happened with your family? That was a dick move on his part, but I thought you two would work it out.'

I shook my head. 'No. That's not it.'

'Did you laugh at his ... you know?'

'His what?' I asked, then it dawned on me what she was talking about it. 'No! What's wrong with you?'

'Where do I begin?' She grinned, then quickly covered her mouth. 'Sorry, I shouldn't smile, but now I know I shouldn't, I can't stop. What's the protocol here? Like, how bad are we talking?'

I pulled the sheet tighter around me. 'Get-the-ice-cream bad. I've stuffed up everything.'

'I thought he'd mucked you around?'

'It's complicated,' I mumbled. 'But I don't want it to be over.'

'Well, that's easy then: don't let it be,' she said. 'It's grand-gesture time. You and I drag-race to the airport to catch him before he flies away forever; or you sprint down the street to his apartment holding a hundred balloons; or serenade him with a guitar — or, if you wanna go super-retro, a boom box — as he watches from his second-storey window. But seriously … what did you do? It can't be that bad.'

And so I told her everything, from the chlorine kiss with Alex in the pool, to the way Edwina hissed at me on the bus and threatened to take me down, and the fact Darlene still hadn't contacted me to confirm Maxxy's appearance at the launch.

Steph didn't say much, just the occasional 'Bloody hell, Alex,' or 'Okay, that's pretty bad'. When I was done, she wrapped her arms around me.

'I should call James right now,' I said. 'Although he said not to …'

'That's not enough,' Steph said. 'You need to do something big, something bold. Do you love this guy?'

I nodded.

'Well, find a way to *make* him believe it,' she said.

20.

It was an MIA sort of morning: Missing Important Answers.

There was no reply from James after I'd tried calling him and texting him (yes, despite him telling me he needed some time). I was a relationship newbie, so my version of 'playing it cool' while giving him space was pacing around the office while motoring through a family-sized packet of jellybeans.

There was no answer from Angel after I'd emailed her to say I needed to talk to her in between all her pasta-eating and bar-hopping, and was half-considering flying her home for a deep-and-meaningful.

No email from Edwina telling me the whole debacle yesterday had been blown out of proportion, so I wouldn't have to bring full combat gear to protect myself at upcoming media events.

Finally, there was no word from Darlene. No email, no voicemail, no text, no carrier pigeon, no smoke signals, no cryptic sign that everything was going to be okay for the launch. Nothing.

And then two little envelopes popped up in the right-hand corner of my computer screen. I had mail. I had freaking *mail*.

The first one was a long, rambling email from my high-school PE teacher who had been forwarded my crazy group message and now wanted to offer me unsolicited sex-ed advice. (Side note: new life, please.)

The second was from the publicist at a hot new fashion label, telling me she'd love to come to the launch and bring a plus one — her celebrity hairdresser friend.

Perhaps this will work out, I thought. Perhaps this could be the best launch ever. Yeah, and perhaps I was about to be 'discovered' and given a six-figure modelling contract.

No response from Darlene meant just one thing: I was screwed. I was going to have to tell Liani that I'd failed to do the most important thing of all — secure Maxxy for our launch. Now it was going to be a failure, and I was going to get fired, and no one would ever hire me again, and I'd end up sitting around all day eating uncooked two-minute noodles and reading bargain catalogues.

Just as I was gazing at Liani at her desk and thinking about how to break it to her (perhaps I could drop the bad news, then soften her by following up with a block of chocolate/puppy/keys to a new car), Sia barged through the office door, late. She dumped her bag on the floor and immediately came over, humming Maxxy's latest song.

'You are amazing,' she told me, squeezing my cheek.

'I am?' I certainly didn't feel amazing.

'I saw you getting your BFF on with Maxxy on Instagram. You did it! We're in!'

'Well, she likes the sound of the launch, but it's not actually —'

'Oi, Liani! Did you see?' Sia called out, before realising Liani was on the phone. 'Oops. Anyway, look at you playing it so cool. I'm totally fangirling, and I know Liani's peeing her giant mama knickers. I don't think I've seen her more proud than when you sent her the email from Lavish. She was on the phone to Mya in seconds.'

'She ... she was?' Well, that made things more difficult.

'Anyway, how was the junket, besides you becoming part of Maxxy's entourage?'

'It was ... well ...' I was hit with flashbacks of Alex kissing me and Edwina threatening me. 'I guess you could say ...'

'What?' Sia asked. 'Are you worried I'll be jealous? Did they give you something incredible? A Tiffany bracelet? A year's supply of shampoo? If you say a new wardrobe of clothes I will literally cry all over you.'

'Food poisoning. That's what they gave everyone.'

Sia's jaw dropped. 'What?'

'Yep. You didn't miss much.'

'Priceless,' Sia said. 'Harrison will have a field day when he hears about it. Anyway, I have work coming out my ears, and I'm sure you do too, but ... like I said, you're amazing.'

'I'm not. Really.' *Really.*

Sia returned to her desk and fired up her computer. I glanced over at Liani, who was now off the phone and eating a blueberry muffin as she scribbled notes in her diary. This was it. This was the time.

I walked towards her desk, but just as I reached it, her phone burst to life again. I began to retreat, but Liani held up a finger, signalling for me to wait.

'Yes, Mya, I know, I know,' she said. 'Plans are going well, only one sleep to go. It's shaping up to be sensational.'

I braced to interrupt her call and tell her right then.

'I know, Maxxy will be incredible,' she said. 'I couldn't have done it without Josie — what a star.' She grinned at me. 'Yep, call you later ... It's going to be a night to remember, I can feel it. Yes, so the announcement's been made? Fantastic. Yes. I'll tell her, yes. I will. And Lavish called? They want to sponsor the night? Incredible! Just what we needed. I'm sure part of it's to avoid a PR disaster, but I'll take it. This is huge for us.'

She said goodbye to Mya and hung up. 'Hey, Jose! I was telling Mya how brilliant you are. She agrees, of course ... especially now that Lavish are on board!'

I saw the sparkle of excitement in Liani's eyes, the warm smile, and didn't want to be responsible for dulling them. Or getting fired. Harrison said he'd seen writers get fired for much less.

I'll give myself another half an hour to hear from Darlene, *then* I'll tell Liani, I told myself. It wasn't like Darlene had actually declined. Maxxy was keen, and she'd said Darlene would sort it out. But the deadline was so close, it was making my hands sweat. I couldn't have been more aware of time running out if there'd been a giant hourglass next to my desk.

'Mya wanted me to tell you that your latest column was superb too,' Liani continued, not realising she was making my confession harder with every breath. 'Put your thinking cap on. I need more like that as soon as possible — relatable, thought-provoking, smart.'

'Sure ... of course ...'

'Speaking of smart — Sia, get your butt over here!' Liani called, pulling up a chair for her to sit on. I perched on the edge of Liani's desk. 'Let's talk panel for a moment. Mya and I have nutted out the details, and Allegra MacGregor and Corrine Spark are locked in. Those names ring a bell?'

'As in *the* women's issues activist and *the* media commentator?' Sia asked, sitting upright. 'Them *and* Maxxy? I'm so proud of us. We're nailing this.'

I didn't say a word.

Liani grinned. 'Sia, if you're feeling up for it, I'd love for you to be on the panel too. I think it's important to give *indi* a voice up there, but I totally understand if —'

'I'm in,' she said. 'Of course I'm in. Me and my little alien bump wouldn't miss it.'

Liani, multitasking as always, cheered as she scrolled through her emails. 'Did I tell you the caterer is making "mini" everything for the night, so there'll be mini sliders, mini hot dogs, mini doughnuts, mini — what the ...?' She froze, scanning an email. She swore. Once, twice, a third time. Then said, 'Josie, sit down.'

'I already am,' I said.

'Well ... *I'll* take a seat,' she said. 'I need a seat.'

'Um, you're sitting too ... what's up? Is it the catering?'

Liani's face was flushed. 'Josie, is there anything you need to tell me?'

Crap. Someone had sent her the big V email. Sia and I swapped looks. I'd been dreading this moment — after all, our epic email-deletion plan had been flimsy at best.

I cleared my throat, ready to offload. 'Well, I've never been that experienced with guys ... There was Pete, whose kisses were like going head-to-head with a windscreen wiper, but James is unlike any of —'

'What are you talking about?'

I swallowed. 'What are *you* talking about?'

'I don't even want to say it in case I make it true,' she said. 'Just look.' She pointed at her computer screen.

I leaned over. And that's when I saw it. The email.

Only it wasn't the email that had been haunting me for two and a half weeks. No. This email was much worse.

At first glance it seemed innocent enough, but as I scanned down I realised why Liani was looking as though she needed to breathe into a paper bag.

The subject line was: *RSVP indi launch*. It started off with a polite, professional intro: *Dear Liani, I hope you're having a lovely day so far.* The part that caused me to splutter was the perfectly worded apology from Edwina at *Marilyn* magazine about how she was sorry she could no longer attend our launch because she had a last-minute cover shoot with Maxxy on the same evening. She hoped we'd have an amazing night, and would be sure to send us a signed copy of the magazine once it was out. The email concluded with a final act of fakery: three neat kisses in a row.

The words 'last-minute cover shoot' and 'same evening' stuck to my brain like glue. I couldn't believe Edwina had convinced Darlene to move the cover shoot forward just to get even with me. And the promise of a signed *Marilyn* mag was a not-so-subtle message to me: 'Take what's mine and I'll take what's yours — and then some'. It was the ultimate, passive-aggressive way to tell me I really was a nobody in the industry.

'So,' I started, before realising I had no idea how to finish that sentence. I tried again. 'I've been meaning to say, there's a *slight* problem. Darlene's been a little incommunicado —'

'This isn't a joke?' Liani said, nostrils flaring.

Turned out saying 'slight' before 'problem' hadn't softened the blow as I'd hoped.

'I'm so, so sorry, Liani,' I stammered. 'I tried to convince Darlene, but she wouldn't return my voicemails or reply to my emails.'

Sia shook her head. 'I'm confused. Didn't you say Maxxy was in? That she was thrilled?'

'That you were taking care of it?' Liani added, her voice measured, but coated with restrained anger. 'When were you going to tell me? When I was about to go on stage and introduce Maxxy's performance?'

'I'm sorry,' I repeated, feeling the heat crawl over my chest, up my neck and wrap itself around my cheekbones. I wondered whether my face was more reminiscent of a tomato or strawberry. 'Maxxy did want to be involved — *does* want to be involved. She told me herself. She loves the idea, the website ... but technically, I suppose, she —'

'Technically, we're screwed,' Liani said. 'Did you ever think she may just have been telling you what you wanted to hear?'

I stared at a stain on the floor, my eyes tracing its rounded edges. Call me naive, call me too trusting, but that thought hadn't entered my mind once.

'You've made me look like a fool,' Liani went on. 'Mya's already made the announcement to our network.'

'What can I do?' I said. 'I'll do anything, *anything*, to fix this.'

'I've half a mind to send you home on the spot,' Liani said, 'and if I didn't have a launch to throw tomorrow, I would.'

'I'm so sorry,' I said again. 'I wish I'd told you sooner.'

'Yeah, me too.' I couldn't tell if Liani was about to cry or scream. 'Josie, you and I are going to talk later — and I mean *really talk* about your future here. But first I have to break the news to Mya. I can't even imagine what the sponsors and advertisers will say ... I suggest you go for a walk. This isn't going to be pretty.'

I'd lapped the block six times before it hit me. Somehow, among all the madness, Liani's words echoing in my mind, the disappointed look on Sia's face, I'd had a column idea. A personal idea that, if I was honest with myself, had been simmering in my subconscious for weeks, maybe even months, maybe even since my father left.

A piece on faking it. That dangerous act of trying to keep your fake-smiling, blow-dried head above water as waves of stress, expectation and pressure crash around you, and your blistered feet paddle for dear life beneath the surface. A piece about what happens when you start to believe in your own phoniness, yet feel like an impostor in your own life. When you hurt someone you love because you've become too entangled in trying to be someone you're not. A piece about trying to find a way out of the mess and learning to be the real you again.

I needed to tell my story.

When I returned to the *indi* office, Sia was at her desk sorting through bags chock-full of beauty products.

'Is the coast clear?' I asked.

'From Liani, yeah. She's popped out for a bit.'

'Okay ...' I walked towards my desk.

'But from me? No way.'

I turned to look at Sia. Her expression was halfway between concern and frustration. 'Why didn't you come to me, Jose? You should have told me something was wrong.'

'I wanted to,' I said. 'But I also wanted to be ... perfect. Then everything happened so fast — with work, and James, and Maxxy — and I wasn't ready, but I wanted to be ready. I got lost in it and ... I just got lost.'

'You want to know a secret?' Sia said. 'No one's ready for most things in life. You think I'm ready for this baby? Liani brought Dylan into the office while you were at Lavish and he screamed the whole time I held him. I'm a bloated baby-repeller and I'm about to pop out a gremlin of my own soon! I'm not ready. But you know what — I ask for help. I tell people. You, Liani, Dad, Scott, my girlfriends. But you go along living life like it's one big game of "Let's Pretend".'

She was right. 'Sia, I know —'

'Perfect doesn't exist. All Liani and I ask from you is that you work hard and do your best. And if you need help, ask. It's okay not to know everything about the world. You're eighteen years old, not eighty, even though some of your cardigans give the wrong impression.'

'I have an idea,' I said, finally managing to get a word in. 'And I'd like to write it for *indi* … if I'm not fired.'

I told Sia my story.

Silence fell over us.

'Damn, hon,' she said. 'I wanna kick your butt so bad right now, but it's like you have an insight into my soul … or something less cheesy. I love it. This is a big piece, a huge piece, so if you can pull this off I'll get Harrison to post it remotely as soon as I've read it.'

'Shouldn't we ask Liani? See if she likes it?'

Sia shook her head. 'You want to survive this weekend unscathed? You don't so much as *look* at Liani for the rest of today.'

'But what if she hates it, or other people hate it, and it ruins tomorrow?'

Sia rolled her eyes. 'We have bigger things to worry about right now. Finish up the launch planning, confirm anything you need to confirm, and write that article. It'll keep you occupied and out of my hair. Trust me.'

I may not have had Maxxy locked in, or James's love, or Liani's respect, but I still had something: I had my writing. I returned to my desk, feeling inspired for the first time in a while.

As I created a new document, it dawned on me what I was doing with this article. Edwina had wanted to drop a bomb on me by exposing my weaknesses, and here I was, helping her pull the pin. I just hoped there was enough good among the debris to counter the fallout.

The cursor flashed. I began to write.

My name is Josie Browning, I'm eighteen years old and I'm a fake.

21.

I lay on my bed with my eyes clamped shut, while Steph and Prue talked in the kitchen. I wasn't trying to be antisocial. I was in hibernate-before-the-launch-tomorrow mode.

Liani had barely uttered a word to me all afternoon, so by the time I got home I was full-blown freaking and considering bribing a doctor to put my leg in a cast to get me out of the launch.

My door creaked open and I squeezed my eyes closed even tighter, feigning sleep.

'I think she's dead,' Prue said, leaning in close. Her breath reeked of onion and cheese, a potent combination. But it wasn't enough to zap me to life.

'Nah, she's breathing,' said Steph. 'Maybe she's meditating. She did go to that pretentious health retreat … *I* think she's actually a robot and her batteries are recharging, or maybe we need to plug her in to refuel her little robot heart —'

'Shut up,' I said, my eyes still closed.

Steph cheered. 'Which part broke you? Was it the little robot heart?'

I opened one eye and glared at her, aware of how ridiculous I looked. 'Leave me alone. Please.'

'What are you doing?' asked Prue. 'Shouldn't you be prepping for tomorrow? I'm sure organising a launch isn't as hard as, say, studying for a medical exam, but don't you have things to finalise?'

'I am prepping,' I said, eyes closed again. 'This is how I prep.'

'Righto then,' Steph said. 'Well, I guess prepping wouldn't go with eating Hawaiian pizza anyway —'

My eyes flew open. 'You ordered Hawaiian? But you never let me order that any more!'

'The novelty wore off after the first fifteen times,' Prue muttered.

'Yes, there is a Hawaiian pizza on the way, but you're only allowed to enjoy it if you tell us what the hell is going on,' Steph said. 'This whole mummified-lying-on-your-bed thing *was* kinda funny at first, but now it's just —'

'Freaky,' finished Prue.

'You want to know what's up?' I said, pulling myself into a sitting position. 'My boyfriend hates me, and my job as a writer is going to be over tomorrow when I get fired ... or maybe worse.'

'Executed?' Steph said in mock alarm.

'I didn't get Maxxy for the launch,' I said, my voice becoming shrill.

There was a pause.

'Well, that sucks, but I'm sure Liani understands,' said Steph.

'I tried everything,' I said, my head in my hands. 'I don't even have a new dress to wear tomorrow night. I ran out of time to go shopping.'

'At least your nails look hot,' Steph said.

'I thought things were going to work out for once, you know?' I muttered.

'But that's life, I guess.' Prue shrugged. 'Sometimes it's a bit rubbish.'

'Yeah, it is … but it doesn't have to be,' Steph said. 'Not tonight. Not tomorrow. Not for you, Jose. Listen, you're a walking catastrophe.'

I raised an eyebrow. 'Thanks.'

'Hey, I'm not judging: I'm broke and living in a room the size of a matchbox,' Steph said. 'But you know what? In the short time I've known you, I've seen you stumble — often literally — from disaster to disaster. Yet you somehow turn things around. *You* work it out. *You* save the day. You're your own knight in shining armour.'

'You've lost it.' I shook my head. 'Liani rescued me when I got the boot from *Sash.*'

'Did she?' Steph pressed. 'Or did you work your arse off and prove that you deserved a job?'

I shrugged. 'I dunno. I guess.'

'You what now?'

'Fine, I worked my freaking arse off. You happy?'

'Well, what's stopping you and that freaking arse now? All this sad-sacking isn't the Josie B I know — and frankly, it's pissing me off!'

I glared at Steph, but she scowled right back, unshaken. A lopsided smile crept into the corner of my mouth. 'Well, well, Miss Stephanie. You give quite the tough-love pep talk. "Your own knight in shining armour" was an especially nice touch.'

Steph broke out into a grin. 'Tell me it worked. Tell me I didn't go off at you for nothing.'

I swallowed. I wasn't ready for my first real job to come to a dramatic end. 'It worked,' I admitted, my mind racing. 'Bugger it, can you guys give me a sec?'

Instead of leaving, my oddball housemates splayed on the bed next to me.

'We live here and we want in with whatever's about to happen,' said Steph. 'Besides, my boyfriend's thousands of kilometres away. You're my only entertainment.'

'Alright …' I said, punching Darlene's number into the phone. I knew it off by heart by now. 'It's ringing.'

'We have no idea what's going on,' Prue said.

I got her voicemail. Again. I'd already sent her several follow-up emails and left two voicemails that day, but still, what did I have to lose? Maybe third time would be a charm (or a good reason to hang up before she took out a restraining order on me).

'Darlene, hi ... it's Josie Browning again, Maxxy's new friend from *indi* magazine ... the bowling *biznitch* girl, if that helps ... Er, probably not ... I can't believe I just said *biznitch* to you,' I stammered, eyes wide.

Steph mouthed, 'Hang up right now.'

'I ... I guess you know why I'm calling ... did Maxxy mention we'd spoken, that she wants to do this? I know she's signed on to do the cover shoot with *Marilyn*, but the launch is tomorrow and — yeah, I pretty much answered my own question, didn't I? The launch is tomorrow ... Look, you know what — *I'll* pay for her expenses. If you can get her there by 6 pm tomorrow, I'll do the rest. Collect receipts and I'll pay you back every cent. I'll sort it out, I'll get a loan, I'll work overtime — well, we don't get paid for that — but I'll get a second job. I just need her there. I don't know what else to say, so ... call me ... please. You have my number.' I hung up.

Steph's jaw was virtually touching her chest. 'Did that just happen?' she said. 'Did you call Maxxy's manager and promise to personally cover her costs? You'd be better off hiring a Maxxy impersonator!'

'If the *real* Maxxy can make it, the *indi* launch will be a success and Liani will be happy,' I said. 'Otherwise I may as well quit now and become a garbage collector.'

'I don't know …' said Prue. 'If they agree, it could cost you hundreds, even thousands, depending on where they put her up for the night. And I have it on good authority you're living on noodles.'

'Shhh, you two, I'm very busy waiting for my phone to ring,' I said. 'I'm eighty-five per cent sure it's all going to work out.'

Steph squeezed my hand.

I swallowed. 'Maybe seventy per cent.'

The doorbell sounded. 'Dinner!' said Steph as she bolted out, with Prue and me hot on her tail.

Steph practically wrestled the pizza out of the delivery man's arms then brought it into the lounge room. I bit into a hot slice, enjoying the stinging taste of tomato and strings of melted cheese getting caught in my teeth. My piece was demolished in seconds, while Steph picked the pineapple off hers, and Prue nibbled at the crust.

I squinted at the clock through strained eyes. It was almost nine.

'I think there's still a forty per cent chance of Darlene calling,' I said. 'Thanks for the pizza, guys, I'm going to bed. These sorts of things happen when you're not watching the clock, you know?'

'Yeah,' said Prue unconvincingly.

'Hey, Jose!' Steph called out. 'Loved your latest article by the way — the one on faking it.'

'You read that already?'

'Timmy-boy and I've been sending it to everyone.' She grinned. 'Everyone thinks you're way too smart to be my friend, but I tell them I taught you everything you know.'

After kissing Steph on the cheek, Prue and I shared an awkward hug goodnight. Then she slipped me one of her classic Post-its. I inhaled, braced for one of her usual passive-aggressive remarks. Only this note simply read: 'It's not over yet, so don't give up … and remember, I'm never wrong.'

Stunned by her gesture, I mumbled thanks and trundled towards the bathroom.

'Ten per cent sure,' I muttered. 'I'm still ten per cent sure.'

But my mind raced with negative thoughts. I had no Maxxy, no loving boyfriend, and no chance of making the launch a success. I fell into a fitful sleep with the words 'one per cent' taunting me over and over.

It had arrived. Launch day was finally here. I stood in front of the warehouse building, playing with my phone while I waited for Sia and Liani. There was still no word from Darlene and no texts from James.

I typed a message to him, deleted it, then retyped the words: *Once upon a time a girl called Josie scored an internship and thought a boy called James was trying to burgle her. Then they ate pizza and she fell in love.*

My finger hovered above the send button as memories came flooding back: the first night we met at Tim's place; the time James loaned me his leather jacket and drove me through the city on his scooter; the time we confessed that we liked each other. There hadn't been any game-playing, or phone tag, or going off the radar. We just … worked.

I wanted us to work again.

I pressed send and instantly regretted it.

Then I reminded myself of my latest article. It was okay to be vulnerable. Okay to put myself out there, to take a chance, to be myself.

There was no time to dwell on it further because Liani arrived with a puffing Sia in tow. Liani gave me an icy hello and a sharp nod, which, coming from her, was the equivalent of screaming in my face.

Sia and I followed her into the building and couldn't believe what we found inside. There was no red carpet, no flowers, no candles, no stage set up. Other than the white furniture and large framed mirrors, the place wasn't decorated.

Sia's face fell. 'You've got a pregnant woman and a rake — no offence, Jose — to help you set up an event for two hundred people? Where's our office-husband?'

'Harrison's coming later,' Liani said. 'He's sorting out the video gear and monitoring the site … something about lots of traffic overnight.'

Sia and I exchanged glances.

'And don't be silly,' Liani continued, 'the event planners will take care of the decorations — the candles, the candy bar, the red carpet, everything.'

'Oh, I could kiss you,' Sia said. 'Sorry, I'm cranky without my daily chocolate fix. Damn baby's gone off it — it's got me craving vegetables of all things. Vegetables!'

Liani put her arm around Sia. 'Hon, go home. I told you to meet us here later.'

'And miss the biggest day in my girl *indi*'s life so far?' Sia teased. 'No way.'

'Well, let me know if you need a rest before the panel,' Liani said. 'If you're staying, we may as well do a practice run before things get too hectic. It'll warm up the old vocal cords and get us pumped for tonight.'

'Perfect,' said Sia.

'Allegra MacGregor and Corrine Spark won't be here until later, but they're old hands so it won't be a problem.'

I cleared my throat. 'Anything I can do?'

Liani paused, not quite making eye contact. 'Goodie bags. You can put them together.'

My trustworthiness was shot, but I couldn't blame her. 'On it,' I said, trying to sound perky.

The front-door buzzer went off.

'That must be the florist with the roses,' Liani muttered.

'She hates me,' I whispered to Sia after Liani had gone to let the florist in. 'And she still doesn't know about the article?'

'Not unless you've told her,' Sia said. 'Anyway, Jose, listen, you've got to distract her for me, okay? I'm feeling weird, but I can't tell her that. Not today.'

'But you said you didn't fake it in life? That you asked for help?'

'Did I forget to mention my disclaimer? I don't fake it unless my boss is on the verge of a nervous breakdown! I'll get through it ... but is my skin green? I feel like I'm green.'

'No, you're washed out though ... Here, take my water bottle.' I pulled it from my handbag and passed it to her. 'Want me to get you something to eat?'

'I think I need to go to the bathroom,' she said, hobbling off in that direction.

I followed her, standing guard at the door like a loyal watchdog. Minutes passed, so I knocked and whispered her name. 'Are you okay?' No reply. I knocked again, and the door creaked open.

'I think something's happening,' she said, clutching her stomach. 'Something bad.'

'What do you mean?'

'There's ... there's blood.'

I froze. 'Oh god.'

'Get help,' she said through gritted teeth.

Without another thought, I ran towards the open door, shouting, 'Liani, come quick!'

Liani stepped into the warehouse buried under a mountain of stunning white roses. The florist and her two fresh-faced assistants followed, bringing in even more.

'Marina, you and the girls have done a gorgeous job,' Liani said, as she placed the flowers on a table. 'I'll put them here for now —'

'Something's happening with the baby,' I said. 'There's blood, Liani! What do we do?'

Liani — as always — was three steps ahead. She rushed to Sia's side and stroked her arm with one hand, while calling her dad with the other.

'We don't have a car,' I realised. 'I'll call a taxi or an ambulance —'

'I'll drive her,' Marina interrupted. 'There's plenty of space now, and my girls can sit in the back.'

Liani hung up the phone. 'St Joseph's Hospital is only five minutes from here, and her dad's already on the way. Thank you, Marina. I'll come with you.'

'Me too,' I said. 'I'll get my handbag and —'

'Jose, Liani … no,' Sia said. 'I love you, but you need to be here.'

'But we want to be there with you … You're scared.' Or maybe that was me.

'Honey, I'm fine,' Sia said, but her eyes misted over, which immediately made mine well up too. 'We haven't spent the past three weeks busting our balls for you guys to call off the launch.'

I squeezed her hand. 'I'll visit as soon as I can. And I'll save you one of those mini iced doughnuts you were eyeing off in the catering brochure.'

'Make it two.' She forced a weak smile, which fell away almost immediately. 'Jose ... what if the baby doesn't —'

'Don't say it,' I told her, clutching her hand. 'Don't even think it.'

Liani and Marina helped Sia out the door, and the assistants followed with her enormous handbag. Left alone, I went up on the stage and took a seat. I suddenly didn't care whether I was hours away from being fired. All that mattered was that Sia and her baby were okay.

Liani walked back into the room wringing her hands. 'If anything happens to that poor baby ... I was not prepared for that.'

'Me neither,' I said. 'Liani, I know everything's a bit nuts right now, but I want to let you know I'll do whatever it takes to make today work. Whatever you need. Whenever you need it.'

Liani's eyes met mine for the first time since yesterday. 'Thank you, but I'm working on a plan. Besides, as if this madness wasn't enough, I need you to deal with our visitor.'

I sat up straighter, wondering if James was pulling his rocking-up-at-my-work stunt again.

'I'll be in the next room going over the panel questions,' Liani said, then called out through the open door. 'You can come in now.'

But it wasn't James. A sheepish, wide-eyed Kat shuffled in, wheeling a suitcase and scuffing the floor with her sneakers.

'Hey, Jose,' she said.

I could have wrapped my manicured hands around Kat's scrawny little neck. I reminded myself I was the older sister and should be mature, but then I yelled my head off anyway. I yelled that she shouldn't scuff her feet on the floorboards because renting this place cost *indi* a fortune. I yelled that I couldn't believe she'd done this to Mum and me, today of all days. I yelled that she was grounded for the next four hundred years.

'I get it — you can make your voice go really loud,' she said. 'What do you want to do today? I was thinking shopping ... or maybe the movies ... When I was at the station I saw an ad for a musical that —'

'How could you?' I said, my voice trembling. 'You can't waltz in here and demand your own tour of the city. I'm working. I have the launch. How did you even know where to come?'

Kat rolled her eyes. 'It isn't a secret — all the info is on *indi*'s website. Anyway, I was kidding. I'm here to help with the launch — and meet Maxxy — but mostly to help out. I should score brownie points for being this awesome.'

I sighed. 'I let you off the hook last time. And forget about Maxxy — she's not coming.'

'What? You're kidding me! Why not?'

'Focus, Kat. I can't believe you did this. You could get me fired.'

I didn't mention that I was pretty close to getting myself fired. How had I ever thought I could pull this off? I was so far out of my depth I should have been wearing floaties.

'Jose, I called Mum from the train,' Kat said. 'She was angrier than that time you and me catnapped the neighbours' pets. But once she calmed down, she said it might be good for me. And you.'

I shook my head and dialled Mum's number.

'I'm grounded for a month, but she says I have to stay with you tonight,' Kat went on.

'*What?*'

'She's working late so she can't pick me up, and she doesn't want me getting the train back by myself at night.'

'Mum?' I said into the phone.

'Love!' she said. 'I'm guessing your package has arrived. I'm sorry, love, but as she's there, I've told her to help you in any way she can.'

'But I —'

'I know, I'm angry too ... but, Jose, she misses her big sister.'

'This isn't like letting Kat join me and Angel at a sleepover, Mum ... this is my work. And there's so much going on at the moment I can't even ...' I trailed off, my mind swirling with Sia, James and Edwina.

'Sometimes you've got to be tough,' Mum said. 'I wish my daughter hadn't run away, I wish I was eating blue cheese right now and I wish I owned a Louis Vuitton bag, but we can't always have everything we want, can we?'

I took a deep breath. 'No … we can't.'

'Love, whatever is on your mind, you can handle it,' she said. 'You've never stopped making me proud, Josie Browning — even that time you pulled down your pants and mooned the other kids at preschool.'

'Mum!'

'I mean it — you mooned with flair!' she gushed. 'That was the moment I knew you were going to be someone special.'

'Yeah, I was special alright.'

Her laughter sang down the line.

'Mum …' I choked up before I could finish.

'I miss you too, sweetie. I'm right here, you old softie, always have been.'

'Everything feels impossible right now.'

'Look, you put that little sister of yours to work, okay? Whatever else is going on, chin up and face it head on,' she said. 'I know you can, so no more doubt, no more hesitation, just do it, my girl. I'll drive up with Rodgie in the morning and pick Kat up. But before her grounding begins, perhaps we could all do brunch? I'm quite fond of brunch these days.'

'Okay. Love you,' I said.

Kat stared as I hung up. 'Well?'

'You're still grounded for life, Rodger's hijacking our family brunch tomorrow, and yes, you're staying with me for one night — one night only.'

'Sweet.' She grinned. 'Rodger's alright, you know. You should ease up on him.'

I didn't reply.

'He taught Mum how to make risotto that doesn't taste like Clag.'

I had to laugh. 'That is a feat. Fine, I'll give him a chance, but only because Mum deserves to be happy and, for reasons that can't be explained, this guy is making that happen. But if she makes me call him "Rodgie", I'm out. And if he so much as —'

'Not every guy's like Dad. Remember that.'

I bit my lip. 'Yeah.'

'I'm right, as always,' Kat said. 'Now, what can I do to help today, and more importantly will I get paid?'

'Paid? No! Come with me and try to stay out of the way. We need to organise the goodie bags.'

Kat's eyes lit up. 'Goodie bags? Cool!'

22.

Fifteen minutes later, Kat's delight had transformed into disgust. 'I hate goodie bags!' she snapped, crossing and uncrossing her legs in search of a comfortable position.

We were sitting on the floor of the storeroom surrounded by lip glosses, eye shadows, biscuits, chocolates, drink bottles, customised *indi* pencils and vouchers — anything we could stuff into goodie bags that would please the media hounds and prevent them from saying anything too terrible about us in their publications.

'How many have you done?' I asked.

'About five. Am I nearly finished?'

'Sure … I've done ten, so we only have one hundred and eighty-five to go.'

'This sucks,' she whinged, packing another bag.

She wasn't wrong. It sucked more than the time my class had to clean the gym locker room after Holly Bentley and her gang egged the school but didn't own up to it so our whole grade suffered. The two of us worked in silence for what felt like hours, methodically placing items into the bags, neatly writing people's names on the tags, and tying it all together with a purple ribbon.

'Kat, I have to ask,' I said, breaking the silence, 'why are you really here? Is something wrong back home? Are you being bullied?'

'What? As if! Jose, you had my back the other week ... I could tell you needed me here tonight so I could have yours. I know when something's up.'

I waited for her to pressure me for more details. She didn't, which made it harder to stay mad at her. I snuck a quick look at my phone. No messages from Sia. No messages from James.

'Whatcha wearing tonight anyway?' Kat asked after we'd filled another dozen or so bags.

I shrugged. What did a person wear while she got fired? I'd brought two dresses with me but wasn't happy with either of them. One was a Sia hand-me-down; the other was an oldie-but-goodie that didn't feel special enough for tonight.

The door creaked open and Liani poked her head into the room. 'Josie, can I ... Whoa, those goodie bags look fantastic.' Kat beamed, soaking in the praise. 'Josie, can I borrow you in the meeting room next door? Alone?'

'Of course,' I said, and got up.

'Oh, and Kat,' Liani added, 'take a bag or two. We always have leftovers.'

Kat thanked her in a polite voice that I'd never heard

before, but as Liani and I walked away, we heard her shriek, 'Best job ever!' At least someone was finally enjoying themselves.

I closed the meeting room door behind me. If Liani was going to go off, I didn't want my little sister to hear it. She knew something was wrong, but I wasn't ready for her to know *how* wrong.

'Any word from Sia?' I asked.

Liani shook her head. 'Not yet ... Look, Josie, without her ... you said you'd do whatever it takes to make tonight work.'

'Of course. Anything. Do you feel like a coffee, or a tea, or a coconut water, or a —'

'Josie, everything is riding on tonight ... everything. I need you to step up for *indi* like you've never stepped up before. Could you be my youth representative on the panel?'

'You're ... you're not firing me?' I blurted out.

'The night is young,' she said wryly. 'Right now, I can't think past tonight. I need someone from *indi* on the panel, and that means you.'

Nerves flooded my body, and I rummaged through every nook and cranny of my brain for an excuse to get me out of it. Nothing.

'We need someone female, someone young and someone who gets the *indi* brand. And Josie ... you really do get the *indi* brand. Your "Faking It" article proves that.'

'You read it?'

Liani pursed her lips. 'I did, after a number of our guests contacted me to say congratulations for leading with such a provocative, raw piece on launch day.'

'Right ...' I couldn't tell if Liani was peeved or impressed.

'Morning, squirrels,' Harrison said, bursting through the door with a coffee in each hand. He passed one to Liani, who kissed him on the cheek. 'I got your messages. Has Sia texted you, Jose?'

I shook my head.

'Well, while we wait, you could start by saying "Thanks for moderating *all* the comments on my article this morning, Harrison",' he said. 'It's had about ten times the hits of your others, thanks to a little retweet from The Social Source.'

'As in ... *The* Social Source?' I asked. It was an online community that shared the hottest stories of the day, and it had hundreds of thousands of followers, many in *indi*'s demographic. 'Are you both serious? About the article? And the panel? This is ... this is ...'

'Hopefully not the dumbest decision I make all day,' Liani said.

'It won't be. I swear.' At least I hoped it wouldn't be. Public speaking wasn't exactly my specialty, but if meant I could keep my job for a bit longer, I'd do anything. 'So ... panellist and youth representative Josie Browning reporting for duty. What do you need me to talk about?

Climate change? Young women's issues? Equal pay? The changing employment landscape?'

'Slow down, Youth Representative,' Liani said. 'We want to put *indi* on the map as the place to go to for real, smart conversations on the things people are talking about, so yes, that includes climate change and equal pay. But it also means tapping into those topics that really resonate with readers, like sex for the first time and faking your way through life.'

'Oh … okay.'

'Anyway, Josie, if you're replacing Sia on the panel, we should go over a few things. Harrison, you can give feedback.' Liani looked around the meeting room, no doubt imagining a heaving crowd dressed in their finest designer outfits.

'Good evening, everyone, and welcome to the inaugural *indi* magazine forum,' Liani said. 'I trust you're having a lovely time. Now, allow me to introduce our wonderful panellists. First up, Josie Browning, our youth representative. Many of you may also recognise her fresh voice from her *indi* column. Next, the fierce and fabulous women's issues activist Allegra MacGregor, plus everyone's favourite outspoken media commentator, Corrine Spark — that's when everyone will cheer.'

Harrison covered his mouth, trying not to laugh.

'Let's begin by throwing to the audience for a question — yes, you, sir, in the navy jacket,' continued

Liani, so realistically I almost looked around to see if there was a guy standing there. 'A question for our youth representative? Of course ... Josie would love to discuss the pressures of sexual expectations on youth today. Take it away!'

I thanked the hypothetical man in the navy jacket for such a great question, then opened my mouth again to answer it and said ... nothing.

I tried again.

Still nothing.

Forget tongue-tied; I didn't feel like I even had a tongue. Five seconds later it felt like my mouth was *filled* with tongue and it was so big, so huge, so disgustingly enormously gargantuan, that it was threatening to choke me. I wasn't lost for words; I couldn't *remember* a single word or letter in the English alphabet — I would have had more luck speaking in Japanese.

'Josie?' Liani said, her eyes narrowed. 'The pressures?'

Oh, I knew about the pressures.

'Um ...' I said. 'Well ... I guess I should start by saying ... um, sex.'

Liani raised an eyebrow, and if the man in the navy jacket had actually existed, I'm sure he would have done the same. I didn't dare look at Harrison.

'Sorry, that's not what I meant ... I meant to say ... sex.' I screwed up my nose in frustration. 'I'm not usually so good at this — I mean, bad at this. Can I start over?'

Liani nodded. 'Please.'

I cleared my throat. 'In this country, young people are often judged and criticised in the media based on the behaviour of a single few.' Liani looked relieved that I'd rediscovered the power of speech. 'And, well ... sex and ... um ... well ... sex is ... sex is a thing that ... I mean, some people want to have sex and ... some people do have sex ... but not everyone ... so there's a lot of pressure ... and pleasure, I guess ... but pressure ... when it comes to ... sex.'

Liani's face looked as I imagined it would if she'd just discovered that her son had smeared poo on her designer rug. I wished for a hole to open in the warehouse's floorboards and suck me down to oblivion.

'Josie, what was that?' Liani asked.

'I'm sorry, I'm nervous. I've never talked about this in front of other people.'

'When you write, you're articulate, you sum up what people feel. You saw the reaction your latest columns have received. People want more, so that's what I'm trying to give them ... but you have to help me out.'

'Liani's right, doll,' Harrison chimed in. 'I love ya, but that may have been the worst thing I've ever seen.'

'Ever?'

He rolled his eyes. 'Fine ... it was top two, only just beaten by my sister-in-law's water-birth video. Liani, we shouldn't risk this ...'

'I'll do better,' I said, devastated that Edwina's curse was coming true, all through my own failings. Even though being on the panel was nerve-racking, being sacked and humiliated would be even worse. 'I can do this, I know I can.'

'Really?' Liani asked.

I paused. 'If you give me the chance, yes. I want everyone to see we're the best online magazine out, and we're going to give the glossies a run for their money. Ask me the question again. I'll do it right this time.'

Liani reached into her handbag and handed me her iPad. 'Memorise your articles instead. Choose your key points and practise 'til they're locked in your brain.'

I scanned the screen. 'You don't want to quiz me?'

'We may be making it harder than it has to be. You have everything you need to inspire our guests inside you already. Talk the way you write, from the heart, and the audience will love you.'

'You're really going to do this, Li?' Harrison asked. 'Take this kind of chance tonight of all nights?'

'You told me yourself — the number of hits she's getting is unprecedented for us,' Liani said, the two of them talking as though I wasn't even there. 'We need to take that strength into the market, lean into it, not stifle it.'

Harrison sighed. 'But if she can't finish a sentence ...' He turned to me. 'Jose, don't take this the wrong way, but we need to do what's best for *indi*. You're a great writer, but —'

Liani cut him off. 'Finish setting up the video recorder, Harrison. This is my call.'

She sounded like she was moments away from ripping off her blouse to reveal a ripped Hulk-like torso.

Harrison walked out of the room, muttering, 'Whatever will be, will be,' but the damage was done. Even though Liani had stood up for me — a surprise in itself, all things considered — Harrison's doubt had shaken my confidence.

'Maybe he's right,' I said. 'Maybe —'

'You told me yes and I'm trusting in that,' Liani said. 'Don't make me look like a fool again. You have your columns. Read them until you know every word. Then, when the launch kicks off, prove to me I was right to hire you. Now, come with me. I want to show you something.'

I followed Liani down the hallway and into the main area. I sucked in a breath when we entered. A soft glow filled the room, giving it the ambience of a romantic restaurant. Tables were covered in white linen and stunning white roses. Tea lights played peekaboo on windowsills, tables and the bar — they even lined the stage. There was a red carpet in the entrance, ready for people to pose on for photographs when they arrived. A huge *indi* sign hung above the stage. All the meetings, all the brainstorming, all the budgeting, all the celebrity-wrangling had come down to this. In an hour we would know if it had all been worth it.

'Well?' Liani asked.

'It's magical, like a dream.'

She exhaled. 'It is, isn't it? There's something else.' She led me over to one of the doors in the wall, and paused before turning the handle. 'I wasn't sure whether I should still give you this, but, the fact is, you helped make this launch a reality — with or without Maxxy. I'm not blind — I've seen how much of your heart and soul you give daily, far beyond the hours you're expected to work. And I know you've had a tough time lately, what with the problems you've been having with your boyfriend, and that email doing the rounds —'

'The email?' I said. 'You know?'

'I was forwarded it forty times that day alone, once from Mya who found the whole thing surprisingly charming. I'm not sure how I missed it the first time though —'

'Mya saw it?' Next thing I'd be hearing about how the prime minister had read it.

'Frankly, I'm impressed by how well you've handled it,' Liani said. 'Although we may need Harrison to give you a lesson on group email functions to avoid any further mishaps.'

I blushed.

'Now, I know you're sorry for not keeping me in the loop about Maxxy, so let's agree to get through tonight and regroup later.'

Before I had a chance to decode what that meant, Liani opened the door to reveal a room filled with racks of gorgeous dresses and shoes, and a floor-to-ceiling length mirror. I gasped.

'I figured you may need something to wear tonight, so Sia and I called in a bunch of outfits via Sophie's new styling business,' Liani explained. 'The rules are, there are no rules: you can try on whatever you like — except that cream dress in the corner, that's mine.'

'Wow ...' I said, stepping closer to the nearest rack to run my hand over the materials. Lace, silk, cotton and leather dresses, each crying out to be worn. There was a backless sequinned dress that would look stunning on the red carpet. I stopped at a coral-red dress with capped sleeves and a cinched waist that dropped into a floaty, dreamy skirt. I held it up to my body and snuck a peek in the mirror. It was prettier than anything I'd ever worn before.

'Don't forget to pick out some shoes,' was all Liani said. 'Okay, next up ...'

'There's more?'

Liani opened the next door along to reveal a smallish room with two middle-aged men in it, both so bronzed they looked like they'd bathed in fake tan. One held a hairdryer and a comb; the other, who was short and stocky, was sorting make-up brushes and lipsticks in a beauty kit.

'Josie, play nice with Paul and Ken,' Liani said.

'Ah, before you go,' I started. 'About Lavish ... did they pull their sponsorship?'

Liani paused. I could tell she was weighing up the pros and cons of telling me the truth.

'No,' she admitted. 'But they're disappointed. They can't afford to be linked to any more PR catastrophes.'

'Sure,' I said, gulping. 'And, as for Kat showing up, I'm —'

She cut me off. 'You read those columns — I don't want your head anywhere but there — and I'll grab you when it's time to greet guests.'

'Thanks ... I don't know what else to say.'

'Just make sure you've worked it out by the time the panel starts. I'm counting on you,' she said, and left the room.

Clutching the iPad, I sank into the chair and looked at my reflection in the mirror, wondering if this was all a dream.

'Darl, we're starting with a head, neck and shoulder massage to get you nice and relaxed,' said Paul, the hair stylist.

I nodded, too overwhelmed to speak. If this was a dream, I didn't want to wake up.

23.

The room was filling up fast. I mentally ticked guests off the VIP list as they flowed onto the red carpet and posed for photos. There were soap stars, singers, reality-show hosts, footy players (all codes), as well as a smorgasbord of the city's media hawks. Newspapers, magazines, radio, websites and blogs — they were all there, each clinging to their own kind.

The Blue Dames were performing an acoustic set, and I'd noticed several men leering at them over the tops of their champagne glasses. Liani, who'd slipped into her cream dress, was air-kissing each guest; Harrison was in videographer mode; and there was still no word from Sia, or James. Kat was nowhere to be seen. Without anyone to chat to, I plucked a hot dog — miniature-sized, of course — from a passing platter, and used my other hand to scroll through my phone's inbox.

And there it was: an email from Angel. She'd been MIA for over a month (I'd convinced myself that she'd been kidnapped by pirates in Europe) so I clicked on the little envelope icon faster than you could say, 'You've got mail, baby!' But instead of the long-overdue account of the amazing adventures she'd been having, Angel had written just a few lines: *Hi babe! Greetings from Berlin. I'm dying for a d-and-m too. But what do you mean you need a case-study call-out from me? Where's my email dripping with filthy gossip about you and James? Miss and love you, bestie.*

I had to laugh. Angel was so far off the grid she'd completely bypassed the email mix-up. There was no time to fill her in on the dramas with James, Alex, Edwina and Maxxy, so I snapped a selfie of me sticking my tongue out with the bustling event behind me and sent it to her with the message *Miss you too. Talk soon xx.*

'That didn't look very professional,' a voice announced next to me.

I turned to see Kat dressed in a mint-green body-con dress, statement jewelled necklace and high heels.

'Wow!' I said. 'Did you go shopping? If you've stolen Mum's credit card —'

'Calm down, worrywart!' she said. 'As a thank you for helping with the goodie bags, Liani took me into that *amazing* room filled with clothes and said I could pick anything to wear. Your boss is so nice.'

I rolled my eyes. 'If this is you being grounded ...'

'I know, right?' She grinned. 'I'm going to Instagram the hell out of this party. Who do you know here anyway?

I met two women called Allegra and Corrine — are they famous?'

'You did? Yeah ... yeah, they are. I know Stevie Q's meant to be coming,' I said. 'And there's a whole group of famous journos in the corner over there, chatting with that actress you love who —'

'Oh my freaking god,' Kat shrieked, then covered her mouth. 'This is, like, the best night of my life. How are you playing it so cool?'

Me? Playing it cool? *Puhlease*. 'Well, maybe I'm maturing and growing as a person and — crap, crap, crap on a hat! It's her, Kat! She came, oh god, she came.'

I ducked behind my sister, who was scanning the room trying to work out who had frightened me.

'Who? Is it someone famous? It's not Billy's girlfriend, is it, 'cos I bet she still hates you.'

No — worse. It was Edwina. She was standing at the bar by herself, sipping a cocktail, all soft, bouncing waves of hair, red-stained lips and attitude. Eyebrow raised, she surveyed the rainbow-coloured lollies and whimsical decorations on the candy bar. Judging by the way she was looking down her nose, she was here to watch us fail and take pleasure in every humiliating moment. Why was she even here? Had she arranged for a bucket of pig's blood to be dropped on my head *Carrie*-style mid-panel? What about the *Marilyn* cover shoot with Maxxy?

'Why are you hiding?' Kat whispered. 'You look weirder than usual, and that's saying something.'

'I'm fixing my dress,' I lied. I glanced at my phone. There was only about seven minutes until the panel started. 'Hang on … where's the iPad? I've lost Liani's iPad!'

'Jose, it's in your left hand,' Kat said. 'What's this panel you guys keep talking about anyway? Is it like a fashion parade?'

'No, it's like … a panel,' I said. 'An exchange of ideas, a debate, a discussion.'

'That sounds worse than school. The guests better drink up because it's going to be seriously dull.'

'You're the expert,' I said. I took a deep breath, trying to compose myself. I needed to get through this with no problems, no distractions, no mistakes — as if my career depended on it. Because, well, it did.

I saw Liani walking towards me through the crowd. Argh, it was nearly time. I willed my legs to walk towards her, then I heard someone call out my name. Filly, bald and beaming, was bearing down on me, a mini taco in one hand and a mini burger in the other.

'Filly!' I gasped. I hadn't invited him, and part of me wondered whether he had accidentally wandered in off the street following the smell of delicious food.

'Surprise!' he boomed, swallowing the mini burger in one bite, then snatching a green cocktail from a passing platter. 'Liani invited me along to see what you've been helping her pull together. It's a marvellous event, simply marvellous.' He took a gulp of his cocktail, which looked like a tiny toy in his swollen sausage-like hands. 'By the way, I've been reading your columns. Good work, Browning. It's been quite a ride teaching you.'

'Thanks, Filly.'

'But you're officially starting second year now, so ...'

'So ...? *Oh.* You won't be my lecturer any more.'

'No, I'll have a whole new batch of little shi— er, students to teach,' he said, chomping his mini taco. 'I'll still be course convener, though, so I'll check in from time to time. Thanks for keeping it interesting between fishing trips.' He winked.

'You too, Filly,' I said. 'It's been great.'

'Who knows, at the rate you're going, you may end up being my boss one day — and a fine one you'd make too. Best of luck tonight.' He patted me on the shoulder and walked off, lunging at a nearby platter to collect three prawns, and chomping them down, tails and all, as though they were sultanas.

'Ready?' Liani said, appearing by my side. 'Harrison's all set up, so let's make it a memorable panel for all the right reasons.'

'I'll come with you for moral support,' said Kat, teetering after me, a soft drink in one hand and a cupcake in the other.

I truly hoped 'moral support' wasn't her code for throwing rotten tomatoes at me while I spoke.

Waiting backstage wasn't half as glamorous as I hoped it might be. Kat's version of moral support was scoffing down cupcakes; Allegra was getting her make-up retouched; and Corrine was taking selfies. Liani was already doing her introduction on stage, which meant I had about three minutes, five at most, to gather my thoughts. You have your columns, you know your material, focus on translating it from the page to the audience, I told myself.

'Jose,' Kat whispered, her voice muffled with cupcake.

'Shhh, I'm trying to concentrate.'

'But there's someone here to see you,' she said, her voice quivering.

'Who could be so important —' I turned to see Maxxy standing there. 'Kat, get a doctor. I think I'm having a stroke.'

'Josie, we got your voicemail,' Maxxy said. 'Actually, we got all *fifteen* of your voicemails.'

'I ... you're ... um ... you're here,' I squeaked. 'I can't believe it!'

Another miracle. Holy crap, maybe Santa was real.

A quick look on stage showed Liani had no idea what was unfolding behind her.

'After the fifteenth voicemail, Darlene was worried I

had a stalker, so she let me listen to a message to see if I knew the perp before she involved the police.'

'She thought I was a stalker?' That was a humiliating low, even for me.

'A little.' Maxxy laughed. 'Okay, a lot. I think she was ready to double my security, but then I heard your voice. I showed her the bowling pic on Instagram, filled her in on our talk at Lavish, showed her the website — she finally caved and moved things around. She'd crammed in a last-minute photo shoot for *Marilyn* for some reason, but we worked around it. Darlene didn't pass on your messages right away, so I'd figured you'd changed your mind and didn't need me any more — it happens all the time.'

My stomach churned at the mention of Edwina's magazine. 'What happened with *Marilyn*? You still did the shoot?'

'Yeah, we brought it forward to this afternoon. But between you and me, it was weird. I mean, it's *Marilyn,* you know, so I thought we'd do something groundbreaking, but it all felt beige and rushed, like no one was prepared.'

Probably because they weren't. Probably because Edwina had organised it as part of her revenge spiral. Rae would be fuming if the shoot turned out to be a dud.

'How ... how did you even get here?' I asked. 'People are going to lose their minds when they see you.'

'Darlene had me brought in a back way to avoid any fuss. I hope your boss likes surprises.'

I took a deep breath. 'I've imagined this moment so many times, but ... now I'm kinda speechless.'

I wasn't the only one. My celebrity-obsessed little sister was staring at Maxxy with her jaw ajar.

'Say when you want me to perform!' Maxxy said. 'I'm ready whenever you need me.'

'Ah, this is awkward, but we had to hire a band,' I said. 'They played earlier, we're up to the panel now.'

She shrugged. 'Is there anything else I can do?'

I'd let Liani down with the launch planning, but if I handled things in the right way now, I might have a chance to redeem myself. An idea clicked into place. An idea that would give Liani what she wanted: Maxxy up on the stage.

'You're pretty opinionated,' I said. 'How would you feel about answering questions on our panel?'

'Sounds easy enough.'

'Yeah ...' I thought back to my epic flop at the rehearsal. 'Well, now you're taking my place. Here are my columns. You can refer to them if you get stuck, but I'm sure —'

'You're meant to be doing it?' Maxxy asked. 'Let's do it together.'

'I can't ... I'm packing it,' I admitted.

'Fifty-seven.'

'What?'

'Fifty-seven — the number of media interviews I've done in the past month alone. Fifty-eight if you count tonight. And you know what? I still get nervous, but I get through it. And you can too.'

'I feel sick,' I said.

'In my first-ever interview I got the name of my own song wrong!' she said. 'My advice? Imagine you're telling one person your opinion, not a roomful. That way it's as simple as having a conversation. It's helped me. And if all else fails, picture them naked.'

I stared at her. 'How are you only sixteen? You have more wisdom in your little finger than I do in all this hair ...'

Maxxy cupped her hand over my ear and whispered, 'I'm actually nineteen. Being sixteen is for my "brand" — but you better keep that quiet.'

'For real?' I laughed. Fake name, fake age, fake who-knew-what-else, yet somehow Maxxy was one of the most genuine people I'd met.

'I'm serious. Now, I've put my trust in you. It's time for you to put your trust in me.'

'I can't believe we're doing this,' I spluttered. I looked at Kat, who mouthed 'Good luck' before stuffing the rest of her cupcake into her mouth. 'Walk out when I do,' I said to Maxxy.

As we waited in the wings, I realised I'd got my miracle after all. Sure, it was delayed — it would have been much better for everyone's stress levels and my future career at *indi* if it had arrived twenty-four hours earlier wrapped in a big red bow, but miracle-beggars can't be choosers. Maxxy was here. My schmoozing assignment was complete.

Liani had wound up her introduction and moved on to presenting the panel members. First, she announced Allegra, who was greeted with an eruption of applause when she walked on stage. Next up was Corrine, who pumped her fists before taking her seat.

It was almost my turn. Almost *our* turn.

'… And last but not least, making her debut appearance tonight is *indi*'s very own writer, commentator and youth representative, Josie Browning,' Liani said. 'Please make her feel welcome!'

Everyone politely clapped — to them, I was about as famous as a ham sandwich. But when I strutted out on stage with my arm linked through Maxxy's, everyone gasped, including Liani, who dropped an expletive into the microphone.

'It's really her!' I heard someone say.

'Marry me, Maxxy!' another voice screamed.

Cameras flashed and the crowd surged forward. I saw Harrison elbowing journalists out of the way — this was the exclusive of his career and he wasn't letting anyone else nab the perfect shot or spoil his recording.

Liani was supposed to start off the panel discussion, but her mouth was opening and closing like a fish blowing bubbles. I decided her shock outweighed my nerves, so I walked over and took the microphone from her.

'Hi everyone,' I began, raising my voice to be heard over the crowd chanting Maxxy's name. The microphone screeched and I pulled it away a little. 'Like Liani said, I'm Josie from *indi*. We told you tonight's launch would be something special, and we meant every word. Please let me introduce Maxxy, our super-secret panel member.'

I didn't know whether it was hearing the blissed-out screaming of two hundred people, or seeing Liani with a grin on her face, but I didn't feel as nervous any more.

'I'm here to celebrate the launch of my favourite new website, *indi*,' said Maxxy into the microphone. 'Now ... someone grab me a chair and let's do this thing!'

The crowd cheered in approval and I wondered if Liani was as close to wetting her pants with excitement as I was.

24.

Allegra finished off her passionate, eloquent answer to Liani's question on the different interpretations of the word 'feminism', while I sipped from my plastic cup and hoped they didn't ask for my input. It wasn't that I didn't have an opinion; I just knew it was better suited to a politics lesson for preschoolers.

I knew I had only one chance to convince everyone that I deserved my place on the panel. There would be no second chances, not with a crowd as cynical as this. By now, at least two-thirds of the guests had their mobiles ready to capture anything great … or terrible. I'd already gone viral once after stacking it during a high-school presentation night, and 'Josie Browning, two-time YouTube sensation' wasn't a claim to fame I was striving for.

I had another sip of water, then wiped my brow. Even Maxxy had a glow on under the lights after answering Liani's questions about the effects of fame, life as a musician, and whether celebrities made good role models, although she somehow managed to look ethereal and gorgeous, rather than strained and steamy like me.

And then I heard my name, loud and clear through the microphone. 'We're thrilled to have *indi*'s youth representative, Josie Browning, here to speak,' said Liani, gesturing to me.

I heard a slight tremor of fear in her voice. She wasn't alone. The words 'sex', 'virginity' and 'faking it' circled on repeat in my brain as I wondered which angle Liani would go for.

'Josie's had a busy week,' Liani continued. 'However, she's still found time to tap into the external and internal pressures that so many young women are facing. Her column on feeling like a fake has resonated with our growing *indi* community in a big way.'

Awesome. I was off the hook. But Liani hadn't finished.

'Turns out, we all feel like fakes from time to time, but nobody talks about it — until now! And that's our aim with *indi*: to encourage girls to have real conversations. If we can give them a platform to do so, even better. So, in the spirit of sharing, let's hear from the girl who touched a nerve this week. Over to you, Josie.'

I thanked Liani and leaned closer to the microphone, suddenly paralysed by the thought of the rehearsal when the only word I'd managed to blurt out was 'sex'.

'Well, hi again. I guess I'd start by saying ... by saying ...'

I looked at Liani, whose lips were locked into a nervous grin. Allegra and Corrine were also smiling, urging me with wide eyes to continue. Pull it together, I told myself. But still the words wouldn't come. I'm not sure how long I was silent for. It could have been five milliseconds or five minutes, but it felt like five hours.

'This is the worst, get her off!' someone jeered, which set off a round of laughter.

I felt Maxxy squeeze my left hand under the panel table. Before I had a chance to acknowledge her by squeezing back, she'd picked up her microphone, setting off a round of applause.

'What Josie's trying to say is … this isn't an easy topic to talk about,' Maxxy began, waving her hand to quieten the crowd. 'But it's a worthwhile one … so let's hear her out. I don't see any of you leaping up here to expose yourselves to a judgemental crowd, so quit the heckling.'

The crowd fell silent.

'Thank you,' she said, and smiled. 'Now, Josie, I'm with you on the issue of faking it. Throughout my life I've gone through phases of trying to give people what I thought they wanted from me, rather than what I wanted from myself … and that never leads to happiness. Is that something you can relate to?'

I nodded and raised my microphone to my lips. 'Yes,' I said, my voice shaky but loud. 'Yes, I can. We're always trying to compete with each other, to one-up each other, and ... it's exhausting.'

'Can you explain that a little more?' Liani asked.

'Sure, um, the goalposts keep changing ... nothing's ever enough because we're all trying to fake these perfect lives to ... I don't know ... impress each other? Feel better about ourselves? And the weirdest part is, no one asks, "Why am I doing this? Why am I trying so hard to be someone I'm not?"'

'Yep, that's exactly the message I was trying to get out with my song "Square Peg",' Maxxy said.

'The lyrics in that sum it up perfectly,' I went on. 'No one ever says "I'm content and happy with who I am". Instead, we keep trying too hard, aiming to impress, and all with big phoney smiles on our faces. Well ... I'm sick of it, so yesterday I wrote an article and said I was tired of faking it.'

'I loved that article,' Allegra said. 'I really did.'

'Me too.' Corrine nodded. 'It hit the nail on the head.'

'I'm just ... I'm tired of trying to be someone I'm not,' I said, relieved I wasn't alone. 'Tired of comparing myself with everyone else and never feeling enough. Faking it is fine with the little things ... You're nervous before a speech? You fake a little confidence to survive. Trust me, I'm doing it now. But when it comes to the real stuff — the big stuff — I'm over faking it. Somebody once told me that being yourself can be harder than being someone else, but it's important to at least try. I don't want to pretend I'm happy when I'm sad, or that I'm too cool for everything in a lame attempt to fit in with people who are probably striving to be cool themselves. I don't want to pretend that I have my life sorted when I'm only eighteen, or that I know the first thing about designer brands when I have no money to go shopping, or that I'm a sex kitten when I'm really a virgin, or that I don't care about my gorgeous boyfriend when I'm really in love with him!'

The crowd gave a collective laugh, and I looked at Liani with wide, panicked eyes. Crap on a cravat. Did I just say all that? Judging by the cameras clicking and red lights flashing, yes, I did. Liani nodded at me, urging me to keep going.

'Well … that wasn't meant to come out,' I said, hoping my face wasn't as beetroot red as it felt. 'But my virginity's out there now … I may as well lay it all on the line. My love for my boyfriend — who may not even want to be my boyfriend after I stuffed up royally this week, but god, I hope he does — is out there. The real me — the one inside this expensive dress, blow-dried hair and layers of thick, itchy make-up — is out there. You know, it took three people to help me look like this: a stylist, hairdresser and make-up artist. If it had been up to me, I'd have come in Cons and a hand-me-down dress.'

Someone in the crowd whistled, and instead of jeering this time I heard a shout of 'You're awesome!'

'You are!' I replied, and everyone laughed. 'Tonight, I'd love for you all to imagine a world where you don't have to fake it. Where you can stay true to yourself. Where you can say what you think without worrying about being judged. Where you can just ... be. Call me naive, but that's a world I want to live in.'

'Hear, hear!' Maxxy cheered, and the crowd joined in.

'My name is Josie Browning, I'm eighteen years old and I'm a fake ... but I don't want to be any more,' I said into the microphone, my voice finally firm and clear. 'Um ... thanks everyone for your time. Any questions?'

The room fell quiet.

'Yeah! You wanna go on a date?' a guy slurred from the back. 'Maybe I could help you out with your little predicament.'

'I'd rather eat my own hair,' I said, as people booed him.

'Security, get him out of here,' Liani called out, before thanking me for talking, then directing everyone to read more from me on *indi*'s website.

The sound of cheers, rather than catcalls or unkind laughter, was so uplifting I felt it could sweep me off my feet and twirl me around in the air.

'Thank you,' I whispered to Maxxy. 'You're a lifesaver.'

'That was all you,' she whispered back.

And, in a way, she was right. Once I got going, it was all me. I was exposed. I may as well have dragged out my family photo album and showed everyone the nudie-rudie shots of me playing with our neighbour's kelpie in the bath. Yet I couldn't have been happier. I was feeling a smidge of what it was like to be the person I'd always wanted to be: honest, confident, strong (mentally, not physically — I still had twigs for arms). Call me lame, call me a nerd, but I was proud of myself. And, by the looks of Liani, Kat and Filly clapping along, those closest to me felt the same way.

It was then, towards the back of the crowd, framed in the doorway, I saw James waving at me. I wanted to fling myself into the cheering guests and crowd-surf my way straight to him. Was he really here? Or was I so high on public-speaking success that I'd imagined him standing there?

I didn't have time to find out. Still waving to her adoring fans, Maxxy took my hand and led me down the steps off the stage, to where Kat and Harrison waited.

'That was brilliant,' Harrison said, kissing me on each cheek, then doing the same to Maxxy. 'Totally TMI, but everyone lapped it up! Oh, doll, I was a bitch. Do you forgive me?'

I smirked. 'I'm sure we can work something out. Guys, can we try to keep the whole public confession of my love for James and the V-plates thing under wraps? Like, maybe we don't tell Mum or —'

'I live-streamed the event on our website,' Harrison said. 'You're global, pipsqueak.'

'And I texted Mum the link two minutes ago,' Kat said. 'Sorry ... Not sorry!'

'You didn't!'

'She did!' Harrison cheered. 'You might catch Oprah's attention, or Ellen's! Now, who is that hunk of man meat by the candy bar? How do I look? Oh, forget it, I know I look great. I'll catch you bambinos later.' He strutted off in the direction of the bar.

My eyes raced around the room, searching for James. Where was he?

'Don't stress!' Kat said, wrapping her arm around me. 'You looked hot and that speech was cool.'

'You're telling me I've reached the impossibly high standards of one Katherine Browning?' I said, eyebrow raised. 'I've achieved the elusive "hot and cool" status?'

'Yep. Until you find a way to screw it up.'

I laughed. 'Fair enough. Anyway, give me a sec — I think I saw —'

'How much of a blast was that panel?' Maxxy said, and I realised I couldn't exactly run off from the famous pop star who'd done me a massive favour. 'I feel like we need to debrief or something! Your boss was asking me some tough questions, but it was so good! *So* good! I don't think even Darlene could disagree with that. And Allegra and Corrine! Wow. Superwomen. I officially love *indi* and I'm not afraid who knows it!'

'You do? Maybe you could work with us?' I suggested, half-joking, half-serious. 'Oh, but you do have that whole super-famous-music-career thing to deal with, right?'

'Yeah, that old thing …' she smirked.

'Maybe you could be *indi*'s ambassador,' Kat piped up.

I looked at her, impressed.

'What do you mean, ambassador?' Maxxy asked.

'You know, you could contribute when you feel like it, and give them all kinds of loving in the press and vice versa … Just an idea, it's probably stupid,' Kat finished.

'Not at all,' I said. 'What do you think, Maxxy?'

Her eyes scanned the room, taking in the happy guests and the big *indi* sign hanging above the stage. 'I'm in. Let's keep it fluid for now and work out the details later. Darlene can deal with it.'

'Okay!' I said. 'Oh, and about payment … would you like me to transfer Darlene some money?'

Maxxy grinned. 'Well, *Marilyn* covered everything for my stay in the city tonight anyway, so consider yourself off the hook. Maybe just remember this little conversation when my next single drops. I am your ambassador after all.'

'You bet.' I exhaled, relieved I'd be able to afford groceries and accommodation for the next few years.

'Josie!' Liani swooped in and pecked me on the cheek. 'Congratulations! That panel was beyond sensational, and ohhhhh … I could sleep for a week.'

'You did it,' I said. 'We're officially launched. It's done. And I'm so, so sorry about the whole virginity thing — it just slipped out.'

'Mya's losing her mind from Dubai over the live-streaming, Lavish want to stay on as an advertiser *and* we're already receiving new enquiries from other brands — we're a hit! Don't give it another thought,' Liani said.

I was thrilled by the response, but not giving it another thought was easier said than done; Liani hadn't just revealed her virginity to the world via the internet.

'Oh, by the way, say hello to *indi*'s new celebrity ambassador,' I announced, drawing Maxxy a step closer to Liani. 'It was Kat's idea. Sorry, I know I technically can't hire anyone because in the hierarchy I'm about as important as an ant, but —'

'Amazing! Maxxy, welcome aboard,' said Liani, giving her a hug. 'It's lovely to meet you by the way — I'm a huge fan. And Kat, are you a little media mogul in the making? You Browning girls sure know how to keep me guessing. Now, if you're half as exhausted as me, you should all head off. Things will be wrapping up here soon.'

'We'll stay, help you pack up,' I offered, as Kat tried to stifle a yawn.

'Already on it,' Liani said. 'The pros will take care of everything. Go on, it's been a huge day.'

I smiled. 'Well … congratulations again. I'll see you bright and early on Monday?'

Liani hesitated, then said, 'No ... I don't think so.'

My heart sank. Maybe the last-minute save with Maxxy hadn't been enough to earn back her trust.

'Let's make it Monday lunchtime,' she went on. 'I'm giving us all a mini long weekend. The pace is only going to pick up from now, so I need you at your best. Although I might double our catch-ups, and talk to Mya about getting some freelance help to make sure nothing slips through the cracks again, eh? What do you say?'

I blushed. 'Of course. Never again. Never ever, ever, ever —'

'I think she gets the point,' Maxxy whispered, as Kat gestured for me to shut up.

'Wow, this is so ... so ... thanks,' I finished.

She grinned. 'Try not to send me grey before I'm forty.'

Then I remembered. 'Hey ... any word from Sia?'

'We'll hear,' she said, her voice softening, and I wondered if she knew more than she was letting on. 'Goodnight, girls — get out of here.' She hurried off to continue schmoozing with the VIP guests.

'I better go too,' Maxxy said. 'Darlene only agreed to bring me here if we popped into her niece's bat mitzvah on the way back to the hotel. I think they'll be a tougher crowd than the media you had here! Hey, pass me your phone.' I watched as she added a number to my contacts list. 'That's my direct line. Apparently I'm the ambassador of the coolest website in the country, so we'll probably have some stuff to discuss soon.'

I could have kissed her. No more of Darlene's voicemail giving me the cold shoulder.

'Yeah, okay. See ya!' I said, waving goodbye and trying not to laugh at Kat's face, which had morphed into a picture of jealousy at seeing her sister being given the phone number of one of the hottest singers in the country.

I scanned the room, but couldn't see James anywhere. People were packed in like sardines, so maybe he'd got caught in the crowd. Or maybe he really was just a figment of my imagination.

'Let's get out of here,' I said to Kat. 'I need to check something on the way out and —'

'Hello, prodigy,' said Edwina, queen bee, protégé of Rae Swanson and my sworn enemy. She had appeared so fast it was as though she'd emerged from thin air.

'You scared me,' I gasped, almost splashing my drink. 'Seriously … what are you doing here?'

Edwina pursed her lips. 'I was invited, remember?'

'I do, but I also remember you RSVPing *no* because of a certain cover shoot with a certain pop star that was mysteriously brought forward for a certain reason. I also remember you overreacting about the voicemail message — which I'm really sorry for, by the way — and threatening to spread a certain rumour about me.'

'Well, don't you just remember everything,' she said.

'I get that you're in the middle of Operation Destroy Josie Browning, but I don't have time right now,' I said, lowering my voice. Kat's eyebrows shot up with interest. 'There's someone important here who I *want* to speak to, so —'

'Josie ... I ... I do need to speak to you ... alone.'

I'd never heard Edwina stumble over her words before. 'If you have something to say, just say it ... here's fine,' I replied in my toughest voice (bolstered by Kat unknowingly playing bodyguard next to me).

'Fine, I'll get to the point — *Marilyn* still needs a new writer.'

I stayed silent. Unfortunately my bodyguard had missed the memo on how to make your frenemy squirm.

'*Marilyn*? *Marilyn* magazine?' Kat said. 'She'll take it!'

'Kat, no!' I hissed, before facing Edwina again. 'What are you trying to say?'

'We need a new writer. Rae wants someone with creativity, someone raw, someone with an edge — and after reading your last few columns and hearing you speak tonight, she thinks that someone is ... you.' Her face was so scrunched up with displeasure, it looked as though she'd bitten into a lemon.

'Rae's here? She wants to hire me?' I asked, not sure that I'd heard properly. 'But she fired me ... And she practically laughed in my face when I wound up at that job interview! And "hate" doesn't even begin to describe how *you* feel about me! How much physical pain are you in right now having to ask me this?'

'Look, Josie —'

'You sent that email to my boss to try to humiliate me, to bring me down, and now you're here doing Rae's dirty work. Unless ... unless this is some kind of prank? I know you couldn't stand the idea of me working with you, with Rae, so what's the plan? Hope I say yes, then take delight in the fact that there's really no job and I'm a big loser?'

She sniffed. 'You said it, not me. I didn't come here to fight about what happened between us ... or with Alex ... But I'm not going to grovel, not for you, not for anyone. I'm offering you a job, and yes, the pain is palpable.' She folded her arms. 'Rae's decided you're perfect for her team. What do you say?'

I followed Edwina's glance over to where Rae stood in the centre of a group of women, dressed in top-to-toe black. Her lipstick was a dark blood-red and her bob looked sleeker than ever. She caught my eye and gave a curt nod, which sent my heart racing and instantly took me back to my days as an intern under her terrifying reign at *Sash*. I tilted my head to nod back, but my neck stiffened and my head barely budged. Rae always had that kind of effect, leaving me tongue-tied or rambling, tripping or rushing, blubbering or hysterically laughing. I couldn't be myself around her or Edwina. Instead, I was always trying and failing, reaching and falling. That was no way to live; no way to work. Especially when I already had a boss like Liani.

'Well, do you want the job or not?' Edwina pressed.

All I'd wanted was for the Raes and Edwinas of the glossy magazine world to accept me. I'd seen them as goddesses to idolise, to worship. I'd aspired to be just like them one day. But now, receiving Rae's approval after months of her looking down her perfect, powdered nose at me rubbed me the wrong way. I was the same person I'd always been: the girl who needed to borrow designer clothes and have someone help her with make-up; the girl who loved working with down-to-earth people — people who valued the same things she did. That wasn't Rae. And it certainly wasn't Edwina.

'Josie?' Edwina said. 'This should be easy to answer.'

'Yeah, you're right, it is. Thanks, but I don't want the job.'

The words hung in the air like a putrid smell. Edwina looked confused, like nobody had ever said no to her before. They probably hadn't.

'Excuse me?' she spat. 'This is *Marilyn* magazine. Girls everywhere would give up *everything* for the slightest chance to do this job, to work with Rae. Hell, to work with me! And I'm offering it to you on a platter! Rae wants you, Josie, and she always gets what she wants.'

'Not this time,' I replied. 'Sorry.'

'Jose, think about it,' Kat whispered. 'This is a once-in-a-lifetime opportunity.'

'I don't want to give up everything for a job — especially a job that involves working for someone like you,' I told Edwina, my heart pounding.

'You spoiled, ungrateful little ... You are done! If you so much as breathe in my direction the next time we're at an event together, so help me —'

'Instead of plotting my demise, I'd suggest you spend your time working out how to tell Rae you've let her down,' I interrupted. 'A little birdie told me she always gets what she wants. I can't imagine how she's going to react when she doesn't. That on top of a crappy Maxxy cover ... *ouch*. Enjoy the rest of your night, Edwina. Oh, and try the canapés — the mini hot dogs are delicious.'

I walked off with flushed cheeks, leaving a stunned Edwina behind me.

Kat rushed to join me at the candy bar, where I scooped handfuls of lollies from the apothecary jars and stuffed them into my mouth. 'Let's go before I faint or change my mind,' I said.

25.

Out on the street, I was startled by the stench of cigarette smoke and the sound of honking cars. It had felt like another world inside the warehouse, like a glamorous oasis in the middle of the city. I released a deep sigh that seemed to travel up from my now-blistering big toes. There was still no James. I must have imagined him standing there in the doorway.

'Let's duck into that convenience store over there,' I said to Kat.

'Dessert?'

'Dessert.' My tastebuds were crying out for ice-cream to numb the uncomfortable churning in my gut that was rising quickly to form a lump in my throat.

My phone beeped. I checked it, hoping to see James's name. Instead it was a picture message from Sia.

'Oh god, oh god, oh god,' I said, my fingers fumbling over the screen to reveal a picture of Sia lying on her back on a hospital bed, one hand pointing at her belly, the other giving me a thumbs-up. The caption read: *Nearly five months and he's already a troublemaker, giving us a scare like that. Everything is okay. I need to rest more and work less (bonus!). My doctor's kind of a babe. It's making things super awks. xox*

I swore with excitement, then called Sia.

'*He?* You're having a he?' I blurted when she answered.

'Did I type that? I don't know for sure, but something's clicked in me — I have this weird feeling he's a little dude. Scott and I are convinced.'

'You've been talking?'

'Yeah ... he's flying up tonight to see me,' she said. I could hear the tiredness in her voice. 'It's not perfect, but ... we'll see.'

I wished I could squeeze her hand through the phone line. 'If you do have a baby boy, he can wear cute little sailor outfits, or cowboy outfits or —'

'Since when was my bump a member of The Village People?' she said.

We both laughed.

'So, you're okay?' I asked.

'The whole bleeding thing? Not ideal, so they're going to keep an eye on me and the mini-mister. But it could have been worse ... so much worse ...' Her voice trailed off. 'Far out, Jose. It's all hit me. I already love this kid too much. Don't tell anyone.'

I beamed. 'Your secret's safe with me, Mama Bear.'

'Hey, Hot Doc's on his way in, I better go. I want to know all about the launch, every single second, so call me tomorrow. Bye, honey.'

I hung up, grinning from ear to ear.

'Hey, so who's Alex?' Kat asked, stopping me outside the convenience store. 'And who was that bitchy girl back at the launch? And why don't you want to work at *Marilyn*? And what was the rumour she was threatening to spread? And who was on the phone? And why are you grinning like a maniac?'

'Ahhh, so many questions, grasshopper,' I said. 'I'll catch you up on all the drama when we get home. You were right though: I did need you to get my back after all.'

'Yeah, well, duh.'

'This ain't a bad way to be grounded, is it?' I gestured to the bright lights of the city shining around us.

Kat giggled. 'Mum knows how to do it in style. Hey, so before we make sweet, sweet love to our junk food, I wanted to say I'm sorta proud of you ... you know, for tonight.'

'Hi, I'm Josie. Have we met?'

'Shut up!' she said, shoving me. 'I was being nice.'

'Well, it's creeping me out!' I said, and laughed. 'But thanks. And me too — that was clever work with the Maxxy-ambassador suggestion. You vying for my job?'

'Definitely!' Kat said, skipping ahead of me into the shop. 'Now, to make up for laughing at my compliment, it's your shout.'

'Get whatever you want,' I said, collecting an ice-cream and some mints and dumping them on the counter. 'Urgh, my feet hurt! Whoever designed these freaking things is a sadist.'

The shop assistant sighed. 'Just the cookie-dough ice-cream and a —'

'Packet of mints, right?' James's voice drawled behind me.

'James!' I turned to see him standing there with a lopsided smile on his face.

'Did you say *James*?' Kat shrieked, rushing out from an aisle. 'He's real? He's actually real?'

'Was that ever in question?' he said.

Kat took a step closer, studying him as though he were an endangered species in the zoo. 'Can I touch you, just to make sure?'

'I guess.' He winced as Kat pinched his forearm.

'Okay, you're real,' she said, which I secretly found reassuring too. 'Sorry, that's going to leave a mark.'

'You came ... you're here,' I said to him. 'And ... I'm here.'

'And *I'm* here,' Kat chimed in.

'This isn't awkward at all, I mean *at all*,' I stammered. 'We're here and we're talking, and you came to the launch and I totally thought I'd hallucinated you because I was so upset. But this is normal and it's not awkward and —'

Kat rolled her eyes. 'I'm officially reneging on your "hot and cool" status tonight. You're down to "hot" only. I'll wait outside and give you two some privacy, but I'll be back in five minutes to make sure you haven't killed each other.' She snatched my ice-cream, tore open the wrapper and left the store.

'Excuse me, miss?' the shop assistant asked me. 'Are you going to pay for that? And these mints?'

'Just a sec,' I said, rummaging in my bag for my wallet.

'This should cover it,' James said, handing over some money. 'Keep the change — I've always wanted to say that.'

He grinned like a dag and I shot a small smile back. 'Thanks ...' I managed to say through my nerves. 'Um, so that was Kat.'

'Figured as much,' he said. 'She's a cyclone, just like you described. So ...'

'So ...' I mirrored, willing the painfully awkward vibe between us to dissipate.

'Steph yelled at me.'

'What? She didn't!'

'Said I was being a sook. That Alex meant nothing to you. That I was lucky to be out of the bad books myself. She even got Tim to have a stern word to me via Skype — he made me listen to them reading your article on feeling like a fake, line for line. For a couple of hippies those two sure know how to dish out tough love.'

'She called you a sook?' I shook my head. 'I didn't put her up to it. Or Tim. I love them, but they're vigilantes, driven mad by a long-distance relationship, frozen credit cards and student debt. I swear —'

'Jose, you were right, in your speech. You did stuff up. Royally.'

I hung my head. 'I know.'

'But Steph and Tim were right too ... I overreacted when you told me about ... *him*. It's just ... the thought of another guy's lips even close to yours made my skin crawl.'

I nodded.

'Then I got your text today,' he continued. 'And ... I've missed hanging out with you. Your laugh, your —'

'No one misses my laugh.'

'I do,' he said.

'This is kinda heavy to talk about in front of the canned vegetables,' I said. 'I feel like the peas and carrots are judging me.'

'Not to mention our old mate at the counter,' James said, steering me into the confectionery aisle. 'Better?'

I nodded.

'I know your speech tonight wasn't for me — and it was brilliant by the way. But when you said —'

'It was though. It was for you,' I said, taking a step closer. 'You're one of the only people I've never had to fake it with. Truly. You know I'm a dork.'

'A brilliant dork … but you didn't even know I was there.'

'But you were on my mind,' I said. 'You always are … Damn it, can't we just forget about everything? Reboot?'

'I want to, but after what happened with Summer, and the thought of you in that pool with him … I can't shake it,' James said.

'It was nothing. Think of me in a pool sipping a pineapple juice. Or doing an epic bellyflop *into* a pool. Or, even better, think of me kissing *you* in a pool.'

'That hasn't happened,' he said. I assumed he meant the kiss because I'd bellyflopped my way into more pools that I'd care to admit.

'Me kissing you in a pool *should* happen,' I said. 'You're my first in all kinds of ways, and I want that list to keep growing. FYI, I'm counting this as my first real relationship fight. This is a milestone. I'm ticking it off the list. James … you're my person.'

'I'm not sure, I'm —'

'You're not sure?' I asked, panicked. 'I might have fancy hair and a manicure for once, but I'm still the same girl you were crazy for all those months ago. The girl you rescued from the nightclub, the girl who accused you of trying to burgle her, the girl you kissed on the couch. You said you missed me.'

James took my hands, his fingers tracing the lines on my palms. 'I tried to stop, but you're like an annoying itch that doesn't go away.'

I burst out laughing. 'Hey!'

'JB … I … you're my person too,' he said, and warmth filled my body from the inside out, spreading from the centre of my chest up towards my cheeks and down towards my toenails. 'If we're going to do this thing, and do it properly, then I want to — need to — tell you that … I love —'

'Daydreams?' I interrupted.

James laced his fingers through mine. 'You've already stuffed this up for yourself once. You want it to be perfect, so let me get it out. I love —'

'Kebabs, right? I know, they're awesome.'

'Josie!'

'I love you,' I said, staring into his big blue eyes. 'So much it aches sometimes.'

'Shit. You just said it.'

I nodded. 'Yep, and now *you're* leaving me in the lurch.'

'You're a giant pain in the arse … but I love you too.'

James leaned down to kiss me, but I held my fingers up to his lips. 'See,' I murmured, 'didn't need a string quartet, or a thousand balloons, or a sky writer. Perfection's overrated. Although I did get your face tattooed on my butt.'

His jaw dropped. '*What?*'

'Kidding!' I said. 'You should have seen your expression just then.'

He shook his head and pulled me in close. 'I still can't believe you told a roomful of strangers that —'

'I know what I said. Harrison's pretty sure Oprah's going to call.'

'J-Bird, there's certainly never a dull moment with you,' James said, tucking a stray curl behind my ear. 'What do we do now?'

'I think you know.'

He raised an eyebrow. 'Does it involve that lingerie?'

'*Once upon a time a girl called Josie scored an internship and thought a boy called James was trying to burgle her. Then they ate pizza and she fell in love ...*'

'But what happens next in the story?' He grinned. 'You always have a plan.'

'Why don't we start with a pizza and see what happens for once?' I said. 'But before you get *too* excited, Kat's crashing with me, so ...'

'I get it: we're on limited time tonight. I can work with that.' James turned to the shop assistant. 'I'm sorry, sir, I'm going to have to ask you to avert your eyes. There's been a report of a potential PDA threat in the vicinity. It's an urgent, high-stakes situation so ... don't say you haven't been warned.'

He lowered his lips to mine in a soft but passionate kiss. I kicked off my heels, wincing at the pain, and stepped in closer, so our lips and tongues and bodies could press against each other once more. I wrapped my arms around his neck, savouring the feeling of being back in his arms. Our bodies swayed as one as James's hands moved from my cheekbones to my waist, and I rose onto my tippy-toes to bring our warm lips together again. All I smelled was a soft hint of cologne, all I heard was the store radio playing, all I felt was ... James's foot crunching onto mine!

I swore and stepped backwards, sending our intertwined bodies crashing into a stand of chocolate boxes behind us. We toppled to the floor, butts first, legs sprawling, both cackling and ignoring the angry shouting from the shop assistant. As I leaned over to kiss James once more, I accidentally squashed a fallen box of chocolates beneath me, causing him to clutch his stomach and roar with laughter, setting me off all over again.

One thing was for sure: we were back, and this time I wouldn't let anything or anyone stuff it up. I'd done enough faking in the last year. It was time to get real, live life and be myself — no heels required.

ACKNOWLEDGMENTS

Here we go again: another book, another incredible ride surrounded by cheerleaders brave enough to fasten their seatbelts for the biggest twists and turns.

First, thank you to my marvellous HarperCollins family: Rachel Dennis, Tim Miller, Amanda Diaz, Matt Stanton, Hazel Lam, Libby Volke, Gemma Fahy, Shona Martyn, Helen Littleton and, of course, my gorgeous publisher, Lisa Berryman, and publishing director, Cristina Cappelluto. Thank you for sending *The Intern* out into the world with a bang, believing in my writing and giving me the freedom to stay true to my voice, instincts and ideas. As always, it's a privilege and a joy to work with each and every one of you.

A special mention to my word-wrangling editor extraordinaire, Nicola O'Shea, who — two books on — knows the world of Josie Browning as well as I do.

Thanks to my best friends, writing buddies, author mates and online community for your emails, tweets, comments, likes, shares, calls, shoulders to cry on, hugs and bowls of hot chips (with extra chicken salt). I know we'll always cheer each other on as we aim for the stars.

And to my dear readers, thank you. Without you, none of this would be possible.

To my family: I feel like the luckiest girl in the world to be connected to such kind, generous, funny and loving people. Your encouragement throughout this ride has been unwavering. Never forget how grateful I am to have you in my life — I never do.

And to my husband and first reader, Jason: once again, I couldn't have pulled this off without your love and support. Thank you for your patience, pep talks and editing eagle eye (and for taking over as domestic god when I forgot to clean the apartment for a year ... or two). You're a weapon with a red pen and I adore you for it.

Bring on the next ride, I say – seatbelts compulsory.

Gabrielle Tozer is an author, editor, journalist and copywriter from Wagga Wagga, New South Wales. Since moving to Sydney almost a decade ago, she has contributed to publications including *Dolly, Girlfriend, Cosmopolitan, TV Week, Bride to Be, The Canberra Times* and *news.com.au.*

Gabrielle's writing has also appeared in the creative anthologies *Take It As Red* and *GOfish* and she is a previous winner of the ABC's Heywire competition. More recently, she was Writer in Residence for the State Library of Victoria's Inside A Dog program. When she's not working on her next book (yes, that's why she *still* hasn't brushed her hair), she loves tweeting, eating chocolate and watching too much television.

Faking It is the sequel to Gabrielle's much-loved YA novel *The Intern*.

Say hello:
gabrielletozer.com
facebook.com/hellogabrielletozer
twitter and instagram: @gabrielletozer

GABRIELLE TOZER

'If you loved *The Devil Wears Prada*, you'll dive right into *The Intern*.'
Lauren Smelcher Sams,
Girlfriend magazine

Find out how Josie got her big break …

Josie Browning dreams of having it all.

A perfect academic record, an amazing journalism career — and for her crush to realise she exists. The only problem? Josie can't stop embarrassing her little sister or her best friend, let alone herself.

Josie's luck changes when she lands an internship at *Sash* magazine. A coveted columnist job is up for grabs, but Josie quickly learns making her mark will be far from easy, especially under the reign of editor Rae Swanson.

From the lows of photocopying and coffee-fetching, to the highs of celebrities, beauty products and by-lines, this is one internship Josie will never forget.

Totally fresh and funny, this debut novel from media insider Gabrielle Tozer reveals just what's behind the seeming glamour of the magazine industry.